T0006249

FUZE

A LEXI MILLS THRILLER

BRIAN SHEA
STACY LYNN MILLER

SEVERN RIVER
PUBLISHING

FUZE

Copyright © 2022 by Brian Shea and Stacy Lynn Miller.

All rights reserved.

No part of this book may be reproduced in any form or by any electronic or mechanical means, including information storage and retrieval systems, without written permission from the author, except for the use of brief quotations in a book review.

Severn River Publishing
www.SevernRiverBooks.com

This is a work of fiction. Names, characters, businesses, places, events and incidents are either the products of the author's imagination or used in a fictitious manner. Any resemblance to actual persons, living or dead, or actual events is purely coincidental.

ISBN: 978-1-64875-387-9 (Paperback)

ALSO BY THE AUTHORS

LEXI MILLS THRILLERS
Fuze
Proximity
Impact
Pressure
Remote
Flashpoint

BY BRIAN SHEA
Boston Crime Thrillers
The Nick Lawrence Series
Sterling Gray FBI Profiler Series

Never miss a new release!
To find out more about the authors and their books, visit

severnriverbooks.com/series/lexi-mills

1

Asking for a corner desk without a window was the best decision Lexi Mills had made since her assignment to the Bureau of Alcohol, Tobacco, Firearms, and Explosives field division in Kansas City eight months ago. The location not only gave her and her partner enough wall space to hang whiteboards, but it also kept them out of the eyesight of the floor supervisor. Unless the ASAC ventured past the moat, as Lexi called the row of industrial copiers and printers separating their space from the rest of the cubicles, she and Trent Darby were free to clutter the walls in blatant violation of the new division chief's policy. In Lexi's view, a plain wall didn't equate to an orderly work environment. It was a sign that someone wasn't earning their paycheck.

Lexi and Darby had summarized everything they'd collected on the Gatekeepers over the last three months on four three-by-four-foot whiteboards hanging over their two desks. Today's addition had convinced her time was running out. The evidence pointed to no other conclusion: this expanding homegrown extremist group was days away from escalation. Their planning and organizing were about to turn into deadly action.

Digesting every picture and scribbling, Lexi leaned back in her chair, crossing her arms in front of her chest. "We need to brave the moat."

"I was hoping you'd say that." Darby stood from his chair, pulling a quarter from his front pants pocket. He flipped it in the air, caught it, and covered it on the back of his other hand. "Call it. Loser does the briefing. The new division chief is going to need a lot of background."

"Heads."

It was tails, but Lexi was the real winner. Though standing up in front of the brass wasn't her favorite part of the job, this investigation was personal. Darby wasn't invested like she'd become and might not present their case for a search warrant with the same intensity as she would. Lexi wouldn't exaggerate the evidence but wouldn't downplay it either.

By three p.m., every special agent in charge at the Kansas City Field Division had assembled in the briefing room. The collection of middle-aged white men was a sad display of homogeneity. And during her and Darby's previous briefing, she'd learned it was subject to groupthink. Since then, the only unfamiliar face was the new division chief with a reputation of proactiveness. He was her and Darby's only hope of steering the group from its default "no" response to approving their request for an interagency raid.

Lexi cued the PowerPoint presentation. The first few slides detailed how this case started. She and Darby had followed up on a shipment of solid nitroglycerin stolen en route from Dallas to a Kansas City pharmaceutical production facility three months ago.

"The security guard killed during the heist was an inside man of" —Lexi flipped to the next slide—"Tony Belcher, the founder of an extremist group called the Gatekeepers. We learned through an informant that Belcher claims a divine message has guided him to form an army of true believers to serve as soldiers in the coming revolution. He's been growing that army for years in a compound near Wichita. Yesterday, that same informant told us that Belcher plans to steal a plane from an aerospace manufacturer in Wichita. We believe Belcher intends to pack the plane with the nitro and use it to take out a target."

The brassiest of the brass swiped his glasses from the bridge of his nose. This ASAC was full of opinions. Opinions the others tended to jump on, but also ones that rationalized inaction when common sense dictated otherwise. "If I'm not mistaken, Special Agent Mills, you have a personal interest in this case, which makes me question if you're unnecessarily sounding the alarm bell."

"I assure you, I am not, sir. At the onset of this case, I disclosed that the guard and I shared a passing friendship a decade ago. And if not for that association, we would have never cultivated the informant."

"Do you have intel on his target?" The division chief's question hinted he'd moved past Brassy's accusation.

"No, sir, but we know Belcher and his brother intend to start a revolution. Introducing a plane suggests a 9/11-type attack, putting regional financial centers and seats of government at risk."

"But why the urgency?" the division chief asked. "What makes you think we need to act now?"

"The informant reports seeing a load of nitro and a schematic of the Airbus plant with a date written on it in big red letters. That date is three days from now."

"That's enough for a search warrant. How do you propose we proceed, Special Agent Mills? I don't want another Waco on my hands." Lexi liked this new division chief. He leaned forward in his thinking and looked to his people for advice.

"Which is why I recommend going in hot with the FBI Hostage Rescue Team. We estimate fifty to sixty men, women, and children live in the compound and expect it to be well guarded and fortified with IEDs around the perimeter. My team can clear a path and dispose of the mines, but the FBI should take point during the breach. Once the compound is secure, the ATF will execute the search warrant."

Without hesitation, the division chief said, "Set it up. I'll notify Washington."

At the rally point, the HRT commander detailed a straightforward plan to breach the compound under the cloak of darkness. Last month's satellite photos revealed that the only gate leading into the area rivaled those at any first-rate military facility. Breaching it would be time-consuming. Time they didn't have. The commander then chose a section of less-fortified fence along the back for its close proximity to residential buildings. IEDs there would likely have a smaller kill zone to avoid friendly casualties.

Lexi and Darby's role was to clear a twelve-foot-wide path up to the fence line. That area had been emptied of trees and shrubs like military bases to lessen the chance of sneak attacks. The terrain closest to the fence was rocky, making the use of robots impossible. They'd have to go in themselves.

Protocol dictated one specialist to clear the path while the other stayed back and kept in radio contact to talk the other through the zone. The problem tonight was timing. They needed to clear a path before people in the residential cabins started their day. That left them with two options. Speeding through the process was a nonstarter, so Lexi offered a solution to have her and Darby work simultaneously without blast suits but staggered enough to provide a safety buffer. If they discovered a device they couldn't circumnavigate, they would don those heavy suits.

Darby voiced his dissent and threatened to can the operation, but Lexi pulled him aside. "Our window of opportunity is small, Trent. If Belcher pulls off a strike because we didn't want to sidestep protocol, blood will be on our hands."

Darby locked on to Lexi's eyes in deep examination. It felt more like an interrogation tactic than a friendly discussion. "I'm beginning to think the ASAC was right. This is too personal."

"Yes, Bobby was a friend, but that was a decade ago."

"He was also the only man you were close enough with to have sex with."

Lexi placed her hands on her hips, arms akimbo, wondering how many times she had to go through this with Darby. Her drunken night of experimentation convinced her of one thing—she was a lesbian through and through. That night had the added benefit of proving the same for Bobby. He was as gay as she was.

"You know very well that meant nothing."

"The sex, no. But the level of trust required for it did. I saw the look on your face when we pieced together that Bobby was working for Belcher. He was more than a failed experiment."

Dammit, she thought. Eight months of sharing an office cubby hole, working a dozen investigations, and deploying on ten bomb threats had made her an open book to Darby. It was a dynamic she'd welcomed until now. Bobby's backstory was complicated, but they didn't have time for a lengthy explanation. Nevertheless, she owed Darby a proper answer when time allowed.

Lexi dipped her head briefly before looking him in the eye again. "I failed him a decade ago. If I'd been a better friend back then, he might not have ended up in Belcher's circle, so this is my chance to make it right. It's a long story that I'll share with you when this is over. But trust me when I tell you I'd make the same argument if Bobby wasn't a factor. I couldn't live with myself if we passed up the chance to save innocent lives."

"All right. That's all I needed to hear. But if we come across anything nasty, the suits go on."

Minutes later, a caravan of black SUVs and two armored HRT vehicles rumbled down a gravel access road eighteen miles northeast of Wichita. To the naked eye, they were traveling in complete darkness. However, infrared LED driving lights on each vehicle and night vision goggles on each driver, including Darby, lit their path.

Sitting in the front passenger seat without the aid of night vision was an exercise in complete trust for Lexi. According to the briefing at the rally point, steep ditches lined the narrow road, and one moment of inattentiveness could send their SUV over the edge. And as the lead vehicle, that would create a disastrous chain reaction. For that reason, she didn't start her and Darby's typical pre-operation banter to settle their nerves. Instead, she put superstition aside, convincing herself that deviating from their routine didn't matter. After all, as the top certified explosives experts in the division, they'd proven their ability to adapt to any circumstance.

Passing a designated landmark, Darby slowed and turned left, stopping inside the tree line of a small patch of woods fifty yards from the compound's perimeter fence. The assemblage of HRT vehicles then lined up, waiting to roll on Lexi and Darby's signal.

Lexi started by donning her helmet with night vision goggles, the ocular lens turning her environment phosphorous green. She then placed two small white rectangular flags, sixteen feet apart, at the head of the path they were about to clear. Subsequent flags would delineate the safe zone and silently relay their progress to the waiting HRT every few yards along the route.

Dark conditions meant the risk of missing a buried device was high, but Lexi remained confident. After all, they'd requisitioned the Cadillac of bomb detectors. The two units were the only handheld devices in their inventory that combined ground-penetrating radar with a metal detector and didn't require recalibration when moving across differing terrain. Talk about a time saver. It was a critical dimension for this operation.

Dressed in matching camouflage uniforms, steel-toed sage boots, helmets, and Kevlar vests, Lexi and Darby ops-checked their radios. The HRT commander gave both a thumbs-up. Then, each turned on their handheld detector, calibrated it to the terrain, and set the screen to night mode to minimize the glow.

Their plan of attack was simple. Darby would start first, clearing a strip eight feet wide. Along the way, he'd mark the right perimeter with white flags and detected devices using a red flag with an X printed in the center. Once he'd cleared the first fifty feet of length, Lexi would start clearing an eight-foot strip to the left. The HRT vehicles needed only ten feet to pass safely, but the six-foot buffer allowed for minor swerving on the rocky terrain.

They'd remain fifty feet apart until Darby reached the wall. At that point, Lexi would retreat, double-checking the safe zone on her return. Meanwhile, he'd complete the final swath on Lexi's side.

Darby started by hovering his detector three to six inches off the ground in a methodical pattern. Lexi watched him through her night vision goggles. His tall and thin camouflaged body glowed green as he moved slowly forward six inches at a time.

"Gretchen was right, you know," Lexi said through her mic.

"About what?" Darby asked.

"You look like the Grinch."

"That's the last time I let you alone with my daughter and my gear bag." Lexi snickered.

Ten minutes later, Darby announced, "All right, Mills, I'm fifty out. Join the party."

"So like you, partying without me." Lexi executed her first swipe.

"How about I buy the tequila when this is over?" Darby continued his search, staying fifty feet ahead of Lexi.

"I'll hold you to it." Lexi let the corners of her mouth draw back. They were fifty feet apart in the dark, but she counted on his night vision goggles to highlight her toothy grin. Darby had once said she could disarm any suspect with her bright smile. She'd have to remember that superpower the next time she was at a bar and had her eye on a beautiful woman.

She mirrored Darby's technique, completing her first eighty feet without detecting a single threat. Then, continuing her search, she swung her detector left over a flat patch of dirt. The handle vibrated in her hand to the sound of a low buzz in her earpiece. She steadied it to get a reading on the visual display. Two seconds later, the detector provided the approximate dimensions and depth of the suspected device.

Lexi knew that, at five inches tall by four inches in diameter and buried one inch below the surface, the device could only be one of several possibilities. Then she remembered their informant mentioning seeing an old crate of explosives with a Nazi symbol stamped on its side. She'd likely stumbled across a German S-mine. These World War II devices were particularly lethal. When triggered, they would launch into the air and detonate three feet from the ground. The explosion would project a spray of shrapnel in all directions and could be lethal up to sixty-six feet.

Lexi spoke into her mic. "I got a hit, Darby. Likely a Bouncing Betty." She pulled a red flag from her right utility cargo pocket and marked the mine. Then, considering the mine's location, she determined the path needed to move. "Shifting the west perimeter two feet to the east."

"Copy," Darby replied. "Shifting two to the east. We shouldn't have to move my side. Double mark it and move on."

"Copy. Double marking." Lexi realigned the west perimeter by placing a white flag at the shift point.

"I've reached the rocky patch," Darby announced. "It stretches ten yards from the fence line."

"Careful, Darby. Footing could be tricky." When Lexi glanced in his direction, he craned his neck toward her, giving her a thumbs-up. He then shifted his stare forward and stepped toward the fence line. His right leg moved oddly, causing him to wobble.

A click came through the mic, the worst possible noise when clearing a minefield.

A bang sounded. Darby flew backward with his legs in the air, landing on his butt.

Two seconds later, a metal cylinder emerged from the ground at the spot where Darby had stepped. "Trent!" Lexi yelled.

In another two, a blinding flash filled the area.

A wave of pressure blew Lexi off her feet. Then, searing pain enveloped her left foot. She hit the ground with a thud, unable to take in a breath. In her earpiece, a voice said, "Brock. Johnson. Get Mills."

The green from her goggles turned black.

2

_____

"Gretchen was right, you know." Lexi watched Darby through her night vision goggles while he swept his detector across the dark terrain.

"About what?" Darby asked.

"You look like the Grinch."

"That's the last time I let you alone with my daughter and my gear bag."
Lexi snickered.

"All right, Mills, I'm fifty out. Join the party. I've reached the rocky patch."

"Careful, Darby. Footing could be tricky."

Darby looked over his shoulder, giving Lexi a thumbs-up.

A blinding light flashed, waking Lexi with a start. She opened her eyes to bright afternoon sunlight hitting her face and the Uber driver standing curbside. He'd opened the rear passenger door, gripping the window frame with one hand and her crutches in the other. "I'm sorry to wake you, miss, but we've reached your destination."

Lexi shook off the fog of her recurring bad dream, but not the accompanying regret. She had the same experience every time she'd fallen asleep for the last month. Her mind would drift to that horrible night and the risky choices she'd made. Going in without the benefit of their blast suits was terrible enough, but she'd added to her foolhardiness with their light-hearted back-and-forth during the critical phase of the operation. Lexi had made an idiotic play, putting the mission ahead of safety. The ATF had cleared her of any culpability, but she knew better. If she hadn't suggested going in light or hadn't joked with him in the kill zone, he might be alive. That guilt brought her here today before she left town for good.

"Thank you." Lexi flung her legs out, letting her right foot hit the pavement. When the driver offered her the crutches, she handed him her small backpack. "Do you mind holding this for a minute?"

"Of course not."

She exited the car, using the technique the nurses at the hospital had taught her. While balancing herself on the crutches, the driver then helped her sling the backpack in place, one shoulder at a time. "Thank you. Your help is much appreciated."

Lumbering up the walkway, Lexi replayed last week's phone call in her head. She'd avoided reaching out since the funeral out of cowardice, but the caller ID had tricked her. She hadn't realized Trent's widow had changed her number following weeks of nonstop calls from the intrusive media. If Lexi had just let the call go to voicemail, she wouldn't have backed herself into the corner she was in now.

But Lexi did answer, and Karla had asked if it was true that the brass was reassigning her to the Dallas office. She couldn't lie, and before the call ended, Lexi had promised to drop by and say goodbye before she left. Now that time had come. Movers packed her belongings yesterday, and another agent would drive her and her SUV to Texas tomorrow. That left only today to keep her word.

Lexi reached the door, mustering the courage to face the monumental consequences of her poor choices from that awful night. Having altered the lives of the people on the other side of the door forever, she tucked away her shame, hopefully long enough to get through the next hour.

Putting on her best game face, Lexi knocked. Soon, the door slowly inched open, revealing a three-and-a-half-foot angel in pink tights and blond curls. The last time this little girl had answered the door in the same adorable manner, Lexi had bent on one knee and issued her the password to coax her into opening the door farther. But that trick was unavailable to her today. So instead, Lexi dipped as low as the crutches allowed, pulling out her brightest smile.

"Hey, Munchkin. Is the password still 'Grinch?'"

Biting her lower lip, Gretchen nodded and opened the door fully. "Where's your foot?" she asked. Her innocence was both endearing and refreshing, making the back of Lexi's throat swell.

Once Lexi had recovered, her amputation became a giant elephant in every room she had entered. No one mentioned it. Not her mother when she'd brought her to her apartment from the hospital. Not her coworkers when she'd gone to the federal building to gather her things from her office. And not the woman in her apartment building Lexi had been sleeping with when she said goodbye. Every adult in her life clearly considered the topic off-limits until Lexi brought it up.

The young girl's question marked the first time Lexi had been asked to explain how she lost her leg, and it caught her off guard. If it had come from a stranger at a bar, she could throw out something vague about the line of duty, but Gretchen was too young to understand. However, she *was* old enough to realize that she hadn't seen her father in a month. That was a topic better left unmentioned.

"I hurt it, and the doctor couldn't fix it."

Gretchen cocked her head to one side, eyeing the area where Lexi's left foot should have been. "Can the doctor get you a new one?"

"Not a real one, but he's making me one out of metal."

Gretchen raised her pant leg, displaying a freshly scraped knee. "I got hurt. Mommy fixed it with a Band-Aid and kiss."

"Well, aren't you the lucky one?"

"Let her in, Gretchen." Karla stepped down the entry hall toward the front door. She carried a dish towel, wiping her hands with it.

Lexi stepped inside, careful not to tangle her crutches on the rug runner fringe or a line of Legos along the dividing line between tile and carpet. In her experience, the Darby house was frequently dotted with toys, but it never appeared this chaotic. Toys, clothes, and blankets were strewn about, looking as if a tornado had hit the room. The only sign of order was a path from the door that extended past the stairs. Karla had clearly done some cleaning ahead of Lexi's visit, but that tiny bit was likely all she could manage.

"It's good to see you, Lexi. I hope you're hungry," Karla said. The strain of losing a husband had undoubtedly taken its toll. Puffy, bloodshot eyes suggested many tear-filled hours. And many strands of her usually perfectly kept hair had escaped her ponytail holder and hung wildly in front of her ears.

"Starved," Lexi replied.

"Mommy's making grilled cheeses and tomato soup." Gretchen tapped Lexi on the forearm and she bent. She extended a tiny index finger at Lexi, encouraging her to lean lower, and whispered, "Can you eat my tomato soup? I don't like it."

Lexi released her grip from the left crutch and fist-bumped Gretchen. "Happy to do my girl a solid."

"Are you okay with the kitchen table?" Karla asked, gesturing toward the rear of the house.

"It will work fine." Lexi hobbled into the kitchen and sat in her traditional guest chair after leaning her crutches low against the table. She then removed her backpack from around her shoulders and rested it against her chair leg on the floor.

"Can I play until lunch, Mommy?"

"It's 'may I play,'" Karla said. "And yes, you may."

Once Gretchen left the room, Karla worked at the stove, stirring the soup pot and grilling the sandwiches. The conversation soon settled on Lexi's hospital stay and how she was adapting to life with one foot.

"Once I get my prosthetic next month, I can start my rehab in earnest. I hope to work my way back to SRT within a year."

Karla brought over a tray of three soup bowls and a plate of five small sandwiches. She then sat next to Lexi, offering a bitter smile. "Why not take a medical retirement? Haven't you sacrificed enough for this damn job?"

"It's hard to explain, Karla, but I'm not done with the ATF yet."

"Well, figure out a way to explain it because I can't see how you can go back to a job that took your leg and my husband."

She could say that staying on the job was a calling, but that was only half the truth—the half only those who wore the badge could understand. So she decided to tell Karla the half that would make sense. "I won't be done with the job until I get the bastard who was responsible for burying that mine."

Karla squeezed Lexi's hand with a look of determination in her eyes. "Get the bastard."

Gretchen returned to the room.

"Hey, Munchkin." Lexi pulled from her backpack a package encased in bright birthday wrapping paper. "I know your birthday isn't for a few months, but I have a present for you."

Gretchen hopped into her chair, sitting tall on her knees and clapping with joyous anticipation. "I love presents." She shifted her stare to her mother. "Can I open it, Mommy?"

"Yes, you may."

Gretchen ripped off the wrapping paper and opened the bread loaf-sized box. Her eyes twinkled like a Christmas tree when she saw what was inside. She pulled out the soft stuffed toy. "Look, Mommy. It's the Grinch. Just how Daddy looked in his funny glasses."

Moisture pooled in Lexi's eyes. She cleared the emotion from her throat. "That's how I'll always remember your father."

3

FOUR MONTHS LATER

Lexi woke in a sweat, her heart still thumping from a recurring nightmare that never changed. Darby would slip, steady himself, and give her a thumbs-up. The second he turned away from her, a blast would blow him backward. Then the ensuing flash would jerk her awake. This morning was no different. If she didn't have to pee, she'd lay in bed for another hour or two until she got bored enough to move to the couch.

Reaching for the bedside crutches, Lexi felt every muscle scream that that was a horrible idea. The thought of peeing where she sat crossed her mind, but if she did, she'd have to change her sheets, and that was out of the question until her replacement prosthetic socket arrived at the end of the week. Out of options, Lexi pushed herself up. She then gripped her crutches and hobbled to the toilet, sorer than she had been in the days following the explosion that had taken her leg five months earlier.

Once done, she hopped to the sink to wash her hands but paused to inspect the bruises on her face. They had reached alarming shades of purple and dark red. She touched the eye socket bone, wincing at the sharp pain. She was lucky Monday's treadmill fall had left her only with bruises, a fat lip, a bloody nose, and two sore hamstrings.

Having realized that showering required too much effort, Lexi splashed water on her face and gingerly dabbed it dry. Besides water, the minty taste of toothpaste was the first thing she'd had in her mouth since the fall yesterday morning. A nauseating stomach gurgle confirmed it.

Hobbling to the kitchen, she chugged a glass of water and tossed a banana on the couch, her destination for the day. Lexi plopped down on her sectional, leaving the crutches leaning against the ottoman. She hated those things. She hadn't needed them since receiving her first prosthetic six weeks after her surgery. Getting that artificial leg had returned her independence to her. But yesterday's accident established that that sense of freedom was only an illusion. Those crutches were reminders she'd be a cripple for the rest of her life.

She'd been fooling herself to think that she could run on a prosthesis. She'd spent two months working her ass off, learning how to walk with a prosthetic leg. Another month to walk without a noticeable limp. And another to learn how to jog. All that hard work would be for nothing if she couldn't meet the ATF's physical fitness standards.

Lexi picked up the banana, preparing to peel it, but then the doorbell rang. She sighed. The only people who came to her apartment were the pizza deliverer, Uber Eats, and her mother. She hadn't placed an order, so that left one suspect. "Go away, Mom. I'm not in the mood today."

A muffled voice came through the door, "Lexi, it's Nita. I was worried when you didn't show for your physical therapy appointment this morning."

Nita Flores? She was the last person Lexi wanted to see today. She didn't want to hear "I told you so" from the very person who had warned her not to push herself too hard too soon.

"Not today, Nita. I'm tired."

"Just let me see that you're okay."

"I'm fine. Now go away."

"I'm not leaving until you open this door, Lexi Mills. I'll make a scene if I have to." Nita had warned Lexi that she possessed a fiery side, but this was the first she'd displayed it in their four months of working together. Evidently, she wasn't lying or leaving.

"Fine. Hold on." Lexi tossed her banana down, retrieved her crutches, and trudged to the door. She flipped the handle, cracked the door open, and maneuvered backward for several steps. "Come in."

Nita walked in, instantly drawing Lexi's gaze to her never-seen-before curves. She'd ditched her baggy maroon medical scrubs for formfitting jeans and a U-neck T-shirt that hugged her body like a lover.

"My God, Lexi. You look horrible." Nita gently stroked the area around Lexi's left temple.

"Thanks for the compliment." Lexi leaned into her crutches, enjoying the touch from her physical therapist more than she should have. But she couldn't help herself because the caress felt anything but clinical.

"You know what I mean." Nita lowered her fingers to Lexi's lower lip, grazing the swelling ever so slightly. "I knew you took a hard fall, but I didn't expect this. I feel horrible about not stopping you."

"It's not your fault that I pushed myself. But falling yesterday showed me my future. I now know that I'll never run again." Lexi's chest tightened at her harsh truth. She wasn't up for more pep talks and worked her crutches, returning to the couch.

Nita followed, laying her purse on the floor and sitting next to Lexi. "Do you mind if I look at your residual limb?"

Lexi shook her head and lifted her leg to Nita's lap.

Nita had been looking at her limb three days a week for five months, following each physical therapy session. She'd taught Lexi how to massage the tissue to promote blood flow and work out the daily edema that would likely stay with her for the first year post-amputation.

Lexi's favorite part of limb care was the lotion. It was soothing and the touch was the same every time, but Lexi had gotten into her head that the care Nita had taken to rub in the special cream was more than professional necessity. Maybe it was more wishing than reality, but Lexi enjoyed the attention, nonetheless.

When Nita touched her skin around the nub, the tension Lexi had felt at the door began to ebb. Nita's gaze followed her hand as it trailed upward toward Lexi's knee and down again on the other side. "I'm glad you wore extra layers of socks yesterday for your workout. They saved you from bruising on the side where the socket snapped."

"You taught me that. Thank you."

Nita used her thumbs to knead the flesh on what remained of her left calf. Her pace was slower than the one she'd use following a physical therapy session. Lexi cautioned herself from reading anything into it, but the longer the massage lasted, the closer she came to assuming the motivation she'd attributed to Nita wasn't merely in her head.

"You had a setback," Nita said softly. "Every amputee does."

"I had more than a setback, Nita." Lexi pulled her leg back, returning it to the couch. "I snapped my socket and nearly broke my other leg. I have to face the reality that walking is as good as it gets for me."

"I agree this was significant, but if you give up, you're not the woman I thought you were. Where is the Lexi Mills who walked into my office five months ago saying that she wanted to run a mile and a half in twelve minutes again to make it back to the ATF SRP?"

"That's SRT."

"*T, P...*" Nita flapped her arms as if she were out of arguments. "It's all crap if you give up."

Lexi snickered. Nita did too.

"I don't like to compare patients because each one has different needs and abilities, but I've never had one work so hard." Nita placed a finger under Lexi's chin, pulling it so they faced one another. "I won't let you give up. I'm going to keep after you until the Lexi I first met comes back."

The silence and unbreakable eye contact that followed gave birth to a recognition of an undeniable mutual attraction. Or so Lexi hoped. Then, there it was. Nita's stare dropped a fraction and focused on Lexi's lips. She wanted to be kissed. Lexi did too. But what were the rules with such things between physical therapist and patient? If Nita's swallow and rapid breathing were an accurate barometer, she wasn't considering the ethical implications of what they were undoubtedly about to do.

Lexi edged her head forward until their lips were inches apart. Steamy exhales mixed in rising anticipation. Nita placed an index finger on Lexi's lips. "If we do this, I can't be your therapist. Is that what you want?"

"I've wanted to kiss you for months."

"But what do you want more? A kiss or for me to get you running?" Nita lowered her finger, setting the stage for Lexi to choose.

4

SIX MONTHS LATER, ONE YEAR AFTER LOSING HER LEG

You got this. Lexi silently willed herself to dig deep and pound the treadmill harder.

Her self-imposed deadline to prove to herself she was ready to return to the Special Response Team by the first anniversary of the explosion was two days away. She'd already been cleared for field duty months ago, after passing the ATF physical fitness test. Yet her boss still had her assigned to a "temporary" desk job. Though Lexi refused to let that dissuade her.

Passing at the women's level wasn't good enough. Since the first day she'd made the SRT in Wichita, she'd met the men's physical standards to keep misogyny at bay. Sure, she'd have plenty of time while waiting for her reinstatement, which was likely months away, but her last day at the Dallas Physical Rehabilitation Center posed the perfect opportunity to put herself to the test.

Lexi increased the speed to seven and a half miles per hour, the eight-minute-mile pace required of the men on the SRT. She kept her spine erect, her shoulders back and directly over her hips, and her arms relaxed for a compact swing. The first eight minutes were a snap, but her residual limb sank lower into the prosthetic socket during the ninth and hit the bottom of it on the interior side. She'd thought the new, smaller socket she'd received after her leg shrinkage had stabilized last month meant her days of wearing layers of socks over her limb to avoid slippage were over, but she was wrong. Pushing herself today proved it would be a never-ending battle.

She dug deeper to ignore the pain, but the discomfort forced her to take in shallow breaths. Thankfully, her legs remained strong without tightening or burning, validating months of squats, lunges, and presses to build strength.

Three more minutes, Lexi told herself. If she could maintain the same pace for three more minutes, she'd meet the men's fitness standard—a challenge she'd tackled every year since joining the SRT for her own satisfaction. Knowing she was as strong, fast, and fit as the men she served with gave her more confidence than the Gold Star Medal the ATF director had pinned on her chest for getting her leg blown off.

Two more minutes. In 120 seconds, Lexi would prove to herself that not being whole didn't matter. That she could manage anything the ATF or the bad guys threw at her.

A slender hand came into view, pressing the downward-speed button repeatedly. "Are you trying to hurt yourself again?" Nita decreased the treadmill speed incrementally to three miles per hour, a comfortable cooldown pace.

"Damn...it...Nita." Lexi took in quick breaths between words.

"The fact that you're wheezing proves my point." Nita pressed a few more buttons on the control panel before crossing her arms in front of her chest. "Now, finish your cooldown and stretch it out."

Lexi mumbled several choice curse words, unsure what needed cooling down more, her body or her temper. It was so like Nita to want to take things slowly. The first day Lexi hobbled into her physical therapy room, Nita had set the bar low in terms of speed. She'd warned that rehab following a below-the-knee amputation would require considerable effort and patience. Nine months later, Nita still didn't understand Lexi's drive. Or she did and refused to encourage it.

The machine reduced the pace to a slow creep, and by the time it came to a stop, Lexi's temper had faded. There was no need to stay mad. She'd have plenty of opportunities to prove to herself she was ready for the SRT.

Her current job, after all, had her chained to a desk. As a result, she only ventured off the floor to use the gym or attend physical therapy, like today.

"Sometimes, I think you don't listen to me out of spite," Nita said.

"For this, I listen to my trainer, not my girlfriend."

"I was your trainer until four months ago." Nita narrowed an eye in a way that guaranteed Lexi would be in the doghouse tonight if she didn't smooth things over.

Lexi stepped off the treadmill, careful to lead with the good foot first, grabbed the towel she'd hung on the safety bar, and buried her face in it. The sound of clanking weights and the whir of other treadmills passed the seconds until she produced a more thoughtful reply.

Lexi looked up and locked eyes with Nita, recalling the first time she'd pulled her from her funk. "Do you remember when I fell on the treadmill because I'd pushed myself too hard?"

"How could I forget? You were a bloody mess. I thought you'd broken your nose."

"I wanted to give up because I didn't think I'd ever run again. But when I missed my next appointment, you tracked me down and wouldn't let me quit."

"You were so stubborn."

"But you kept chipping away my walls." Lexi scanned the room, ensuring no eyes were watching them, and linked their pinkies.

"We both had walls." Nita squeezed her pinky before letting go. She lowered her smock sleeves that had been rolled up to her elbows, covering the intricate pattern of tattoos on her arms. The history that ink hid had served as a glowing neon road map for Lexi to break down Nita's defenses. "I'm glad you found a way around mine."

"It was the best damn bit of navigating I'd ever done."

Nita checked her surroundings before lowering her voice. "Navigating your way into my heart may make you the perfect girlfriend, but staying on the slow and steady path of rehab would make you the perfect patient."

"Samuel already thinks I'm the perfect patient." Lexi slung the towel over her shoulder, confident Nita was projecting. Her model of slow progress had worked well in her own journey, but Lexi had grown past it. "I love that you still look out for me, Nita, but I know my body. I can do a sub-twelve-minute mile and a half."

"You need to learn patience." Nita pointed toward Lexi's legs. "Now stretch before Samuel barks at you."

"I'd like to take this thing off first." A sheepish grin formed on Lexi's face, predicting what her following words would trigger. "I'm a little sore."

Nita threw Lexi the "I told you so" look before leading her to the locker room. She waited silently while Lexi retrieved her crutches and sat on the padded bench to doff her prosthetic limb carefully. Lexi then rolled down the neoprene sleeve and removed the socket and the liner encasing her leg. Letting the skin there breathe felt as good as removing her bra after a long, tiring day.

"It looks a little red." Nita grimaced. "You might get some swelling today." Lexi began rubbing it, but Nita softly cupped a hand over hers. "Let me." Lexi responded with a silent nod.

Nita massaged Lexi's limb gently, starting at the surgical tip. Her touch was clinical, applying the proper pressure to promote blood flow into the area. "You're not fooling me, Lexi Mills. I know why you're pushing yourself, and a running test is only half of it."

"What's the other half, Miss Smarty Pants?"

"Guilt." Nita's touch became lighter, more tender. "And it's unwarranted. Even the ATF agrees. I wish I could convince you that nothing you said or did that night made Darby's foot slip. You said it yourself. As the senior agent, he took point that night because the terrain near the fence was dangerous."

"You weren't there." Lexi rubbed her temples. They throbbed with the frustration that manifested whenever that night became the topic of conversation. Despite the audio and video recordings and witness testimony, Internal Affairs had no way of getting into Darby's head. Lexi knew her partner and their routine. Blast suits weren't required for reconnaissance, but they'd always worn them before. They'd reserved bantering for the pregame, not the show. But that night, they'd done things differently, costing Darby his life.

"I don't have to be shot to know it hurts. Some things are simply intuitive, such as the likeliness of a foot slipping on a jagged rock on a cold, wet night."

"I don't want to argue with you, Nita. Not this week."

Nita stopped her massage to place her hands on Lexi's outer thighs. It was an intimate touch that was more reassuring than sensual. "I know this is a hard week for you and that being assigned to a desk job is making it worse."

"I should have been assigned to field investigations months ago, but the brass has been dragging their feet." Lexi pounded a fist on her bad leg. "I don't need to be coddled. I'm in better shape now than I was before I lost my leg."

"It's not the visible injuries they're concerned about. You may have passed your psych eval"—Nita briefly placed a hand over Lexi's heart— "but you and I both know you still haven't healed in here."

"And you know I have a rich history of locking away my emotions and getting on with life. This is the same thing." Growing up gay and half Black in small-town Texas meant facing narrow-mindedness every time she walked out the door. Her very existence was an abomination to many in that town, even in her own house.

"I'm no psychologist, but I know facing homophobia and racism isn't the same as facing the guilt of causing a friend's death, albeit unwarranted."

"I really don't want to talk about this, Nita." Lexi rubbed her temples again. "I should shower and get back to the office."

"I'm sorry, Lex. I didn't want your last day of physical therapy to end on a negative note." Nita lifted Lexi's chin with a hand and drew her head closer until their lips pressed together in a brief kiss. When they pulled back, moisture had pooled in Nita's eyes. "I'm going to miss seeing you here. These sessions remained the best part of my week even after Samuel took over."

"It's not like I won't see you again. We live together, for goodness' sake."

"You're right." Nita straightened her posture, wiping her lower rims dry. "I'll pick up dinner tonight. Chinese?"

"Extra orange chicken?" Lexi asked, wide-eyed. Leftovers were in her future because her favorite entrée was Nita's least favorite.

"Of course." Nita rolled her eyes. "I better get ready for my next patient."

Lexi kissed Nita goodbye and hopped to her wall locker, holding her prosthetic. Resting it on the floor against a neighboring locker, she opened hers and grabbed the mesh bag containing shower necessities. Then, something about her exchange with Nita gave her pause. Nita was right about the guilt facet of her motivation, but that wasn't what had caught Lexi's attention. Nita wasn't a crier. Like Lexi, she'd learned to compartmentalize her emotions to get through the day. Something was bothering her girlfriend, and it had nothing to do with Lexi completing physical therapy.

Her phone vibrated against the flimsy metal of the bottom of the locker, creating an echoing clank. She flipped the phone over to read the number. The area code and three-digit exchange meant the call was from the Dallas Federal Building. She debated picking up, dreading another call from another agent telling her they couldn't find the notes or emails she'd asked for. Being the unit's grandmaster for the weekly and monthly reports to the division chief felt more like punishment than a "cushy desk job," as several agents had labeled it. Lexi should have been in the field, not chained to a desk, pushing paper. Nevertheless, work was work.

Lexi swiped the screen and pressed the speaker button. "This is Mills."

"Special Agent Mills, this is Jack Carlson."

An adrenaline rush nearly knocked Lexi from her crutches. There was only one reason the Dallas division SRT commander would call her personal number. She countered the lightness in her chest by firming her stance and grip on the crutch handles. "Yes, Special Agent Carlson, how can I help you?"

"I'm calling to tell you that your application for reinstatement to the Special Response Team has been approved. Our on-call explosives expert has been activated for National Guard duty, so I need you to fill in."

Lexi's lungs filled to their fullest with deep, satisfied breaths. Only once when she'd earned herself that bloody nose had she taken her eye off the prize, and now her hard work and persistence had paid off. "Thank you, sir. I won't disappoint you. When do I start?"

"Have you been watching the news?"

"No, I haven't." Lexi glanced at the television mounted on the wall in the corner of the room. The volume was off, but she didn't need the closed captioning to explain the images on the screen. A breaking news clip showed the emergency response to a collapsed tunnel at the border in Nogales, Arizona.

"Be in my office in an hour for a mission briefing," Carlson said.

"I'll be there, sir." Lexi disconnected the call, prouder than the first day she pinned on the badge. She pumped her fist once, strong and firm. "I'm back."

5

Lexi exited the elevator on the fifth floor of the Dallas Federal Building with an extra pep in her step. She'd been assigned to the ATF field office there for eleven months, but this was the first time she'd walked into its inner sanctum feeling like an agent. Compiling reports and requisitioning and inspecting equipment were necessary to keep the operations running smoothly, but Lexi had trained for something intrinsically more critical— explosives detection and disposal.

Two years of classroom and range training to become certified, as well as the week-long recertification course she passed six months ago, had been wasted until now. Despite the agency having a limited number of explosives specialists, some GS-15 had her filling out forms all day because he wasn't willing to accept the blowback if something went wrong after she returned to the field. That was, until his back was against the wall. Thank goodness for small favors.

She strode past the supply clerk's desk, slowing long enough to give Ronald a toothy grin en route to her cubicle next door. That little rectangle of space had served as a home away from home since her first day in Dallas. Its tucked-away location was ideal for limiting foot traffic and uninvited visitors—she had none. Only she and Ronald ventured this deep past the equipment closets. However, the isolated location had created an invisible barrier.

If not for her diligence in contacting the other agents face-to-face instead of exclusively by email or voicemail, they likely wouldn't recognize her. Lexi supposed if she hadn't slid in her expert opinion at every opportunity, they might have forgotten she was a contemporary and assumed she was a clerk.

The moment Lexi opened her top side drawer to retrieve her notepad, Ronald stuck his head around the corner and grinned before stepping farther inside. "What's up, Mills? I haven't seen you smile like that since the Chiefs got their asses handed to them in the Super Bowl."

Lexi pushed the drawer shut and hunted around her desk for a pen. "I've been reinstated."

"Fieldwork?"

"Better than that." Pen found. She looked up.

"SRT?" Ronald's smile dropped a fraction at her affirmative nod. "That's great." Clearly, he considered her good news his misfortune. Strangely, Lexi would miss his quirkiness and affinity for quoting Marvel characters, but she was meant to be partnered with an agent, not a logistics clerk. Even the best damn one she'd ever worked with.

She leaned her butt against the edge of the desk. "It's what I've wanted for a year, but I'm delighted I got to work with you. Good people like you make it possible for the agents to do their jobs. It's not easy getting the right equipment to the right place at the right time. Speaking of that"—Lexi leaned her head out of the cubicle to ensure no one was close by—"do you think I can get one of the new vests that came in yesterday?"

Ronald retrieved a mechanical pencil from his shirt's breast pocket and tore a piece of paper from Lexi's notepad. "If you want to do something right, you make a list."

"Tony Stark?"

"Ant-Man. Now, what else does my favorite customer want?" After reviewing the list of the standard gear for explosives experts, Ronald suggested several unique additions. "I'll make sure you have the newest of everything. When do you need it?"

"My mission briefing is in ten minutes."

"I better get hopping." Ronald returned his pencil to its proper place. "I should have your go bag ready in thirty."

"You're the best, Ronald."

Lexi knocked on the casing of Carlson's door two minutes before her hour was up. She silently thanked her father for breeding punctuality into her since she was old enough to tell time. Being on time, he'd taught her, was the first sign of respect.

She'd walked past this office when the door was open several times since her arrival but had never given it a thorough inspection until now. Carlson's was relatively tame in terms of "I love me" walls full of awards and citations. She swore the brass at the Kansas City office had a competition going as if the more awards they displayed meant they were that much better as an agent. In Lexi's experience, the opposite was true. The good agents worked under the radar.

"Good morning, sir." The lack of other personnel in the office left Lexi perplexed. She'd been on the SRT long enough to know that each deployment was different, but every time, she'd been part of a team. Sometimes she was part of a large contingent of a dozen, other times a small unit of three, and everything in between.

Carlson waved her in, gesturing toward the guest chair in front of the desk, not the small conference table near the window. "Right on time, Mills. Have a seat."

Once settled into the chair, Lexi pushed out her prosthetic leg a few inches to ease the pressure on the sore spot.

Carlson briefly glanced at his laptop screen, scrolling the tethered mouse several times. "Your fitness tests, weapons qual, and psych eval all say you're ready for duty. But reports don't tell me the most important thing."

"What's that?"

"Why do you want to return to SRT?"

"This is what I've trained for. I want to get back to what I do best."

"Cut the BS, Mills. That's the same line of crap you fed the bureau shrink. You can still do your job right here in Dallas. Why SRT? If you're going to work for me, I want to know what makes you tick."

Plainly, sugarcoated answers wouldn't work on Carlson. Only one person knew the unvarnished truth, and that widow would be devastated if

Lexi didn't do everything possible to make it back to SRT. If the truth wasn't enough, she'd find another way.

"All right." Lexi leaned forward. "Cards on the table. I promised Trent Darby's wife I'd get the son of a bitch responsible for planting the mine that made her a widow. My best chance of doing that is by going where the action is. And that means SRT. I won't rest until Tony Belcher is behind bars or dead."

Carlson's half-cocked grin meant she hadn't shot herself in the prosthetic foot. "I've been an SRT commander for five years, and that's the best damn answer I've heard."

He turned his laptop around so Lexi could see the screen. He pressed play. The cobbled-together video clips from local media documented a devastating scene, including rescuers carrying out two lifeless bodies. Border Patrol and county subterranean camera footage in the sewer system paralleling the tunnel showed no unusual activity near the point of collapse.

"The Nogales Fire Department pulled out two survivors. One reported a coyote was ferrying a group of twelve through the tunnel at the time of the collapse. The fire chief suspects a gas pocket formed from a leak in the nearby sewer system and somehow ignited. The location of the collapse puts the investigation under the jurisdiction of the local police department. They have a well-trained detective squad, but until now, their primary focus has been drug and human trafficking. With the number of dead, and media attention, the police chief wants to get this investigation right and has asked for our help in ruling out an explosion."

"Ruling out? It sounds like the police chief is asking us to rubber-stamp his detectives. I won't do that."

"That's what I like to hear. You'll be the ATF liaison, assisting in the investigation. Do you have questions?"

"Just one. When do I leave?"

"As soon as you can pack your bags. Have Logistics book your flight."

Lexi walked out of Carlson's office ambivalent about her assignment. An SRT deployment should have her riding a wave of excitement, but serving as a one-person liaison wasn't what she'd envisioned for her first job back in the field. The Dallas office had an entire cadre of part-time SRT agents, including crisis negotiators, tactical operators, snipers, medics, and canine handlers, yet Lexi was going alone. At this rate, she'd never get to know her teammates and prove her worth to them.

"Baby steps." Lexi repeated the words of advice Nita had doled out when she first put on her prosthetic. She'd meant them both literally and figuratively. That learning to walk with an artificial leg required forgetting everything she knew about walking on two feet as if she were right out of the womb. Only then could Lexi take her first unsteady baby step.

Lexi reached the privacy of her cubicle before repeating the words and dialing Nita's cell. While the phone rang, she unzipped the go bag Ronald had assembled for her. It contained the best of everything on her Ant-Man list.

Her girlfriend answered on the fourth ring, using a playful tone. "Miss me already?"

"Always when I'm not with you," Lexi said. "I gather you're not with a patient."

"Nope. We had a cancellation, so I'm done for the day. I'm in the break room, studying sign language for a new patient."

"Even better. Can you meet me at home in an hour?"

"My, my. Special Agent Mills wants to play hooky for a little afternoon delight."

"We might have time for that, but first, I have wonderful news."

6

Nita gripped her cell tight after disconnecting the call. Lexi's news had left her more numb than after the call she'd received from her mother with the revelation her father had died unexpectedly from a heart attack. But she was stronger now than she was at sixteen. When she was younger, grief had launched her into a spiraling depression and earned her the scars below the ink on her arms. She pushed up a smock sleeve, rubbing the reminder of what rock bottom was like and why she'd promised herself to never go there again.

"This is a good thing," Nita said to herself, plopping down in the break-room chair and burying her head in her arms atop the table. For seven months, she'd built up Lexi's strength, agility, and confidence before handing her off to Samuel. All of that work was meant to get Lexi to this point. So why, then, wasn't Nita happy for the woman she loved? She should be popping the apple cider, but that was the furthest thing from her mind. In the forefront was worry about two things, both troubling her equally.

First, relationships with former patients often ended in disaster. Nita knew the risks going in, and now she was facing the foreseeable ending. Twice, she'd witnessed the aftermath when a colleague missed emotional transference despite the reassurance that their former patient's feelings were genuine. In both cases, the patients inevitably fell out of love once they'd gotten back to the life they'd had before losing a limb. And Lexi fit the mold. Both former patients who left their therapists were the strong, silent type with macho jobs.

Second, there was the constant danger. If they beat the odds by some quirk of fate, Nita doubted she could live in constant fear that the job might put Lexi in the morgue one day.

"Are you okay, Nita?"

She popped her head up, finding Samuel, the office empath and Lexi's now-former physical trainer. He had a gift for reading everyone's emotions better than Deanna Troi. The only time his talent worked against him was during a failed attempt at matchmaking at the clinic Christmas party. It had ended in a broken heart and him taking an eggnog shower.

"Oh, that face has girlfriend trouble written all over it," he said.

"In spades."

"What did my favorite butch do?"

"She healed."

"Ahh, and you're thinking you'll end up dumped like Sylvia and Layton."

"Why shouldn't I? The batting average around here stinks."

Samuel waved her off as if she were absurd. "Those two were desperate to find love and dove in headfirst without diagnosing the situation. But you were leery and slowly dipped your toes in."

"That I did. The U-Haul didn't appear until last month. That's a record in lesbian circles."

He laughed and pointed at the intricate reminder of her self-destructive past on her arm. "That's because you know the dangers of dependency. Neither you nor Lexi depend on the other to realize your worth in the world. Yet you make the other stronger. That's love."

Nita hoped his special intuition was working and that Lexi's love for her would last beyond her triumphant return to SRT. "Thanks, Samuel. I needed to hear that."

"But I haven't convinced you, have I?"

"Maybe if I had more time, but I have to go." While not totally persuaded by Samuel's pep talk, it was enough for Nita to put on her happy face. She kissed him on the cheek and rushed out the door.

Nita took in one more reassuring breath when she put the key in the lock of her apartment door. Maybe this assignment would turn out to be a simple consult, as Lexi had framed it. Then she'd come back, and they would begin working on Lexi's emotional healing.

She pushed the door open. The set of keys in the ceramic bowl atop the entry table solved the mystery of whether Lexi had made it home before Nita. Then rustling from down the hall confirmed where she was.

Stepping inside, Nita paused to take in the one room in the cramped apartment with Lexi's touch. From the big-screen TV to the sectional couch with the guacamole stain from a Super Bowl party years ago, this was Lexi's room and her preferred location to fall asleep. If Nita didn't insist on her coming to bed with her, Lexi would sleep there most nights.

Laying her backpack on the couch, Nita walked to the bedroom and leaned a shoulder against the doorframe. She watched silently while Lexi rifled through her dresser, pulling out stacks of T-shirts, cargo pants, and underwear. Her balance was nearly perfect on her new socket. The slight imperfection was likely due to her residual limb bothering her from this morning's treadmill session.

Lexi scooped the load of clothes in both arms and turned around. "Good. You're here. Do you remember where I stored my travel bag? It's not in the closet."

"Under the bed." Nita approached.

"That's right." Lexi transferred her clothes to the mattress and knelt on the floor before Nita could offer her help. Since the day Lexi learned to run on a prosthetic, the day before they shared their first kiss, she stopped acting like she was handicapped. She learned to perform nearly every task through rigorous training and repetition the same way she did before the amputation. Some required more modifications than others, like showering, but Nita was happy to help with that lesson.

"There it is." Lexi came up with her soft-sided tote and sat next to Nita on the bed, smelling like dust. "I only have an hour and fifteen before I have to leave for the airport."

Nita pawed at the number of clothes Lexi had gathered—a ton more than was required for an overnight consult. "How long do you expect to be gone?"

"Probably a day or two, but I learned a long time ago to pack for a week. I won't have time to wash on the road."

"Can I help with anything?"

"A new toothbrush in the package would be great. Oh, and a fresh travel razor."

"Sure." Nita went to the bathroom, collecting the toiletries Lexi would need for a freaking week on the road. She could occupy herself for two evenings, maybe three, without letting her worry get the best of her. But a week would be torture. To be on the safe side, she made a mental note to look up locations of nearby NA meetings every night this week.

Nita paused and stared into the mirror after placing the items into Lexi's travel kit. Samuel had helped with one aspect of her doubt but not the other. Until now, Lexi had an office job, and the most dangerous thing she faced was a paper cut. Then Nita remembered the horrific scene Lexi had related to her about the night she'd lost her leg. Today her girlfriend was about to walk headfirst into the same danger.

"I don't know if I can live with the worry," she whispered.

Lexi appeared through the doorway and stepped behind Nita, staring into the mirror. She wrapped her arms around Nita's midsection and rested her chin on a shoulder. Their short heights were complementary, with Lexi four inches taller. "What has you worried, Nita? I felt you pulling back this morning before I got the call."

"It's just me being silly." Nita wriggled from Lexi's hold, snatched up her toiletry kit, and returned to the bedroom. "This is what you've worked toward for the last eleven months. I'm happy for you."

Lexi followed and pulled on Nita's sleeve, encouraging her to sit with her on the bed. "If I know you as well as I think I do, that was the first time you've lied to me." She narrowed her eyes in apparent concern. "Talk to me, Nita. I could sense something was bothering you in the locker room today. I'll be worried about you the entire time if you don't tell me what's going on."

Escaping wasn't an option. Lexi had expertly cornered her into revealing her deepest insecurities about their relationship. If she didn't come clean in the next hour, Lexi might not have a clear head in the coming days when she needed it the most.

Nita couldn't change the dangers of Lexi's job, and other than quitting, Lexi could do nothing to abate her fears. That was something Nita would have to work through herself, so she decided to reveal the fear Lexi could allay. Nita started by lowering her head to a weighty sigh. "Samuel and I did our jobs, and now you're back to your old life."

Lexi lifted her chin with a hand until their eyes met. "And you think that means my old life doesn't have room for you?"

"Yes." Nita's lips trembled, but she refused to cry. Foreseeable ending or not, she knew the risks going into this relationship.

Lexi gently gripped Nita by the upper arms, her furrowed brow forecasting a heartfelt reply. "Get this straight, Anita Flores. I love you, and until I take my dying breath, I will want you by my side. I came to you physically and emotionally broken. You refused to let me quit when I'd thought I'd reached my limit. You called me on my bullshit, and every time I pushed you away, you pushed back. But ultimately, you made me whole." She pulled Nita's hand to her heart. "And filled this in a way no woman ever could."

Nita raised her hand to Lexi's lips and ran her fingertips across them. "I know you believe that."

"Down to my bones." Lexi let a wry smile emerge. "And it doesn't count any less because I have thirty-one fewer bones than you."

"Technically, twenty-nine. Two are now a third of their original length."

"One good thing about this assignment: I have an excuse for not attending your cousin's bachelorette party tomorrow night." Lexi snickered and eased Nita flat on the bed. "Now for that afternoon delight before my Uber arrives."

7

Lexi had checked in her bags and cleared through the law enforcement officer TSA checkpoint before settling into a seat near the wall of windows several feet from the agents' counter at her gate. Pulling out her agency-issued tablet, she connected her wired earphones. Lexi then opened the briefing packet Carlson's secretary had emailed her on the way to the airport. The opening paragraph detailed that the local chief who had requested ATF assistance hadn't provided a point of contact for Lexi once she hit the ground. His instructions were for her to go directly to the tunnel scene and report to the lieutenant in charge.

She clicked on the first document—the Nogales Police Department incident log detailing the initial 911 call. A local resident whose property was less than fifty feet from the international border on the rural outskirts of town reported hearing an explosion at 4:55 a.m. The embedded audio file revealed no specific information other than the caller's name and address and that the blast had rattled his windows. A separate Border Patrol video from camera station 1432, equipped with a night vision lens, reflected a vibration at 4:55:18. Then a second later, a plume of smoke or dust rose a quarter-mile in the distance.

Lexi moved on to the Nogales Fire Department on-scene commander's initial incident report. Station 1 had rolled with the police to an unspecified location, using only geocoordinates from Border Patrol as a general guide. CBP reported it had sent a roving patrol to investigate, which radioed more precise coordinates directly to the responding units. Fire units had arrived on the scene at 5:04. Two CBP agents then directed firefighters to a three-foot-wide tunnel entrance located among desert shrubs and reported a suspected collapse. The on-scene commander then sent in a two-person rescue team, confirming the failure and bringing out two injured survivors. One, a suspected human smuggler, remained silent while the other reported a dozen were still trapped. The on-scene commander's end-of-shift report detailed gruesome findings before another station had relieved him and his crew. The first two bodies recovered were those of a mother cradling her infant daughter.

Lexi paused long enough to clear that horrifying image from her head.

She then opened her web browser to stream live local news from Tucson, the city with the nearest network television station. The tunnel collapse had made every national news outlet. Networks were streaming reports from their regional reporters with film clips of rescue crews moving in and out on a continuous loop. But that wasn't what Lexi needed. Instead, she wanted to hear reports from the locals who knew the inner workings of the city and the border traffic.

One local station was interviewing a man whose name matched that of the 911 caller. Either he wasn't affiliated with the traffickers or he was and didn't know better than to show his face on TV. He made one interesting comment about his property being near a sewer washout that connected the two Nogales cities on either side of the international border.

A tap on Lexi's left shoulder drew her attention. She removed her headphones and shifted her stare, finding the attractive gate agent she saw when she arrived. "Yes?"

The woman leaned in and whispered, "Agent Mills, right?"

"That's right."

"We should begin preboarding soon. The captain has asked that you board first."

"Did he say why?"

"She likes to greet all armed LEOs before her flights."

"All right." Lexi repacked her things into her backpack and followed the ticketing agent to the gate door.

"Enjoy your flight, Agent Mills," she whispered.

A warm sensation spread in Lexi as she walked down the gangway. The simple greeting and special request made her feel more like an agent than the eleven months she'd spent at the Dallas field office. Getting back to actual investigative work was like being called back up to the big leagues. She'd spent the last year on injured reserve, and this assignment was her big break. If she proved herself capable, her injury wouldn't matter, and Carlson would throw her bigger bones in the coming weeks.

At the cabin door, a flight attendant greeted her. "You must be Agent Mills. You can take your seat. I'll let the captain know you've boarded. She'll come out to see you when she's completed the preflight checklist."

"Thank you." Lexi nodded at the other attendant tidying up a seat row as she passed. She stopped at her assigned row, lowered her backpack from her shoulder, and shimmied across to the window seat.

The moment Lexi sat, her service Glock dug into her left ribs, so she adjusted it for better comfort. As a sworn officer, she'd worn it every day at work in Dallas, but that was mainly for show. With no field action, the only time she'd removed it from its paddle holster was for range training and cleaning.

She then retrieved her tablet again and settled into watching more local interviews to get a flavor for the area. Minutes later, the pilot appeared at her row. She extended her hand. "Agent Mills, I'm Captain Mason. I'd like to welcome you aboard our flight."

Normally, Lexi would stand when greeting someone, but the narrow row made it impossible to observe social graces. So instead, she reached across and shook the pilot's hand. "It's a pleasure, Captain. If I may ask, why did you invite me on board early?"

"To shake your hand, Agent Mills. My crew is based out of Kansas City, and I recognized your name on the LEO alert from the news reports last year. I wanted to thank you personally for your service and sacrifice. The crew knows we have a real-life hero aboard and are prepared to treat you like royalty today, so please take advantage." She winked. "Ask for the whole can of Coke."

"I think I will."

"Is there anything we can get you before takeoff?"

"If there's a chance we can get into Tucson any quicker, I'd be grateful. I'm eager to get to work."

"Where are you headed?"

"Nogales."

"The tunnel collapse?" Lexi replied with an affirmative nod. "Heart-breaking. I'll see if I can shave off some time." Before the captain returned to the flight deck, she pointed toward Lexi's row and added, "By the way, we made sure the middle seat was empty."

"I'll be damned." Lexi grinned. She could get used to the royal treatment.

Soon, passengers began an entertaining parade of juggling overstuffed carry-on suitcases over their heads to Tetris the hell out of the limited storage bin space.

The local news reports on her screen had repeated the same video, so Lexi returned her tablet to her backpack and stowed it beneath the seat in front of her. Soon, the trickle of passengers slowed, giving Lexi a decent chance of having a row to herself for the two-and-a-half-hour flight. With any luck, she could get in a proper nap and hit the ground refreshed.

The thumping toward the front of the craft meant the attendant was closing the hatch. One late-boarding passenger wobbled down the aisle, carrying a final Tetris piece. He zagged past Lexi, giving her cause to release a tiny grin. Then seconds later, Late Larry appeared at Lexi's row.

"Damn connections. My last flight landed fifteen minutes ago in terminal C. Do you mind if I put my laptop bag under the middle seat?"

"Not at all. Knock yourself out." *Impressive*, Lexi thought. This man deplaned, navigated between terminals, boarded here, and buckled in fifteen minutes, and he barely broke a sweat. His long legs clearly played a part. Also, the high-and-tight haircut, muscular trim, and destination suggested he was Army. Those guys were accustomed to hustling under pressure.

Minutes after takeoff, when the attendant announced the all-clear to use electronic devices safely, Late Larry leaned to retrieve his backpack, but his height and thick muscles made it difficult to maneuver in the tight space. When he lifted the strap, the laptop slid out, striking Lexi on the prosthetic shin.

"My gosh. I'm sorry. I'm such a klutz." He picked it up and returned upright in his seat. "Did I hurt you?"

"No worries." Lexi formed a fist and tapped her plastic polymer socket. "Prosthetic."

"Thank goodness for small favors. Let me make it up to you. Can I buy you a drink when the beverage cart comes?"

"Thank you, but I'm on duty."

"Cop?" He lowered his tray table, placed the laptop on it, and pressed the power button.

"Federal."

"Line of duty?" He pointed at Lexi's leg and continued after her confirming nod. "And you're still on the job? I'm impressed." He extended his hand. "Rick Ferrario."

"Lexi Mills." She shook his hand before pointing at the computer screen. It had booted up to a red-and-white emblem with a castle in the middle and the word "Essayons" at the bottom. "Army?" she asked.

"Retired. I'm now a combat engineer instructor at Fort Leonard Wood."

"Is that what you did in the Army?"

"Yep. For twenty years, and a wake-up call."

"Is that like the Navy's Seabees?"

"Sort of. Those guys mostly build and do a little demolition underwater. Combat engineers spend most of their time destroying things to clear a path for the infantry and then building up defensive positions."

"Did you like it?"

"I loved it, except when I'd come across IEDs. Those EOD guys who came in to disarm the mines either had a screw loose or were the bravest sons of bitches on the planet." Rick clicked the touch pad on his laptop a few times. "How about you, Lexi? What agency are you with?"

"I'm one of those people with a screw loose. I'm an explosives expert for the ATF."

"Well, don't I feel like the fool." He pointed at Lexi's prosthesis. "Is that how you earned the leg?"

"Yep. A year ago."

"And you're already back working? That makes you one of those sons of bitches in my book. What happened? If you don't mind me asking."

"My partner and I were supposed to clear a path so the FBI rescue team could breach a compound full of some pretty bad guys, but he tripped a Bouncing Betty."

Rick grimaced. "Ouch. Those things are vicious."

An image of Darby looking back at her and giving her a thumbs-up in slow motion made its way to the front of Lexi's mind. The memory of him being blown backward and the Bouncing Betty rising behind him would forever haunt her. Lexi swallowed back the guilt of pushing so hard that night to go after Belcher. She should have insisted on taking point to absorb that blast.

"My partner wasn't so lucky." Lexi forced the emotion back down her throat. "He never made it home."

"I know what you went through. Two of my buddies never made it home either. Others had their arms and legs blown off like you." Rick shifted his gaze to an unspecific point in the air with a distant look. He then steered his stare directly into Lexi's eyes, almost seeing right through her, as if he had been there that night. "Consider yourself extra lucky. My best friend lost both arms and a leg in that hellhole. He took his life last week. I'm on my way to his funeral."

"I'm so sorry."

"How did you do it?" Rick closed his laptop and shifted to better face Lexi. "How did you bounce back after your injuries?"

Recovering from her visible injuries was a long road, one every amputee faced. And, like her, combat veterans faced the lasting trauma of being in the line of fire or the kill zone. Lexi didn't have to think about her answer. She had eventually tucked away the emotional damage for two reasons. "The love of a good woman and revenge."

"Love, I understand, but revenge?"

"I know who was responsible for planting the mine that killed my partner, and I won't rest until I get him."

"I get that. You're giving your loss meaning. Maybe that's why Ben gave up. His sacrifice became meaningless when we gave up every inch of hard-fought land, packed up the embassy, and left last year. I wish I could do more for those still struggling and help them make sense of it all."

"In the end, they'll have to find their own path," Lexi said, "but I'd say you're doing plenty to give meaning to their sacrifice."

"How do you figure?"

Lexi shifted in her seat to emphasize her next point. "You're teaching others hard-learned lessons. You're doing everything possible to ensure no one makes the same mistakes your comrades did. If your teachings save a single life or one limb, you're honoring their sacrifice."

The flight attendant dragged the beverage cart closer before offering Rick and Lexi a napkin. "Would you care for something to drink, Miss Mills?" The vanilla greeting, minus Lexi's title, was clearly intentional. It served as a reminder that she was queen for the day while keeping her identity confidential.

"A Coke for me, and I'd like to buy this man a drink. He's a genuine hero."

"We seem to be among several today," the attendant said. "What can I get you, sir?"

"Thank you, Lexi, but it's not necessary."

The attendant leaned in. "Drinks are on the house for heroes today. What will it be, sir?"

"Ben would've liked tequila."

Perfect, Lexi thought. Trent would have approved too.

"Coming up." The attendant distributed the drinks, including the whole can of Coke for Lexi and extra snacks.

Lexi raised her fizzling cup of ice and soda. "Here's to Trent and Ben. May their sacrifices have meaning."

Rick clinked his cup with hers. "And here's to keeping your eye on the prize, Lexi Mills. Godspeed in catching that son of a bitch."

8

The pilot kept her promise and landed the flight at Tucson International Airport fifteen minutes ahead of schedule. Deplaning was orderly, and Lexi and Rick walked through the busy terminal, side by side, after exchanging phone numbers.

"How long are you in town for?" Rick asked. "My old squad is getting together at Willy's tomorrow night after the funeral. If you're around, let me return the honor and buy you a drink."

"I'd like that, Rick, but I'm heading to Nogales as soon as I get my rental car."

"Ah, the tunnel collapse. Do the police suspect foul play?"

"It's too early to tell, but that's why I'm here—to fine-tooth comb the scene." Riding the escalator to the lower floor, Lexi said, "I have to get my bags first, but I'd be happy to drop you in town."

"Thanks, Lexi, but an Army buddy is picking me up." At the bottom, Rick shook her hand. "It was a pleasure meeting you, Lexi Mills. If you ever find yourself in the middle of Missouri, look me up."

"It was a pleasure, Rick Ferrario. The same goes if you're ever in Dallas."

They parted ways, leaving Lexi with a good feeling. Their chance meeting made her realize she *was* luckier than most explosion survivors.

She had Nita to lift her whenever she was low and had her thirst for Belcher to keep her moving forward.

After retrieving her bags and signing for her rental car, Lexi loaded up and entered the geocoordinates of the tunnel collapse into the phone maps application. Once on Interstate 19, she took the first highway exit for fast food and to load up on a case of plastic water bottles and comfort snacks. Back on the road, she settled into a comfortable highway drive for the next sixty miles. It was a race to see if she could make it to the border town before the last slivers of the setting sun slipped behind the western horizon.

The glow of red and blue emergency lights hailed Lexi for the past mile, but she couldn't get to the location from the highway. Her phone navigation assistant directed her through town, bypassing the US Customs point of entry. It led her to International Drive, paralleling the United States and Mexico border.

The red-and-blue glow grew brighter. Soon, she came across two Nogales Police Department vehicles parked at the turnoff to a gravel road heading north, away from the border. It was the exact location her phone app instructed her to turn right, so she came to a slow, creeping stop and rolled down the driver's window. When an officer approached her vehicle and shined a flashlight in her face, she showed him the ATF badge she had dangling from a chain around her neck.

"ATF Special Agent Lexi Mills. Chief Hernandez should have added me to the access list."

"Credentials, please, Agent Mills," the officer said. Lexi had her credential case ready in a cup holder in the center console. He then annotated something on a tablet, snapped a picture of Lexi, and waved her forward. "Follow the tracks. You can't miss it."

When she drew closer, dozens of police, fire, Border Patrol, sheriff, city works, and media vehicles were lined up in relative order. No one controlled parking, so she pulled in even with a sheriff's cruiser. She then popped the trunk, unzipped the go bag Ronald had assembled, and first donned her helmet and dark blue ATF windbreaker, and strapped on her kneepads. She then loaded her cargo pants pockets with a flashlight, five sets of latex gloves, tweezers, a utility pocketknife, and a wad of clear evidence bags. She also filled the black backpack marked *ATF* across the front with her tablet, a high-power digital camera, extra ammo magazines, two different handheld detectors, swab kits, water bottles, snacks, an N95 particle mask, and goggles.

Double-checking the shoelaces on her boots, Lexi set off on foot toward the action. Stanchions, yellow police tape, and strategically positioned officers along the perimeter delineated the controlled area to keep onlookers and the media at a safe distance. Flood lights lit four distinct locations. Media vans, field reporters, and camera operators congregated in one area outside the tape. One wouldn't realize it by the streams of cables running from the vans, but in Lexi's experience, the news crews had an unwritten agreement of organized chaos. No one crossed the other's lines, and no one poached another's broadcasting location.

After identifying herself at the entry control point, a deputy asked for her credentials. He entered information into a tablet, snapped another picture of her, and asked her to sign the log. Inside the tape, portable lights flooded three areas. Farthest out, about fifty yards in the distance, was the incident site. Closer in was the comfort station with portable johns, a mobile canteen, and a tent likely filled with cots for rescue workers. The third was the command post with a single canopy and too many pieces of electronics to be mistaken as anything else. She headed there.

Lexi stepped close enough to make out the group of personnel under the well-lit canopy. The collection of bars on their collars suggested she'd come to the right place. Most were talking in pairs, but a deputy monitoring the radio equipment lowered his headphones and looked up. "Can I help you?"

Lexi tightened her grip on her backpack and pointed at her badge dangling chest level. "Which one is the on-scene commander?"

"Lieutenant Martinez." The officer pointed to the one with a good start on a middle-aged beer belly.

Lexi nodded her thanks and continued toward Martinez, whose arm patch identified him as Nogales police. He was talking to another man, whose insignia identified him as a Nogales fire lieutenant. She waited for an appropriate pause in their conversation. "Excuse me, Lieutenant Martinez, I'm Special Agent Mills from the ATF. Chief Hernandez asked for our assistance."

Martinez eyed Lexi up and down as if sizing her up for which curb to kick her to. "You're wasting your time here, Mills. Our guys are more than capable of investigating this scene."

"I'm sure you have an excellent team, Lieutenant, but your chief asked for an extra set of eyes. I'm here to provide whatever help I can."

He took in a chest-expanding breath, sucking in his belly a fraction. "Suit yourself. Follow directions and stay out of the way."

"That I can do." Lexi turned her attention to the other lieutenant, glancing at his name tag. "Are you the ranking firefighter, Lieutenant Sanchez?" She continued following a yes and a handshake. "What's your assessment?"

After explaining about the smuggler tunnel running parallel to the cross-border sewer and the human trafficking aspect, he continued, "We've pulled out ten bodies so far. Four were children. The birth certificate found on the mother said the youngest was eight months old. According to a survivor, there might be two more, so we're still in rescue mode."

Lexi clenched her jaw to hold back her emotion. Any loss of life was horrible, but the death of children made it especially heartbreaking. "Can you tell me more about the sewer system?" she asked.

"The entire system is aging, especially on the Mexican side. It leaks, gets clogged in the rainy season, and drug traffickers cut holes in the walls like it's Swiss cheese. Six months ago, we found the bodies of three smugglers in another tunnel collapse about a mile from here. The city has its hands full, keeping up with repairs, monitoring the methane gas pockets, and creating new vent points. Our best theory going in was a buildup of methane that ignited from someone in the group lighting a smoke."

"Thanks, Lieutenant. I appreciate the insight." Lexi returned her attention to Martinez. His tight expression suggested he still didn't appreciate her presence. "I'd like to walk the site. Who should I report to?"

"Detective Noah Black. You can't miss him. He sticks out like a sore thumb."

Lexi crossed the uneven desert terrain toward the other set of floodlights. The smell of cooking grease wafted in the air from the canteen tent. A half-dozen men in hard hats milled about a crane that had been brought in. Two dumped wheelbarrows full of debris into piles. Lexi made a mental note. Unless they marked each load with the grid location where they pulled it from, any forensic evidence found would have diminishing value.

She approached the closest worker without a shovel. "Where can I find Detective Black?"

"He's at the sewer through the secondary access point," the man said.

"How do I get there?"

"It would be easier if I show you." The man gestured east. "Stay behind me. You don't want to disturb a snake nest."

Shit, Lexi thought. She wasn't afraid of many things, but a snake was one of them.

The escort led, using a flashlight to illuminate their path. He stepped them around shrubs of various sizes for a hundred yards until they reached a concrete storm washout. He shined his light at a tree five feet from its edge. "You can use the rope to get down there. About twenty yards north, you'll come across a maintenance door to the sewer system. The officer there will point you in the right direction."

"Got it. Thanks." Rappelling was on Lexi's to-do list to practice with her new socket, but she had yet to get to it. Nothing like trial by fire.

She lowered herself down the eight-foot slope, using a hand-over-hand method. The section of residual limb she'd irritated on the treadmill this morning ached all the way down. The pain reminded her she'd have to apply another sock layer on her limb the first chance she got.

At the bottom, Lexi made out the officer several yards down before pulling out her flashlight to illuminate the muddy, debris-filled path. The stench from the puddles of liquid suggested they weren't formed by storm runoff but by the nearby sewer. Tiptoeing the best her prosthetic would allow, she reached the police officer guarding the entrance and displayed her badge.

"ATF. Which way to Detective Black?"

"Hang a left inside and follow the lights. You can't miss him." The officer was the second person to make that point. Now her curiosity was piqued.

The concrete tomb was lit inside with strings of temporary shop lights every fifteen feet and stank ten times worse than the washout. The path zigzagged her twice and then straightened out. Water, she hoped, dripped in several spots, adding to the creepiness of being in a sewer.

As she stepped farther down the path, two workers came into view. They were installing metal support struts that reached the ceiling near a rough opening in the wall about six feet in diameter. She approached. "Detective Black?"

"Upstream, so turn left. You may need a flashlight."

This had to be the most complicated route Lexi had to take to a crime scene, making her realize she should have padded her socket at the comfort station. That was her first lesson learned since returning to duty with a prosthetic.

Using her flashlight as a guide through the dark, narrow tunnel wide enough to only walk single file, she aimed for a faint glow in the distance. A radio squawked from that direction. As she closed in, one figure came into view. She directed her light toward the ground to not blind the person. "Detective Black?" Lexi called out.

He rose from his crouched stance and turned. "Yes?" Surprisingly, his height and build were average, even with his helmet, police windbreaker, and well-worn boots. Neither would make him stand out, as she'd been led to believe.

"I'm Special Agent Mills from the ATF. I believe you've been expecting me."

"Wow. I put in the request only six hours ago. Your agency is quick." He approached and extended his latex-gloved hand. "I'm Noah."

"Lexi." She squinted to make out his features. The skin on his face appeared blotchy, but she attributed it to the dim lighting.

He bobbed his head left and right, looking behind her. "Where's the rest of your team?"

"Your chief made it sound like he only wanted another set of eyes on your findings, so the Dallas office sent only me."

A breathy exhale. "I should have expected as much. The chief fought me tooth and nail about bringing in the feds. This must be his version of placating me while covering his ass."

Noah's spontaneous comment confirmed that Lexi's earlier assessment of the lieutenant was spot-on. She'd have to tread lightly around the local brass and stick close to the one person who seemed to want her here.

"Well, I'm here and eager to get to work. Can you show me what you've found so far?"

"Follow me." Noah gestured his chin farther upstream and cast his flashlight in that direction, stopping after twenty yards. He pointed the beam to a ledge cut deeper into the wall of the six-foot-tall tunnel, illuminating an eclectic collection of church candles.

"I recognize the ones in the center. Those are for the Virgin of Guadalupe, right?" Lexi said.

"Good eye, but those aren't what caught my attention. See the three on the left? Those are for Jesús Malverde. He was Mexico's version of Robin Hood around the turn of the twentieth century. In recent years, he has become the patron saint for Mexican smugglers. That suggests at least three narco-traffickers come through here regularly."

"And the one on the right?"

"That's for St. Jude, the patron saint for Mexico City's down-and-out class. That tells me at least one migrant being ferried through this tunnel came from there. It's relatively fresh and appears to have been burned recently." He pointed farther upstream. "The tunnel goes on for another twenty-five yards. By the way, you're standing in Mexico."

Impressive, Lexi thought. Noah was obviously well versed in the local culture and paid attention to the finest detail. "That's some good detective work. Where does the other end lead to?"

"A bedroom closet in a single-family house owned by an aunt of a suspected member of the Sinaloa Cartel."

"What's your take on the collapse?"

"I'm not buying the fire lieutenant's theory of a methane gas pocket."

"Why not?"

"It needed an ignition point."

"Couldn't someone have lit a cigarette like the lieutenant theorized?"

"But why? The tunnel isn't that long. And based on the location of the altar, the group stopped here to pay tribute before moving on. It only takes a few minutes to get from the altar to the collapse point. So why would someone light up for a smoke in a tunnel when they'd be aboveground in the US in another minute?"

"You make a good point. It makes little sense. I'd like to see the collapse site and get some readings."

"I can take you, but you won't get anything valid. I tried earlier, but the sewer gasses gave us nothing but false readings. So all I can tell you at this point is that the debris isn't radioactive. That's why we're bringing it up aboveground."

"I saw them hauling up the first loads. I'd still like to see the collapse site, though." Lexi paused, debating whether to ask her next question, but she had to be thorough. "Based on what I've seen so far, I think I already know the answer. Now, don't take offense, but I have to ask. Are the workers marking the grid location before bringing it up?"

"None taken. You're just orienting yourself to the scene. Yes. I created a grid, and the watch sergeant is supervising the excavation."

"Top notch, Noah."

"There's nothing to see from this side of the collapse," he said. "But I'd like to take some readings from the rubble our crew has brought up before I take you to the other side."

"Would you mind if I use ATF detectors?"

"By all means."

Once they reached the temporary lights, Lexi got a better look at Noah. The blotchiness on his face was more prominent. His skin appeared to be two different colors. Most of his face was darker toned, making her think he was of Hispanic heritage, but the skin around his mouth and chin and below his eyes was pale white like the keys on a piano. She wouldn't exactly describe him as a sore thumb, but he indeed appeared different.

Once outside, down the muddy washout, and up the slope with the aid of the rope, Noah led Lexi back to the other end of the tunnel, where his team was gathering debris for testing. She lowered her backpack to the ground and pulled out the Fido X4, the most advanced handheld explosive trace detector on the market.

Noah issued a whistle, demonstrating his appreciation for the device. "I've asked for one of those, but it's not in the budget."

"It's my favorite."

After putting on latex gloves, Lexi stepped to a pile. It had a cardboard marker, showing they had recovered the debris from grid area D-3. She then swabbed a few rocks and inserted the test strip in the detector. While waiting for the test to cycle, Lexi moved several stones, looking for one that might have scorching and possible explosive residue. Near the bottom of the pile, she noticed the tattered edge of something white half-buried beneath a rock. Lexi carefully extracted it with her tweezers and brought it closer to her face for examination. It was a playing card, but it appeared different—a red ace of spades.

"Hey, Noah. I have something." He approached. Lexi turned the card over. On the back was the word "Border" crossed out with a red *X*. "What do you think it means?" she asked.

"I don't know, but I think you may have found the bomber's message."

Her Fido detector beeped. The onboard screen lit up with a red message. "Was your detector picking up nitroglycerin earlier?"

"No. Why?"

"Mine just did."

9

Lexi snapped a picture of the playing card before placing it in an evidence bag and annotating when and where she found it. She then uploaded the rubble test results via Bluetooth to her phone. Finally, she prepared a text message to her SRT commander and the only intelligence officer at the Dallas division she trusted but paused before hitting send. She'd walked through many minefields in her career, but the most frustrating ones were political. Accordingly, her instinct to notify her chain of command had to take a back seat to her primary role.

"I'm your liaison, Noah, so I'll follow your lead. Who gets to know our findings first?"

"The person who will help us the most."

"And who is that?" she asked.

"It's definitely not my lieutenant or chief," Noah said. "So that puts the ball in your court."

Lexi hit speed dial on her phone, the call connecting on the third ring. "Agent Carlson, this is Mills. I have a critical update."

"What do you have?" A flush sounded in the background, forcing Lexi to hold back a laugh.

"I picked up trace residue of nitroglycerin from debris brought up from the tunnel site." She pressed send on her message. "I'm texting you the test readings right now." A ding sounded over the phone.

"How many samples tested positive?"

"I've taken six samples so far. One showed trace."

"That could mean a victim was carrying nitro pills at the time of the collapse. We'll need more than one reading to justify sounding the alarm."

"We also found what we think is a calling card." Lexi brought up the pictures and texted them to Carlson. "The message on the back makes it seem like the bomber is crossing off a checklist of targets, so I sent a copy to Kaplan Shaw in Intel."

"Dammit, Mills. You should know better than to jump the chain of command."

"My apologies, sir. The Kansas City team did things differently. We kept everyone in the loop in real time."

"Which is why many agents jump to conclusions. They get unfiltered information without it being vetted. From now on, everything goes through me. It's my job to decide who gets the information from the field."

"Got it," Lexi replied, biting her tongue. But policy was policy, and like a good soldier, she would follow orders, even if her SRT commander was a control freak.

"Good. We need to do this one by the book. So keep at it and find us a second sample to confirm. Until then, stay in place and give your advice."

"I will, sir." Lexi hung up, her mind focusing on the nitro and playing card. Calculating how little explosive it would take to cause that much damage in the tunnel made her cringe at the sentiment behind the playing-card message. So much more of the nitro was likely still out there.

The amount of nitro stolen and unaccounted for in the last decade would make every man, woman, and child quake in their shoes. And the last documented theft in this region of the country involved the man she hated most in the world—Tony Belcher. And every fiber of Lexi's being told her she was onto his scent.

A new sense of purpose built in Lexi when she turned to Noah. It was the same drive that had her walking again and running a treadmill every day. "Our intel unit will work on the playing card." She handed the evidence bag to Noah. "My gut tells me we're onto something and that the tunnel is only the beginning."

"Mine too. Care to help me convince my bosses of it?" Noah removed his helmet, revealing stringy dark hair that reached his chin, about the same length as Lexi's. A distinctive inch-wide white streak that split in two ran down the center of his head like a skunk. The sore-thumb comment suddenly made sense, but she liked it. The white spots and streaks made him different. Like she was—female, gay, and half Black.

"Let's do it." Lexi returned her equipment to her backpack and removed her helmet, strapping it to a loop on her pack. She then snatched a bottle from the side pouch, dumped a little water in her hand, and splashed her face before running her hands through her hair, hoping it was enough to tame the goofy hat hair she was prone to.

"You look fine, Mills. No one would guess you traipsed through a quarter-mile of sewer tonight."

Activity around the tunnel access point picked up. Then Noah's radio clipped to his waist squawked again. "Send down two more lights. One large. One small," someone broadcasted.

"Shit." Noah sighed. His defeated reaction suggested the radio call wasn't talking about lights.

"Bad news?"

"Yeah. The media have been monitoring our channels. 'Lights' is code for 'bodies.'"

"And 'small' means they found another child." Lexi's heart shrank a fraction more. That made five children senselessly killed. Whoever did this needed to be brought to justice.

Lieutenants Martinez and Sanchez approached with radios in hand. Then camera lights came to life from the other side of the perimeter tape. If the media hadn't figured out the code yet, the activity and arrival of the on-scene commanders had likely clued them in that something was afoot.

More firefighters from the comfort station double-timed over, securing their helmets as they jogged. Two pushed a gurney with containers of medical supplies in case the person recovered was still alive. But based on the amount of rubble down in the tunnel, they were more optimistic than realistic.

Lexi and Noah settled in next to the lieutenants while the crane slowly brought up its length of cable. Moments later, the top end of the cage emerged, rising vertically from its underground tomb. A worker latched onto a rung and gently guided it safely from the hole as the crane slowly swung in that direction. The moment he brought the cage to rest, the two paramedics with the medical equipment rushed forward. One checked the body for signs of life but shook his head, acknowledging what was apparent to everyone with eyes on this horrific scene.

The medics unlashed the body from the cage and lifted it out. A wave of nausea struck Lexi when she realized the bloody, tattered body was that of a young girl. She dug deep to not let the sight overtake her, but the back of her throat swelled nearly shut. The young girl was no taller than Gretchen when Lexi had said goodbye to her last year. A three-year-old girl, seeking a new life in America with her mother or father, had died for what? So some madman could leave his calling card? Taking the life of innocents never made sense and made Lexi that much more determined to find whoever did this.

The lieutenants shifted as if preparing to go back to their command tent, but Noah placed a hand on Sanchez's arm. "We found something you two should see." He retrieved the evidence bag with the playing card from his windbreaker pocket. "Agent Mills found this among the debris we brought up." He handed it to Martinez. The lieutenant inspected then returned it. "She also detected trace amounts of nitroglycerin, but it wasn't of enough quantity to say that caused the blast. Everything we've found so far leads me to believe this might not have been a methane explosion as first suspected."

"'Might not' isn't enough for me to up-channel this. When can you complete documenting the scene?"

"That's hard to say while we're conducting rescue operations. But, as soon as we switch to recovery, I can accelerate my team sifting through the debris and bring up enough samples to get a definitive reading on the presence of nitro."

"With the media coverage, that won't happen for a while. The chief doesn't want us giving up prematurely, so we'll be in rescue mode until we break through to the other side." Martinez turned the volume down on the chirping radio he was holding. "Go home, get some sleep, and come back in the morning."

"All right, sir." Noah returned the evidence bag to his pocket and stepped away with Lexi. "Want some chow or coffee at the canteen?"

"Thank you, but no. If I drink coffee now, I'll be up all night. I should check into my hotel and get a few hours of sleep."

"Where are you staying?"

"The Holiday Inn Express."

"Good choice. Most of the hotels in town are dumps. I'll call ahead and make sure they didn't cancel your reservation."

After exchanging phone numbers and agreeing to meet back here at seven in the morning, Lexi stowed her gear in the trunk of her rental car and drove to her hotel. She feared if she paused for even a minute, the weight of the day would overpower her.

In the parking lot, Lexi assessed her surroundings. She was traveling alone, albeit armed, in a border town not historically friendly to law enforcement. Those circumstances dictated precaution, so she removed her ATF jacket, stuffed it into her go bag, and took everything into the hotel in one trip.

The room was better than most she'd stayed in while on SRT assignments, sometimes settling for the back seat of an SUV for a bed. But this bed looked too good. Lexi dropped everything except the limb ointment she'd dug out of her bag and rested her service Glock still in its paddle holster on the mattress. Sleep was calling, but she still needed to take care of her leg and mental health. Pulling out her phone, she dialed Nita, put it on speaker, and laid it on the bed. While it rang, she removed her shoe from her good foot, lowered her pants to her knees, and sat on the bed. Nita picked up.

"Hey, you," Nita said. "I'm glad you called. How are you holding up?"

"I got to my room a few minutes ago, and the only things I can think about are you and sleep."

"What about your limb care?"

"I'm starting it right now." Lexi unzipped her pant leg, rolled down the neoprene sleeve on her thigh to the top of her socket, pulled the whole prosthetic through the bottom of her pant leg, and placed it on the bed. She then kicked her pants to the floor with her good foot. The flesh and tendons around the nub felt instantly relieved. Walking on the uneven surfaces getting to and inside the tunnel had taken its toll.

"How was the flight?" Nita asked.

"Great, actually." Lexi removed her single sock layer, making a mental note to add a second layer in the morning for extra cushioning. "I met an Army vet who worked with explosives when he was overseas. Talking with him made me realize how lucky I am to have you."

"If that happens every time you travel, I might get used to you going away for a few days." Nita laughed.

Lexi then rolled the liner off, releasing a loud sigh of relief.

"Was that your liner coming off?" Nita asked.

"You know it." Letting the skin breathe after being encased all day was the best part of doffing her prosthetic. Though seeing her cut-off leg was the ultimate reminder of her injury, having her skin exposed to the air made her feel like her old self when she was whole.

"How's the investigation going? Can you talk about it?" Nita asked.

Lexi squeezed a small amount of prosthetic salve into her hand. It was made of a soothing combination of ingredients, including beeswax and coconut oil. She then gently massaged it into the skin everywhere the socket touched.

"It's slow. You wouldn't believe the workforce required to extract tons of rock from a collapsed tunnel."

"I've been watching the news. I heard they pulled out more bodies tonight. Were you there?"

"Yes." Lexi slowed her massage when the smudged, bloody face of that dead girl flashed in her head. "It was rough, Nita. She couldn't have been more than three."

"I'm so sorry you had to witness that, Lex. In my line of work, I see children who have been injured every day, and that is hard enough to get through."

"I don't want to think about it anymore tonight." Lexi was quickly losing her battle with exhaustion and let a yawn escape. "Can you fall asleep with me?"

"I'd love to." Nita's voice took on a calming tone. "Lie down and curl up with a pillow like you do at home."

Over the next few minutes, Nita talked about the rest of her day, the progress she'd made in learning American Sign Language for a new patient, and how the air conditioner was acting up again. Soon, Lexi's thoughts drifted, focusing on nothing but the sound of her girlfriend's voice and the softness of her pillow. She relished this twilight state between sleep and consciousness. Her day had been filled with unspeakable sights, and if the past year was an accurate predictor, her night would be filled with horrible memories.

Lexi held on for as long as she could before sleep returned her to the night she wanted to forget the most.

10

"Stack them over there, fellas." Retired Army Major Jamie Porter pointed toward a sectioned-off area of the Texas warehouse. The men dressed in brown shirts and matching shorts then began the tedious task of unloading fifty cases of meals ready to eat.

On the fifth trip from the truck, one delivery man asked, "What are you preparing for, the apocalypse?"

"Something like that." Fifty cases of MREs were enough to feed one man for a year or fifty men for a week, but these guys didn't need to know which scenario Porter was preparing for.

He signed for the delivery, walked the men out, and lowered the warehouse door. Then, snatching the two-way from his belt clip, he pressed the mic. "Squad One, you're up."

A door leading to the interior offices opened. Six men dressed in nondescript tactical uniforms filed out and expertly loaded and lashed down the cases onto two pre-positioned pallets. Porter didn't have to check their work because he'd trained them himself. He did, however, recount the load before crossing it off his checklist.

"Thank you, men. The mission briefing is in fifteen minutes."

The squad leader acknowledged with a "Yes, sir" before leading his team to the interior offices.

Porter returned to his clipboard, reviewing the long list of equipment and supplies. The MREs represented the last item needed for the most significant mission of his life and that of the other forty-eight men waiting for him. Those brave men were why he didn't take his role as second-in-command lightly. Like him, they all had an ax to grind with the Army or the direction political leaders had been taking the country in. But thanks to one visionary patriot, they were the tip of the spear that would return the United States to the right track.

A triple honk from outside the warehouse door signaled the visionary had arrived. Porter pressed the button on the wall, raising the door to allow the SUV inside. He closed it when the driver pulled up even to the newly stacked pallets.

The front doors opened, and two men dressed in the same tactical uniforms piled out. One held the rear passenger door open for the man responsible for everyone and everything in this warehouse and the adjoining one.

Major General William Calhoun was a legend in the United States Army. Porter was there when he earned that label and his famous nickname. He had been assigned to Second Platoon of Bravo Company under Captain Calhoun's command. When his platoon had been cut off in Basra and was pinned down by one of the few Iraqi units that had fought back, Calhoun stepped up. He'd manned a Humvee-mounted .50-caliber machine gun. He'd flattened the enemy's stronghold, two clay buildings, in less than a minute, saving all thirty men, including Second Lieutenant Porter.

Fifty, as the men liked to call him when toasting to his good health, stepped onto the floor with the swagger of John Wayne. "Is everything in place, Major Porter?"

"Yes, sir." Porter straightened his posture, proud of the work the men had accomplished. "The last of the supplies arrived today."

"Excellent. None of this would have been possible without your extraordinary effort, Major Porter."

"Thank you, sir. I've assembled the men for your mission briefing."

Despite revering the general, Porter cringed at his title. Topping out at major was an insult for a man who had spent a lifetime training for war. His only fault was focusing on the mission, not his career. If he'd known kissing the right ass was a prerequisite for making lieutenant colonel, he would have resigned his commission years ago and not waited until last year to swear allegiance to the one man who understood the meaning of sacrifice.

Porter walked to the general's left down the hallway, taking mental note of his last-minute instructions for tomorrow's final dry run. "Considering our limited supply of JP-8, I recommend using only Eagle Two for the exercise. They need the practice the most."

"I've seen your report, Major, but I want a complete run-through tomorrow. We'll get only one shot at this, so I suggest you come up with more fuel."

"Yes, sir." Porter swallowed the lump in his throat. He had two days to produce another two hundred gallons of military-grade jet fuel without leaving a paper trail.

Calhoun pushed the converted break-room door open and stepped inside.

Retired Sergeant Major Sanders announced, "Room, ten-hut." Forty-eight uniformed men, each with a rich military history, snapped to attention from their seats. It was so quiet that a mouse scurrying across the linoleum floor could be heard.

"Take your seats." Calhoun approached the podium to a chorus of creaking folding metal chairs. Behind him was the flag of the United States on the left and the flag of the state of Texas ten feet to the right. The banner of the Red Spades was stretched between them, reflecting the merger between them and the Gatekeepers and Aryan Brotherhood of Texas.

"Loyalty. Courage. Determination. Each of you is here today because you have lived up to those sacred words under fire in defense of your country. You have faced the enemy and defeated the bastards with honor. But you are also here because the country for which you sacrificed your innocence has lost its way. It has fallen into the hands of the weak."

Several men mumbled, shaking their heads and fists. Similar words last year had convinced Porter that the great "Fifty" Calhoun was a visionary. That he was the type of leader this country needed. And the day Porter agreed to help him assemble an army to make his vision a reality, his life suddenly took on meaning. Looking at the fruits of his labor, Porter was proud of the men he'd recruited. Each believed that if this country had any hope of survival, it had to change leadership now, not at the next election.

Calhoun continued. "You have seen it firsthand. They have thrown up the white flag of surrender and made our once-great country the laughing-stock of the world. They have done the unforgivable. They withdrew from the hard-fought land our brothers and sisters spilled their blood and lost their lives defending. That cowardice, my fellow patriots, must come to an end. Earlier today, we made our first strike." He turned to Porter. "What have you heard?"

"The red spade card was located. Federal agents are looking into us."

"Excellent. By tomorrow, our second strike will instill fear in the sheep of this country. They will demand the borders be closed, and our feckless leaders will have no other choice but to give in to the panic. But that will play right into our hands. The stage will be set, and we will light the fuze of revolution. Tonight, I ask you one question: Are you prepared to fight for your country?"

In unison, the men called out, "Yes, sir!"

"Then I promise you this. When we take control, we will return the United States to its rightful position on the world's stage—at the fore-front." Calhoun paused for the roaring cheers of the men who would walk through fire if he gave the order. Porter counted himself among them. He'd dedicated his life to a man and a cause worth fighting for. They all had, but many of the men in this room wouldn't live to see the results of their sacrifice. Many, he feared, would die in the battle. That was his only regret.

"Then, tomorrow, we rehearse. I expect nothing less than perfection," Calhoun said. "Dismissed."

The sergeant major called the room to attention when Calhoun left the podium. Porter followed steps behind down the hallway. Before they reached the SUV, Calhoun's cell phone rang. He answered. "Yes...? What is the agent's name...? What do you suggest...? If she gets too close before we deploy, you need to neutralize her... There is no going back at this point. If you don't see to it, I'll send someone else who will... Anybody who stands in our way will find no mercy."

Calhoun returned the phone to his cargo pocket with a look of determination. He pivoted to Porter. "The ATF is moving too fast. We'll need to misdirect them tomorrow."

When Calhoun brought Porter in the fold, he'd said he needed a man who could think on his feet and make things happen. He was about to prove the general had made a wise choice. "Then we will need sacrificial lambs."

"Who do you have in mind?"

"The Aryan rejects." Porter chose those men not for their expert skills but for the likelihood of failing. Like the men in the tunnel, they were the lost souls of Calhoun's army—nameless and expendable. "We already know they are unstable. Their tattoos will have the alphabet soup of agencies looking into the Aryan Brotherhood, not us. That should buy us the time we need."

"Excellent. Make it happen." Calhoun entered the back seat of his waiting SUV. "Are we ready for phase two?"

"Our two-man team is rolling as we speak."

11

"Careful, Darby. Footing could be tricky."

Darby looked over his shoulder, giving Lexi a thumbs-up. His face morphed into Gretchen's, losing its green glow through the lenses of her night vision goggles. Both had the same ocean-blue eyes that swam with emotion in the light, though hers danced with the carefree innocence of youth. But then smudges appeared on her cheeks, making them lose their smiling glow. Her expression turned long and sad before transforming into the face of the girl from the tunnel. The flesh on her face turned sunken and ashen. Her eyes had become a dark abyss.

"Spades aren't supposed to be red," the girl said.

"Did you see the card?" Lexi asked.

"The mean man did. He said it was a bad sign."

"A sign of what?"

Noise close to Lexi's ear shook her from her dream. It took her a second, but she recognized the familiar sound. The cell phone she'd placed on the nightstand in the middle of the night was vibrating against the wood surface. She opened her eyes, discovering the bedside light was still on. Her gaze shifted to follow the buzzing sound, but by the time she reached out for the phone, it had fallen to the floor. "Of course," she griped. Then, blindly feeling for metal on the carpet, her fingers finally located the device. She swiped the screen without reading the caller ID.

"This is Mills," she croaked. Even to Lexi, her voice sounded groggy.

"Sorry to wake you, Lexi. This is Noah. We have another incident."

"Another explosion?" The fog of sleep cleared instantly at the thought of a second bomb going off.

"No, a fire. But I think you should come. We don't get many major incidents in Nogales, and two in as many days makes me suspect they might be linked. How quickly can you come down? I'm in the lobby of your hotel."

"Give me ten minutes."

After disconnecting the call, a glance across the room confirmed Lexi hadn't unpacked a thing other than her ointment. That now seemed like a good choice. She hopped the few feet to her suitcase and dragged it back to the bed. She then changed underwear and put a sock on her good foot and two socks on her residual limb over a fresh liner. There was no telling how long she'd be in her prosthetic today, and yesterday's lesson had taught her to be overly prepared.

After donning her leg, weapon, and jacket, Lexi had a quick round with her toothbrush and hairbrush. Then, deeming herself presentable, she commenced the bag drag to the elevator. The extra sock covering her limb liner was a wise choice. The rubbing and pressure she'd felt yesterday were gone.

Lexi stopped at the front desk, turning in her card key to the clerk. "I'm not sure if I'll be back, but please don't check me out yet. I'll call if I don't need the room tonight."

"No problem, Miss Mills. I'll mark you for a late check-out by one. After that, we'll have to charge you for another night."

"Thank you."

Noah approached, carrying a coffee and a handful of pastries from the hotel breakfast bar. Still dressed in his police windbreaker and boots, he'd traded in his helmet for a wide-brimmed black fedora. "I hope you like bear claws and one sugar, one cream."

"It will do." Lexi re-slung her backpack over her shoulder and grabbed her overnight and equipment bags. "I'll eat it on the road."

Once through the main entrance, Lexi peered into the dark sky. A ribbon of purple over the eastern hills announced sunrise would be upon them soon. The air was chilly but no more so than last night at the tunnel site.

At Noah's unmarked SUV, Lexi stowed her bags in the back. Following a rental car break-in during her first assignment and spending three days in the same clothes, she'd learned to never separate herself from her bags outside of a controlled area.

Once buckled in, Lexi sipped her coffee.

Noah tossed his hat onto the back seat and put the car in drive, flipped the emergency lights on, and rolled code two without the siren. "You should know rescue workers broke through to the other side. No more bodies were found, so we're now in recovery mode. My team is continuing to pull up debris, but we have yet to get another hit on nitro."

"I'm starting to think my boss might be right. What we found last night could be trace from medication."

"Don't close the book on that until we check out this fire." Noah navigated down the business highway on the east side of Nogales.

"Where are we headed?" Lexi asked.

"A Catholic church east of town."

"Has this happened before?" A church burning typically surrounded a hate crime, not a terrorist attack, as Lexi and Noah suspected was behind the tunnel collapse. However, both crimes usually yielded the same result —fear instilled in the community.

"Not since 2015, but that was minor damage caused by a disgruntled parishioner. This is much bigger."

"How big?"

"Judge for yourself."

Noah turned from the main highway, away from the buildings blocking the eastern view, revealing a chaotic scene awash in red flashing lights. Fire trucks and hoses crisscrossed the city street. A dozen firefighters dressed in bulky black suits with fluorescent stripes around their arms, legs, and torsos were dousing the last of the flames and poking at the ashy debris with long metal rods.

Noah parked short of the cordon but close enough for Lexi to make out the complete devastation. Nothing was left but the building's charred skeleton, glowing orange against the dark backdrop. She opened the car door, taking in the fire's calling card—the overpowering smell of smoke.

"Was it occupied?"

"I hope not." Noah exited the SUV, joining Lexi near the hood. "Next door is the Catholic Academy." Those words were a direct stab to Lexi's spirit. The thought of another child dying for some lunatic's cause cut her heart to shreds.

Other than a police officer standing guard near the yellow tape, there were no signs of police or firefighters establishing a command post. Noah retrieved his hat and headed toward the officer, where a group of people had gathered. Stepping closer, Lexi saw those people were a half-dozen nuns huddled together, each clutching a Bible or rosary beads.

Noah approached the one standing at the front of the group. "Sister Agatha, did everyone make it out?"

Sister Agatha released the grip she had on her beads and held out both hands until Noah clutched them. "Otro, I'm afraid Father Marco didn't make it out. We thought he hadn't returned from the tunnel collapse yet, but they found him in a closet in his rectory. It was a miracle, I tell you. It was the only untouched room of the church."

"So he's alive." Noah released her hands.

Sister Agatha gestured toward the rescue vehicle with the back doors open. "They're about to put him in the ambulance."

"Thank you, Sister." Noah jutted his head in that direction, inviting Lexi to join him. He then walked at a fast clip. "Maybe he can tell us what happened." Medics were readying to load a gurney into the back of the ambulance, but Noah called out, flashing the badge he had dangling from a chain around his neck. "Wait. Is that Father Marco? I need to talk to him."

The medics continued to prep the gurney for loading into the back. One looked up at Noah. "He has smoke inhalation. I doubt he can speak."

"He doesn't have to speak to provide me information," Noah argued. The monitors attached to the priest showed he clung to life. Surprisingly, his face looked swollen and bloody, as if he'd recently been beaten. But why would an arsonist beat up a priest? Most firebugs were methodical and carefully cased a place before lighting it up to avoid surprises. If the priest surprised him after he'd lit the fire, a professional arsonist wouldn't leave a witness to chance. Instead, he'd kill him and let him burn. This was the work of an amateur or someone who wanted Father Marco found.

The skin on his face and fingers had turned a frightening bluish-gray. The last time Lexi had seen someone that color, they had died within the hour. Then, coughing through the oxygen mask strapped over his nose and mouth, Father Marco lifted his hand and pointed an index finger toward Noah.

Noah leaned in closer. "Father, what happened? Did someone start the fire?"

Father Marco raised his head a fraction, but a gut-wrenching hacking fit forced him back. The medic adjusted the oxygen mask that had slipped from its proper position. "We need to get him to Mercy."

Father Marco shook his head vigorously, clutching the medic's arm with one hand and tapping the breast pocket of his shirt with the other. Noah reached inside, pulling out a pristine playing card. The face of it was a red ace of spades. The second one in two days.

The priest's body went limp to an ear-piercing alarm from a monitor attached to leads strung from his chest. "He's in V-fib," one medic shouted, pushing Noah out of the way. He began chest compressions, bouncing Father Marco's torso up and down to a rapid rhythm.

The other medic prepared the defibrillator. "Charging to one-fifty." A rising machine sound marked its progress. "Clear." He pressed the paddles against Marco, one high on his right pectoral muscle and the other at his lower left rib cage, but the monitor didn't change. He repeatedly tried, raising the charge higher each time, but there was still no change.

The first medic resumed chest compressions for several minutes, but when his effort failed to restart Father Marco's heart, the other medic rested a hand on his shoulder. "It's no use. He's gone."

The first one stopped, hanging his head low. "No one was here to give him last rites." He looked up, eyes glistening with tears. "My wife will be heartbroken. He married us and baptized our two boys."

"We'll take good care of him." The other one loaded Marco's body into the ambulance and headed out.

Lexi stepped even with Noah and stood silently with the sun rising at their backs. "Did you know him well?"

"Does anyone ever really know their priest?"

"I'm sorry for your loss, Noah." Lexi didn't know what might be more consoling at a time like this. Since childhood, she hadn't been comfortable around priests, ministers, nuns, or any church figure. The ones she grew up with had preached that her very existence was an abomination. She was a triple threat—a half Black, half white gay woman who dressed primarily like a man—and had many Sunday sermons directed at her as if they were a form of conversion therapy.

"Thanks, but Father Marco wouldn't want us to mourn. He'd want us to live." Noah straightened his spine and rolled his neck several times as if shaking off the scene that had played out moments earlier. He then flipped over the card Father Marco had to its back. The word "salvation" was written and crossed out with red ink.

"What do you think that means?" Lexi asked.

"I don't know," Noah said.

"First the tunnel. Now the church. Maybe whoever did this is trying to tell us that Father Marco won't be able to save the rest of us from something that has yet to come. He won't be there to lead us to salvation."

"We need to talk to Sister Agatha. She and Father Marco were close. And nothing goes on at the academy that she doesn't know about." Noah returned to the group of nuns, approaching her directly. "Sister, I have sad news."

"We saw, Otro, but the officer wouldn't let us pass." She tried to appear stoic, but anyone could plainly see she was devastated. "Was he in pain?"

"I don't think so. He went quickly." Noah paused while she made the sign of the cross. "This is now a murder scene, Sister. Are you up for some questions?"

Sister Agatha stood taller, releasing a long sigh. "Yes, of course."

"Did any of the sisters see what happened here tonight?"

"I'm afraid not. They were in their quarters asleep."

"Can you think of anyone who had a grudge?"

"Everyone has grudges, Otro. It isn't our place to judge those who do."

"I understand your reluctance, Sister, but I'm not here to judge. My job is to see that Father Marco's killer is punished for his crime."

"I cannot betray a trust, even for you, Otro."

Noah pursed his lips. Lexi hadn't spent enough time with him to recognize his moods, but his stiff posture had the earmarking of impatience. He ushered Sister Agatha several feet away from the group. Lexi followed.

"Sister, if you're trying to protect Father Marco," Noah said, "you should know that I've looked the other way regarding his extracurricular activities for years. I never wanted to know specifics. All I needed to know was that he was doing God's work. But I need to know now. So please, for his sake and for those he's helped find a new life, if you know anything, you must tell me."

Sister Agatha's expression softened, signaling that Noah had won the battle of wills. "Of course you knew, Otro. You are too observant to deceive." She glanced at Lexi before giving Noah a questioning look.

"It's okay. Agent Mills isn't Border Patrol or Immigration. She's ATF and has been helping me investigate the tunnel collapse. We think it wasn't an accident." Noah held up the red ace of spades he found minutes ago. "Father Marco took his dying breath showing me this card. We found one like it in the tunnel debris. That tells me both killings are connected. Now, tell me about the railroad."

"We work with our sister church on the other side of the border, using the narco tunnels."

"Did you work with the cartel?"

"Heavens, no. We had one rule: no narcos or coyotes. The two churches communicated via carrier pigeon. When Father Marco got word of a group of travelers coming, he'd head out to the desert alone with the church van. A guide from the other side would lead the group through the tunnels and meet him out of view of the Border Patrol cameras. Father Marco would bring them here. They'd stay for a day or two until another van picked them up."

"What can you tell me about the second van?"

"Only that it's old and white. Each stop on the railroad only knows about the one before it."

Noah rolled his neck, which Lexi had deciphered was his tell of frustration. "Was there anything out of the ordinary recently? Did Father Marco have any unexpected visitors?"

"None that I know of, but I must tell you I wasn't completely forthright with you earlier."

"Was that when you were playing coy with me, Sister?"

"Guilty as charged." An impish grin enveloped Agatha's lips. "Earlier, you asked if any of the sisters saw anything tonight. Well, you failed to ask if I'd seen anything."

"What did you see?"

"I went to see if Father Marco had returned from the tunnel site around midnight, but the light was off in his rectory, and he didn't answer the door. Returning to my quarters, I walked past a car parked on the street between our buildings. It was odd because only church visitors park there."

"Can you describe it?"

"It was a black SUV. I remember laughing at the plate on the back. It was from Texas, I think, and started with *G-I-G*. I took it as a sign because Father Marco always ends his sermons by saying God is good."

"Thank you, Sister. This is very helpful."

The tunnel collapse and church burning had been connected by Father Marco. The red spade cards proved it. But who was leaving those cards? And most importantly, what was next on their list?

By the time firefighters declared the scene safe for investigators, a media frenzy had gathered at the perimeter now guarded by extra police. Some reporters shouted questions to Noah and Lexi while they geared up for a walkthrough of what was left of the building.

"Detective Black! Was it arson?"

"Detective Black! Does this have anything to do with the tunnel collapse?"

"Is it true that Father Marco was killed?"

"Was anyone else hurt?"

"Was Father Marco involved?"

Noah ignored the barrage until the last question. His dark eyes narrowed at the accusation before he turned toward the reporter. "That was out of line, Joe. Father Marco was a good man." He formed a fist, taking a step in Joe's direction.

Lexi blocked him, placing her hands on his chest. "Let it go, Noah."

He rolled his neck—definitely his sign of irritation. "You're right. Let's talk to the fire inspector."

Lexi slung her backpack loaded with evidence-collection supplies over her shoulder and followed Noah into the debris field, where smoke rose from charred timbers. Footing in her boots was precarious at best. Halfway through the pew remnants, Noah slipped. Lexi lunged on instinct. She caught him, but his weight and the speed of his fall forced her right leg to twist a fraction inside the socket of her prosthetic. She'd have to correct it before they continued.

"Thanks," Noah said.

"Give me a second. I have to fix my leg."

His gaze lowered to Lexi's askew left boot. "Jesus. Are you okay?"

"I'm fine." She rapped her knuckles against the hard plastic socket. "Prosthetic. It needs a quick adjustment."

"I never would have guessed."

"Normally, I'd lean against a wall or sit to do this. Can I lean against your back?"

"Sure. Tell me what to do."

"Just don't let me fall." Lexi had spent months strengthening her right leg and developing a keen sense of balance on it. Consequently, falling made her feel incapable. That she wasn't strong enough or agile enough to do things for herself.

Lexi retrieved a hex key from her front pocket and leaned against Noah as leverage, taking the weight off her prosthetic. She then unzipped her pant leg past the knee, gently shifted her socket back into place, and tightened two screws. Thankfully, the extra sock layer kept her residual limb from pinching. She then inspected the socket and ankle for further signs of damage but found none.

Rezipping her pant leg, she righted herself. "All fixed. Thanks for the assist."

Noah responded with a crisp nod and continued his trek to the fire inspector combing through the debris. "Morning, Juan. Have you located the source yet?"

Juan turned around. "Oh hey, Noah. An accelerant was used." He gestured toward the burnt, crumbled pews. "Whoever did this splashed it in nearly every pew, creating an intensive, fast burn."

"Do you know what they used?" Noah asked.

"At first, I thought it was kerosene, but my field test confirmed it was jet fuel, specifically JP-8."

"That's military-grade fuel." Lexi noted Juan giving her a curious look.

"This is Agent Mills," Noah said. "She's from the ATF."

"ATF? This is an NFD scene. We have no reason to think explosives were used." Juan's defensive tone gave Lexi pause, but Noah placed a calming arm over his shoulder.

"She's not here to take your case, Juan. We're following up on a lead. We think this is related to the tunnel collapse."

"If that's the case, we're looking for one evil bastard."

Lexi and Noah walked the scene for hours, taking readings at several points but detecting no presence of nitroglycerin. Lexi didn't expect any other result, but she had to be thorough and prepared for her daily update with Carlson. After she explained about the church burning and the appearance of a second red ace of spades, Carlson agreed the incidents were related. He said the intelligence officer Lexi had prematurely notified was already researching the data she'd provided and would call her within the hour.

"It's past lunchtime. Are you hungry?" Noah asked.

"Starved."

"I know a place that makes the best burritos and salsa in the state."

Back at the SUV, Noah started the engine.

Lexi's muted phone vibrated in her jacket pocket. She routinely kept it on silent to not disrupt discussions when working in the field. Pulling it out, she recognized that the area code and exchange number on the caller ID belonged to the Federal Building in Dallas. "This is Mills."

"Hi, Lexi. This is Kaplan." Her voice contained a sense of urgency. "Sorry I didn't call back last night, but Agent Carlson gave me an earful about following the chain of command and running everything past him before I called you."

"He gave me the same speech."

Kaplan Shaw was the only agent in the Dallas office who treated her like a contemporary, not as dead weight and the reason they were always one agent short. Lexi had taken up an armed agent's position for a year but hadn't stepped foot into the field until yesterday. That didn't matter to Kaplan. She encouraged Lexi along her journey to reinstatement as much as Nita and Ronald had.

"Let's get to it," Kaplan said. "I understand you've come across the symbol of the Red Spades."

"Twice now. What can you tell us about it?"

"The red ace of spades is the symbol for a white supremacist group called the Red Spades based in central Texas. They hit our radar three years ago when Army General Bill Calhoun made a divisive speech at a political rally that bordered on inciting insurrection. Two men guarding him were dressed in paramilitary uniforms with the symbol on their arm patches."

"Why haven't I heard of them before?" Lexi asked.

"They've been quiet since that speech, but Calhoun is a living legend war hero with charisma. He's the type of leader who could amass a private army. What concerns me is a classified report that a massive weapons shipment was stolen from Fort Hood six days ago."

"What was taken?"

"Everything from .50-cal machine guns, to rocket-propelled grenade launchers, to armored troop vehicles."

"You think the Red Spades were behind it?" Lexi asked.

"I can't prove it, but it makes sense. And if I'm right, Calhoun's army has enough weapons to start a war."

"Can you do more digging, Kaplan? These guys are knocking off items on a list, and my gut tells me the tunnel and the church are just the beginning. We need to figure out what might be next on their list."

"I'll scour the dark web. If there's any chatter about the incidents or the Red Spades, I'll find it."

"I trust you will." Lexi finished her call with Kaplan and turned to Noah. "This is bigger than we thought. A domestic terrorist group on our watch list is likely involved."

"Then we need to head back to the station. We'll get breakfast to go."

12

As early as his private contractor days in the sandbox, Kevin Grimes had long considered learning the names of his team members a waste of time. Hired guns had rotated in and out every few weeks, and by the time he'd learned someone's name, another took their place. Within six months, he'd come to not care if the person next to him was Bob or Mary Jane. All Grimes cared about was whether the person he was paired with could do the job and pull the trigger when necessary.

Today should have been the exception. Major Porter had given him a job this morning—a bank heist—telling him that Cotton, Jenkins, and Epperson would be on his team. Those names had meant nothing to him. After all, they were merely warm bodies who knew how to handle a gun. But once he walked into the room to arm up for their mission, Grimes realized he'd have his hands full. The men Porter had provided him were jittery as hell and likely on something to give them chemically enhanced courage. If they didn't have in common the collage of Aryan tattoos across their arms and chest that spoke to a blood oath, he would have walked. But that wasn't an option. Porter had laid out that the money was critical to funding the next phase of General Calhoun's vision. And Grimes had to trust that whoever reconned the place wasn't Cotton, Jenkins, or Epperson.

Grimes went over Major Porter's instructions in his head. "Employers in that part of town pay their day laborers cash on Fridays, so the bank should have one-point-two million dollars on hand," Porter had said. "Be in place by ten hundred hours. That's shift change for the police precinct in the area, so that will put the nearest unit eight minutes out."

"I plan to be out in six," Grimes had replied.

Grimes ops-checked the M4 carbine rifle Porter had issued him for the operation. It was the same model he'd used for years in Iraq. He knew every facet of this nearly perfect weapon, could field strip it if jammed, and have it repaired within a minute. One glance at his team members had him doubting they knew the difference between the magazine and the pistol grip. Though, if nothing went wrong today, all they had to operate were the safety and the trigger.

He finished loading his magazine clips and popped one into his M4. "Load up," he shouted to his squad. The four piled into a black SUV stripped of plates and identifying manufacturer emblems.

Cotton designated himself the driver since he visited a cousin in that part of town when he lived in Dallas. Grimes saw no point in arguing the assignment. That meant Jenkins and Epperson would enter the bank with him. Unfortunately, the back-seat fidgeting during the thirty-minute drive was not a good sign. Whatever those two had taken to build up the nerve to rob a bank had fully kicked in.

Cotton parked on a side street, facing away from the main road, when they reached the neighborhood where the bank was located. The corner location made this locally owned, small-town community bank an ideal target. The after-lunch vehicle traffic was light. Foot traffic was also minimal with only four pedestrians—two middle-school-aged kids, a mom jogging with a stroller, and a dog walker with three mutts entangled in leashes.

Because their target was a community credit union, not a regional or nationwide bank branch, the in-place security was likely not robust. The likelihood of having a well-trained guard on duty was low.

"When we get inside, I'll fire a single round to get everyone's attention." Grimes shifted in his seat, directing his following words to the ones in the back. Their pupils were dilated, suggesting they were definitely on something. "Do not fire, and keep your finger off the trigger. Jenkins, you guard the door. Epperson, you stay on my six and help me with the money. We'll need to establish calm after the initial shock. Remember, we're here only for the money, so follow my lead." He knew better than to ask if either had questions. He would never hear the end of it if they had doubts. "Masks on. Safeties off."

Grimes, Jenkins, and Epperson covered their faces with full ski masks. Three metal clicks.

Three car doors flew open. Rifles were at the ready. The crew double-timed in a V-formation. Boots clomped against the pavement along the bank facade, and wallet chains from Jenkins and Epperson clanked to a fast beat. *Idiots! Who brings ID to a robbery?*

Grimes was first through the door, gripping his weapon with both hands, pointed safely at the ceiling. A bank official sat at a desk near a street-side window. Three tellers were behind a counter and plexiglass, each serving a customer. Two other customers stood in line. An armed guard stood at the end of the counter, keeping his eye on a busty teller, not the door.

Grimes peeled off a single shot. Not one head turned. Instead, everyone crouched as if doing so would shield them from a whizzing bullet. A teller let loose with a high-pitched scream.

"This is a holdup. If you do as I say, no one will get hurt." Grimes used a firm, steady voice. The guard inched his hand to the butt of the pistol holstered at his waist. Grimes then leveled his rifle at him. "Don't be a hero. Federally insured dollars aren't worth your life."

The guard twitched his hand once but then crept it chest high, splaying his fingers in surrender. A quick scan confirmed that the other employees and patrons had followed the guard's lead and either stood frozen or shaking in submission.

"This will be quick." Grimes gestured his chin toward his wingman. Epperson then ran to the counter and slid a well-worn pillowcase to each teller through the trough at the bottom of the plexiglass. Grimes then pointed his rifle at the bank officer. "Come here." She trembled when she walked to him. "Do as I say, or she dies. Tellers, gather the cash into the bags."

While the tellers emptied their registers and Epperson held his

weapon, bouncing on his heels, Grimes jabbed the rifle into the bank officer's back. "Reserve cash. Now or die."

The bank officer moved toward the secured area. Her hand shook when
she entered the code on the lock. It buzzed. Grimes pushed her inside and
shouldered the door open, revealing a cart with the big prize—ten stacks of
one-hundred-dollar bills banded in ten-thousand-dollar bundles. One
million dollars was sitting there for the taking.

Grimes retrieved a pillowcase from his cargo pocket and loaded it with
the hundred stacks of bills.

A shot rang out.

"What the hell?" Until that moment, Grimes was calm. If they were
caught, he'd face five to ten years behind bars and would likely serve only a
fraction of that sentence before being released on parole. But that gunshot
meant the circumstances had changed. One of the meth heads had gotten
itchy and turned a heist into a murder rap.

Grimes shooed the bank officer into the main room. The security guard
was lying motionless on the linoleum floor with a puddle of dark red blood
growing at his torso. Meanwhile, Jenkins paced like a caged animal five feet
from the main door, holding his M4 in one hand and rubbing his bald head
with the other.

"You idiot," Grimes yelled. "I told you no shooting."

"He went for his damn gun." Jenkins's pacing increased in speed and
intensity. "I had to shoot the asshole." He darted toward the guard, nearly
straight-legged, and spat on his lifeless body. "You dumb cocksucker."

"We need to get out of here." Grimes slung his overstuffed bag of booty
over his shoulder and angled toward the door. However, Jenkins remained
fixed to his position, hovering over the dead guard, cursing at the corpse's
stupidity.

Epperson approached and clutched his fellow meth head by the collar
with his free hand. "We gotta go."

They didn't have time to deal with a man who had cracked under pressure. Their six minutes were up, and Grimes was sure a teller had hit the
silent alarm the moment he fired the first shot.

"Drag him or leave him," Grimes grumbled. He and Jenkins shared a
brotherhood, but that fraternity stretched only so far. "I'm leaving."

The faint sound of wailing sirens poured into the bank when the main door flew open. Cotton appeared with his M4, shouting, "Cops!"

The thought of handcuffs and a five-by-ten cell had Grimes's heart thumping harder at his limited options—outrun the police, negotiate with them, or fight his way through. He stepped toward the glass door. Two police cruisers barreled through the intersection near where Cotton had parked and came to a screeching halt across the street from the bank. Outrunning them was no longer an option, and a standoff would bring too much publicity on the eve of the Red Spades' big attack. That left him with what he did best—fight.

"I'm not going back in," Jenkins yelled. A wild, determined seething filled his eyes. Grimes had seen that look only once when a suicide bomber took out a checkpoint leading into the Green Zone. Seeing that look on Jenkins told him all hell was about to break loose.

Jenkins blew past Grimes, grunting like a ferocious beast and leveling his M4 at the door. A long burst of bullets shattered the glass into thousands of pieces. He then dashed through the metal frame, shouting, "I'm not going back."

The unmistakable sound of rapid M4 gunfire filled the air. If Jenkins didn't release his trigger finger, he'd be out of ammo in seconds. Grimes had done his share of killing in the past but only when the situation called for it. There was no reason for tellers and customers to pay the price for his failure. He yelled to the people in the bank, "Everyone down."

A second of silence.

A hail of handgun fire shattered the street-side window where the bank official had been sitting earlier. Piercing screams emphasized the panic inside and the urgency to get to the SUV before police reinforcements arrived.

"Get to the car," Grimes yelled. "I'll lay down suppressive fire." He released the safety on his M4, placing it on semi-auto because ammo conservation was imperative. He acquired his targets—the two officers who had taken position behind the quarter-ton of metal of their cruisers. He fired one round at each target one second apart. One instantly fell to the ground. "Go. Go. Go." He continued to fire in single bursts.

Epperson and Cotton hopped through the metal frame, crunching glass shards with each step. They got off a few rounds and dashed left toward their waiting SUV. Grimes followed, laying down fire as he quickstepped. His men finally reached the corner of the building.

Voices called out, "Stop. Police."

Epperson and Cotton turned toward the voices from around the corner and fired. A flurry of shots rang out. Their bodies convulsed with the force of bullets ripping through their flesh, blood spraying in the air for one second. Two. Three. And four. Both men then fell limp to the pavement, tumbling as if they were toy soldiers being upended from the flick of a child's hand.

Grimes was trapped. The only choices left were to die like his men or surrender and spend the rest of his life in prison for their deaths. He chose the latter. Life, even if caged, was better than death. He raised his weapon to surrender and turned toward the officers barricaded behind their vehicles.

A shot.

Searing pain and heat tore through the right side of Grimes's torso. He lost his grip on his rifle and bag of money, letting both fall to the ground. *So, this is what it feels like to be shot*, he thought. Grimes had shot many men himself and patched up several of his buddies who had caught a stray bullet in his eight years in the Army and six as a private contractor. Still, he'd gotten through it all without a scratch until now. Sadly, Barney Fife did what some of the most vicious mujahideen couldn't—put a bullet in his gut.

Grimes fell to his knees, placing a hand over the hole in his midsection. Warm liquid coated his fingers, signaling the end was near. He was power-less to defend himself or to flee. His mind was telling him he still had some fight left in him, but his body was giving up.

His surroundings wobbled as if he were drunk off his ass. The midday sun had begun to fade when an officer pushed him down, smashing his face into the concrete. A knee in his back made the pain ten times worse, but then he felt nothing, and everything went black.

13

Noah Black navigated his SUV through the southeastern part of town where street signs pointed toward the pedestrian border gate. A block shy of the busy border passage, he turned down a narrow alley between a taqueria and a duty-free store, parking in an employees-only slot.

"I thought we were getting food to go," Lexi said.

"We are." Noah turned off the engine and invited Lexi inside. He opened the back door to the taqueria, revealing a chaotic kitchen. Pots on the stove were boiling. The countertops were lined with vegetables, eggs, tortillas, and other ingredients. Four workers were preparing plates at a feverish pace. One was yelling something in Spanish. And the entire place smelled like grease and spices.

"Buenos días, Tía." Noah kissed the one who was yelling on the cheek. Lexi spoke little Spanish, but she understood Noah had greeted his aunt.

"No tengo tiempo, Otro."

"We're in a hurry, too," Noah said. "Can I make us some breakfast burritos to go?"

"Sí, sí." His aunt waved a hand in the air before wiping it on her apron and yelling at another worker. She then turned back to Noah. "You'll like the salsa. I found heirloom tomatoes today."

"I like your salsa every day." Noah dipped a tortilla chip into a large metal bowl of the stuff sitting on a prep table and took a bite. "Mmm, this *is* good. Tía, I'd like you to meet Lexi Mills. She and I are working together today."

His aunt eyed Lexi up and down as if sizing her up for in-law material. "Huh, you could do worse."

"That's her way of complimenting you," Noah said to Lexi before returning his attention to his aunt. "We're just partners on a case."

"We'll see. She has a nice smile." His aunt winked.

Noah rolled his eyes. When he did, Lexi realized the skin right below them was equally white. *Funny*, she thought. After spending six hours together, she'd already become accustomed to his skin condition. They'd been so focused on the job that she hadn't had the time to give it another thought until now. But now that she had, she came to one conclusion: his lieutenant was an ass. The man judged Noah based on his skin, not his ability.

Noah slipped between two workers and assembled two overstuffed burritos like a pro. He then filled a small cardboard bowl with salsa and handed it to Lexi. "You're going to love this batch."

Back in the car, Lexi ate while Noah drove. Between bites, she asked, "Did your aunt teach you to cook?"

"She taught me everything. She's raised me since I was ten after my parents couldn't deal with me anymore. I worked in her kitchen nearly every day until I became a cop."

Lexi stuffed down the last bite of burrito, washing it down with water. Noah wasn't kidding about the best burritos in the state. "That was great. What's the secret?"

"Fresh ingredients." Noah's tone contained a sense of pride. "She crosses the border every day to buy vegetables for her salsa. Nothing is canned or frozen."

"She's spoiled me," Lexi said. "Bottled salsa will never do."

"We're all spoiled in this town. Half of the produce in the United States passes through the port here. That has made Nogales on the other side of the border a major retail hub for northern Mexico. We never have food shortages, which is why the chief and my lieutenant aren't eager to declare these incidents terrorism. Doing so could mean closing the port here, which would have a rippling effect throughout the country. No one from here to Washington DC is willing to shut down the engine of commerce."

"If more of these incidents happen and the body count continues to climb, they might not have a choice until we capture whoever is behind them." Lexi hoped it wouldn't come to that.

Noah parked in the official parking lot of the Nogales Police Department. He stuffed down half of his burrito and tucked the rest into its foil wrapper, leaving it on the dash to bake in the late morning sun. He pointed out, "It works better than my aunt's food warmers at the taqueria."

Lexi's cell phone vibrated. The caller ID belonged to the general Dallas Federal Building. "This is Mills."

"Lexi, it's Kaplan." Her tone was low, barely above a whisper. "Carlson would tan my hide if he knew I called you first."

Lexi's interest piqued, and her trust in Kaplan grew exponentially. "What do you have?"

"There was a bank robbery in a Dallas suburb an hour ago. Three suspects were killed, and the fourth was injured and taken into custody. One of the first officers on the scene ran the serial numbers of the weapons used in NCIC. I then got an alert. They were part of the shipment stolen from Fort Hood."

"What can you tell me about the suspects?"

"I called the officer. He said that all four had Aryan Brotherhood tattoos, which makes little sense. The chatter I found on the dark web said that the Red Spades had been looking to buy military-grade weapons for months, but their search suddenly stopped a week ago."

"And you think that's because they heisted the shipment from Fort Hood."

"I'm convinced of it. Two of the men driving the hijacked trucks were under Calhoun's command in Iraq when he earned his Medal of Honor. The men from that unit are die-hard followers."

"So, what's with the Aryan Brotherhood? Could they have joined forces?"

"I doubt it. They're mostly associated with drug trafficking and murder-for-hire. This would be the first connection I've found between them and the Red Spades. Maybe I'm wrong about the weapons shipment. Maybe the Aryans *were* behind it."

"Hey, don't doubt yourself." Kaplan had the instincts of a lion in the wild. Sitting on the sidelines for a year, Lexi watched this woman's uncanny ability to unearth and put together puzzle pieces of obscure data where others had failed. "I trust your gut more than I trust most people's educated guess. Keep digging."

"In the meantime," Kaplan said, "I'll send you everything I can find on the suspect and ask the Dallas PD for a complete report."

Lexi finished the call and told Noah about the bank robbery and the possible ties to the Aryan Brotherhood and the Red Spades. He rolled his neck. "You might be right about a rising body count. We need to interrogate the suspect."

"I was thinking the same thing. How do you want to play this with your chief?"

"By forcing his hand."

"Let me lay the groundwork." Lexi then called Agent Carlson and outlined a case for returning to Dallas, adding a slight exaggeration to protect Kaplan's butt. "I'd signed up for NCIC alerts for the stolen weapons Agent Shaw had suspected might be related to the Red Spades. I got a hit." She explained about the bank robbery and the suspect being taken into custody. "We think the robbery is linked. Detective Black should be there when I interrogate the suspect. He knows the border in a way that I don't."

"Fine. Take the next flight home," Carlson said, surprisingly without objection or need of further explanation.

"Thank you, sir. You'll make my girlfriend happy. I might actually make her cousin's bachelorette party at the Beebo Club tonight." Lexi wrapped up the call and turned to Noah. "We're on."

Noah then escorted Lexi into the Nogales Police Station. For a small town, it had an impressive facility. They walked past the reception desk that also doubled as the dispatch center. The two workstations were equipped with flat-screen TVs showing security camera feeds from around the city and computer terminals displaying up-to-date dispatching software. The hallway led to a squad room with the same modular furniture at ATF facilities. Clearly, federal assistance dollars had found their way here in recent years.

Noah removed his hat and knocked on an open door leading to a private office. The nameplate on the wall read *Police Chief Jose Hernandez.* "Got a minute, Chief?" Stepping inside, he waved in Lexi. "Sir, this is Special Agent Lexi Mills from the ATF. We need to brief you on our findings today."

The chief stood and shook Lexi's hand. "It's a pleasure, Mills. I understand you've uncovered evidence supporting the theory that the tunnel collapse was intentional."

"That's right, sir." Lexi paused until the chief returned to the executive chair behind his wooden desk. Some things never changed. The rank and file used cheap modular furniture, but the brass sat behind solid wood. It proved the adage that rank had its privileges. "We also believe this morning's church burning is linked." She explained about the playing cards and the ATF intel on the Red Spades organization, including the stolen military weapons shipment. "Four of the weapons were used in a bank robbery outside of Dallas this morning. Three suspects were killed. One was wounded and taken into custody. I'd like Detective Black to accompany me to Dallas to interrogate him tonight."

"Texas is outside of our jurisdiction." Chief Hernandez shifted in his chair, creaking the wheels against the linoleum floor. "I don't know what Detective Black could provide."

"Insight. He knows the border and the players. That's expertise I don't have when time is of the essence. Bottom line: you need both of us to solve this case."

"Fine. Two days." The chief leaned forward. "Check with Sally to book your flight. But the hotel is on you."

The hum of jet engines had Lexi hovering on the edge of sleep. She usually could nap on a plane like a baby, but images of the little girl from the tunnel and the dying priest from the burned-down church kept her from slipping under. In her seven years as an ATF agent, only two investigations haunted her: the Gatekeepers and this one. Like the Tony Belcher case, this one had her feeling as if she were chasing ghosts. Unlike drug gangs driven by profit, the Red Spades were clearly motivated by anonymously instilling fear. That made them exponentially more dangerous.

The Belcher case had gone cold, but this one was hot as mercury. Lexi kept her eyes closed, mulling over the pieces. Border. Salvation. Tunnels and churches. What was next? What was the end goal? Despite the allusion to Aryans, Lexi was confident the bank robbery was the work of the Red Spades, but to what end? A half-cocked, failed heist wasn't the mark of a disciplined militia recruited and trained by General Calhoun.

Motion in her seat row jerked Lexi from her thoughts. She opened her eyes, discovering Noah had returned from the restroom. "Sorry I woke you," he said, buckling in.

"You didn't wake me. I was thinking about the case." Lexi sat straighter to clear the fog in her head.

"I was too. We need to catch these bastards before more innocents are killed." Noah's expression tightened at the heartbreaking nature of the case. The deaths of the children in the tunnel and Father Marco at the church had clearly made this personal. "But I feel like whoever is behind these events is three steps ahead of us, ready to move on to the next target."

"Then we need to dig deep," Lexi said.

"Huh?"

"Just something my girlfriend says to me when I've hit a wall."

"Tell me about her."

"I met Nita a year ago. She was my physical therapist and helped me rehab after losing my leg. She challenges me, calls me on my bullshit, and" —a warm sensation formed in Lexi's chest—"makes me feel whole."

"She sounds like a good fit for you." Noah gestured at her leg. "Lose it on the job?"

Lexi nodded. Rehashing that night and Darby's death would surface too many emotions when she needed a clear head. She then pivoted. "Why do Sister Agatha and your aunt call you Otro?"

"It means 'other.' Sister Agatha was my first teacher after my parents sent me to live here. She started calling me Otro to make me feel good about being different. She said that God made everyone different, but that he must have considered me special because he spent extra time to make me stand out from the others."

"Did it help?"

"Not really, but the nickname stuck. I got into a lot of fights when the other kids called me Skunk or Pepé Le Pew. If not for Sister Agatha, I would have been expelled."

"I know what it's like being different. I was too white for the Black kids and too Black for the white ones, so I had no friends growing up."

"And I'm guessing being gay made things worse."

"Not as much as you think. Besides my short hair and preference for pants over dresses, I don't wear my sexuality on my sleeve. Though, like you, I couldn't hide my skin."

"Otherness can be very isolating," Noah said.

"Which is why I spent my childhood working in my father's garage."

"As a mechanic?"

"A certified NASCAR mechanic." Lexi added a hint of pride to her voice. She knew her way around a racecar as well as she knew explosives. She could tear down and reassemble an engine in her sleep.

"NASCAR? Wait. Is your father Jerry Mills? I saw him race once at Phoenix Raceway."

"Then I was there, either in the garage or on the pit crew."

"That's quite a leap, going from NASCAR to the ATF."

"You'd think so, but it was an easy decision for me. One of our drivers blew an engine during a warm-up lap and was burned badly. We thought it was because of a mechanical failure, but it turned out a rival driver had placed a small explosive device set to blow the brake when in a hard left turn. Seeing how the ATF agents stepped through the investigation made me think about going into law enforcement."

"Well, I'm glad you did. Thanks to you, we might gain ground on the Red Spades."

14

The elevator door in Lexi's apartment building swooshed open to the third floor. Noah positioned himself in its path to keep it from closing while Lexi re-slung her backpack and grabbed her equipment and overnight bags. Leading him down the corridor, Lexi felt exhaustion creeping up on her, but she hadn't had the time to give in to it. A quick shower and an energy drink would give her a needed jolt to get her through questioning the robbery suspect.

After unlocking the door, Lexi tossed her key in the entry table bowl and called out, "Nita! I'm home." When no answer came, she turned to Noah. "You can leave your overnight bag in here. By the way, the couch is yours if you don't want to spring for a hotel. Give me twenty minutes to dump my gear and take a quick shower. Then we can take my car to the hospital. Help yourself to anything in the fridge while I'm getting ready."

"I think I will, thanks."

Lexi continued to the bedroom and tossed her bags on the mattress. The shower was running in the bathroom, solving the mystery of her girl-friend's location. The faucet clanked off, cueing Lexi to hurry if she wanted to enjoy a few minutes of her favorite hobby—watching Nita dress.

She eased the door open, and a rush of steam kissed her cheeks. Water stains and drops on the shower glass partially masked Nita's body but left nothing to the imagination. Each curve and slope was visible, giving credence to Lexi's initial assessment of her girlfriend's body—sizzlin' hot. Dating a physical therapist came with its benefits, namely toned muscles. But those were only the appetizer. Nita's bronze skin was a perfect complement to her own, but hers was smooth and as sweet as honey, not bumpy like Lexi's.

Leaning her hip against the counter, Lexi crossed her arms in front of her chest. She watched Nita pat herself dry with a cotton towel, focusing on her every movement.

Nita finally stood tall, wrapping the towel around her torso. "Enjoy the show?"

"Always." Lexi opened the shower door and pulled Nita closer for a passionate kiss. Every kiss, whether the peck goodbye in public or one with tongue in the throes of making love, held meaning, this one especially. The last time they kissed, Lexi was still unproven in the field. But she returned, having gained the trust of Noah Black and Agent Carlson. Lexi was an agent again in every sense of the word, and she had this woman to thank.

Nita deepened the kiss, and Lexi nearly succumbed to the tingles it generated, but she pulled back. "You are very tempting, woman, but Noah is in the living room."

"That didn't stop you when my cousin was here."

"That's different. She's family." Lexi reached inside the shower and turned on the water. "I only have a few minutes to shower and change before we head off to the hospital to interview a suspect."

Nita grabbed her second towel from the wall hook and soaked up the excess water from her hair. "Do you think you'll make it to the Beebo Club tonight?"

"I'll try, but I'm running on fumes." Lexi sat on the toilet and removed her right shoe and sock before taking off her prosthetic. "I don't think I'm up to dodging the maid of honor tonight."

"Zoe will tire of chasing you. But if she tries something, she'll find her up-do in the toilet."

"I'd love to see you give her a swirly." Lexi chuckled.

Nita pushed back some unruly strands of Lexi's bangs with a finger.

"You look tired. I know you can't talk about the case, but I heard on the news that the tunnel collapse might be a terrorist attack."

"And the church burning this morning."

"Goodness. No wonder you're exhausted. I'll tell Jenny you're working."

"Thanks, Nita." Lexi removed the rest of her clothes, hopped into the shower, and before closing the door, said, "Don't leave without saying good-bye. I want to see you in your little black dress."

Refreshed and in a set of fresh clothes, Lexi entered the hallway and was met by the smell of garlic and onion. Steps into the living room, she stopped dead in her tracks at an unexpected sight. Noah was flipping something in a frying pan at the stove, and Nita was watching beside him, putting on an earring. Nita wasn't much of a cook, but neither was Lexi. In fact, she couldn't remember the last time either of them cooked rather than heated.

The little black dress didn't disappoint. The tight fabric hugged every curve. Nita would have to fend off every lesbian and bi woman in the club tonight. Lexi sidled behind her, wrapping her arms around her midsection. "You look beautiful. Maybe I *should* go tonight. Every woman in the joint will have their sights on you."

Nita melted into Lexi's embrace. "It won't matter because I have eyes only for you."

Lexi fixed her gaze on the perfect omelet Noah was preparing. "Do you give lessons, Noah?"

"I'd be happy to give you two a few pointers before I return to Nogales. Are you sure you don't want an omelet before you go, Nita?" Noah asked.

"I'm sure, but I will hold you to the lessons." Nita patted Lexi's forearm. "I should get going. Jenny will bite my head off if I'm late. I'm the designated driver for everyone."

Walking Nita to the door, Lexi told her to have fun and kissed her good-bye. Before Nita left, she locked eyes with Lexi, grazing a fingertip down her cheek. "Be careful, Lexi Mills. I love you."

After saying, "I love you, too," Lexi returned to the kitchen, where Noah had plated two fluffy omelets and poured two glasses of water at the break-fast counter.

"I hope you don't mind that I helped myself to your kitchen like this, but I figured you were hungry too."

"I am. You and your aunt are definitely spoiling me." Halfway through her meal, Lexi pulled up on her phone an email Kaplan had sent her while she was in the shower. It contained information on the robbery suspect. "Kaplan ran a background check on Grimes. He spent three years in the Army, most of which was in Iraq, before receiving an 'under other than honorable conditions' discharge for slugging his lieutenant." She read further. "He then spent six years as a private contractor over there, doing classified work."

"Any criminal record?" Noah asked.

"Two arrests for bar fights but no convictions." Lexi scanned more of the email. "His older brother was a member of the Aryan Brotherhood, but he was killed the year before Grimes enlisted in the Army."

"It sounds like he traded one nightmare for another."

"How do you think we should approach the questioning?" Lexi asked.

"Lives are at stake. We need to go at him hard."

"Then we don't leave until we get answers." Lexi wasn't sure what "going at him hard" meant in Noah's book, but she was prepared to follow his lead.

15

The second floor of Memorial Hospital on the suburban west side of Dallas was bustling with a dozen uniformed officers. Most were nursing cardboard coffee cups, and others were engaged by their cell phone screens. Lexi looked for the uniform with the highest rank and zeroed on a portly man with lieutenant's bars. She showed him her badge and credentials and asked to speak privately. They then stepped down the corridor, out of earshot of staff and other officers.

"Lieutenant, I'm Special Agent Mills from the ATF. This is Detective Black from the Nogales Police Department. I believe my supervisor called ahead." The lieutenant stared at Noah too long to be taken as anything but gawking. The man clearly needed to learn manners. Lexi snapped her fingers inches in front of his face to get his attention. "Over here, Lieutenant."

"Yeah, he did. What do you want to know?"

"First, I understand an officer was shot during the robbery? How is he?"

"Officer Moreno made it through surgery. He's in ICU. The next twenty-four hours are critical, but his chances of survival are decent."

"That's good to hear. Now, about the suspect your officers took into custody."

"We've already questioned the perp, but he's not talking."

"Has he lawyered up?" Noah asked.

"Not yet." The lieutenant resumed his stare.

"Care to tell us where you're holding the suspect?" Noah asked.

Lexi pressed the number five on the lighted elevator control panel. "I'm sorry you had to go through that, Noah. He was an ass."

"I'm used to it."

"But you shouldn't have to be. We shouldn't have to tolerate people who judge or make a spectacle of someone's otherness."

"I've learned to pick my battles and only worry about the asshats who are worth educating or the satisfaction of kicking *their* ass. He's neither."

"That I can agree with."

The elevator door opened to the disinfecting bright hallway lights. The two uniformed officers standing guard in front of a door thirty yards down broadcasted which room housed the robbery suspect like glowing neon lights. Anyone who passed by knew a prisoner was inside.

Lexi approached the nearest officer, introducing herself and showing her badge and credentials. "What can you tell us about the suspect?"

"He's a walking billboard for the Aryan Brotherhood in terms of hidden tats. Otherwise, his high-and-tight makes him a model for an Army recruiting poster."

"I hear Officer Moreno's prognosis is looking good." Lexi gestured her chin toward the door the officers were guarding. "Does he know that?"

"We haven't told the prick a damn thing."

"Good." Lexi had been through this before. Thinking he might be a cop killer could be a source of leverage. "He might be connected to the terrorist attacks at the border, so we'll need some time alone with him."

"Are you both armed?" the officer asked. Lexi replied with a nod. "Then you won't mind covering us for a bathroom break." He winked.

"Not at all."

After the officers disappeared around the corner, Lexi and Noah entered the hospital room. The first thing to hit Lexi was the smell. All hospital rooms had the same pungent antiseptic odor. A monitor on a rolling stand beeped, and the numbers on its screen suggested that Kevin Grimes was in no immediate danger of succumbing to the gunshot wound on his side. Grimes was asleep with his head slightly raised and his wrists and ankles shackled to the metal railings on the bed. The cardiac leads and wound bandage covered a portion of his chest but left enough skin visible to make out the white power tattoos. They confirmed his allegiance to the Aryan Brotherhood.

Lexi shook Grimes's lower leg until he opened his eyes. She'd left her badge dangling around her neck so that it would be the first thing he saw. "Mr. Grimes, I'm Special Agent Mills from the ATF. This is Detective Black." Grimes didn't have to know Noah's place of employment, only that he was a law enforcement officer.

Grimes eyed Lexi up and down disapprovingly before casting his stare at Noah. "What the hell are you?"

"Your worst nightmare." Noah narrowed his eyes. "Your Army friends have brought their crazy shit to my neighborhood, and I'm pissed. Baby killers get no mercy in my book."

"Child killer? I didn't kill a kid."

"You might not have, but the Red Spades did," Noah said. "That tunnel explosion rained down on fourteen people. Twelve are dead, including four children, and I was there when they brought up a mother's corpse still clutching her dead eight-month-old daughter. Whoever had a hand in that bombing deserves the same fate, and we won't stop until everyone responsible is in a casket."

"I couldn't give a shit what a half-breed and a human skunk think."

Lexi moved forward. "You might when those cops outside your door hear you've killed a brother officer. Do you know what Texas does to cop killers? Those who aren't shivved in the gut while in gen pop end up with a needle in their arm." Lexi gripped the lead to Grimes's IV bag between a thumb and index finger, sliding her hand down the plastic tube several inches. "Just like this one. Once the state doctor squeezes pentobarbital into your IV, you'll have about thirty seconds to think about your impending death. Thirty seconds to make peace with whatever God you believe in unless you help us. You don't owe the Red Spades your allegiance, just like you didn't owe the Aryan Brotherhood after your brother was killed. Both abandoned you. If you help us bring down the Red Spades, you could get life, not death."

"I'm already dead," Grimes sneered, wincing when he shifted on the mattress. "The Red Spades have a long reach in and out of prison, and they know I've failed."

That was the confirmation Lexi needed. Grimes tied the stolen weapon he'd used during the robbery to the Red Spades, and the calling cards left at the scenes connected them to the events in Nogales.

"Then tell us where we can find them," Lexi said. "We can put you in protective custody. Where are they, Grimes?"

"I'd rather take my chances with them than with a half-breed cop."

Noah stepped closer and pressed his knuckles onto the bandage on Grimes's midsection. The prisoner balled up and moaned in apparent pain. He reached for the nurse's call button, but Noah swiped his hand away. "She asked you a question."

Grimes deserved the death penalty for what he did today, but that didn't justify physical torture. Not in Lexi's book. Not ever. Those who enforced the law had to be better than those who broke it. At the same time, she couldn't show weakness in front of a suspect. If she did, he'd never give them the information they need. *Damn you, Noah, for boxing me into a corner*, she thought.

"If you're in pain, we can get the nurse after you tell us where we can find the Red Spades."

"I'm not telling you a damn thing," Grimes said through gritted teeth. Noah pressed harder without letting up, causing Grimes to lurch and scream in agony like a wounded animal caught in a trap. A piercing monitor alarm went off, and the screen showed his life signs had spiked wildly.

Noah had crossed a line, one Lexi had promised herself to never flirt with from the day she took her oath as an agent. Her gut told her no matter how many lives might be saved, this wasn't right. She tugged hard on the back of his jacket, enough to relay her disapproval but in such a way that Grimes couldn't see. Noah finally relented and stepped back.

A nurse burst through the closed door, striding directly to her patient. Her gaze shot to the monitors that still showed elevated levels. She then flipped a switch on the monitor, silencing the deafening alarm, before checking his drainage tube and bandage that had become blood-soaked.

"You may have opened your wound."

Grimes continued to moan. "Not me. Him. Damn ACAB."

The nurse shot her stare at Noah, whose expression remained unchanged. "What did you do to my patient?"

Noah remained silent.

"I'm going to sue your asses for police brutality," Grimes groaned.

"I have to ask you to leave, officers." The nurse's tight tone and stern expression left no room for negotiation. "If you don't, I'll call security, which will raise attention. The last thing you want is your faces splashed all over Twitter."

"I can't wait to hear from your lawyer." Noah led the way out the door.

"This is only the beginning, asshole," Grimes yelled. "Only the beginning."

The uniformed officers had returned but said nothing to Lexi and Noah about the screams likely heard from several rooms. One remained sitting in a chair, scrolling through something on his cell phone. The other was leaning against the wall, gnawing on a well-chewed toothpick. The chewer asked, "Did you get what you need?"

Noah clenched his hands into fists without breaking his stride down the corridor. "No."

Lexi's anger built while she rode down the elevator and walked out of the main hospital entrance. What Noah had done was unforgivable. By the time they reached her car in the parking lot, she couldn't contain her temper. She gripped Noah's coat sleeve and flipped him around abruptly, shoving him into the tailgate of her SUV. "What the hell was that, Noah?"

"It's called interrogating a suspect." Noah threw off Lexi's hold.

"Grimes was right. It was police brutality."

"I didn't figure you for being uptight, Mills."

"So it's Mills now." Lexi placed both hands on her hips to contain the urge to knock some sense into Noah. "Look, I get that you encounter the worst of the worst enforcing the law at the border and have to employ different tactics, but you don't work under a different constitution. You may call it uptight, but I call it doing what's right. I refuse to lower myself to their level. The day I can't hold my head high doing this job is the day I turn in the badge."

"I can respect that, Lexi, but you wouldn't last a week at the border. The men I deal with are evil and only respond to pain or the certainty of death. But, having said that, there is a line I won't cross, and what I did tonight was the closest I've come to crossing it."

"I like you, Noah, but I can't stand for anything like that again."

"I can respect that." Noah's response, while polite, wasn't a guarantee. But his softer tone suggested she might have gotten through. "Want to stop for some coffee and figure out our next step?"

Questioning Grimes had given Lexi a second wind. Sliding into the driver's seat of her SUV, she checked the time on her phone—eight o'clock. She could make a respectable appearance at the bachelorette party and show her girlfriend her support if she left now. Though alcohol wasn't Nita's primary addiction, it contributed to it, and hanging out at a nightclub after six years of sobriety couldn't be easy.

Once Noah settled in the passenger seat, she asked, "Would you mind if we went to the Beebo Club? The party I'm supposed to attend is being held there. We can talk, and I can earn some brownie points with Nita by showing up for an hour."

"I can think of worse ways to spend a Thursday night than in a club full of beautiful women."

"It's a bachelorette party for a lesbian wedding in a lesbian bar, so don't get your hopes up."

"With this face, I never do." Noah's self-deprecating comment was likely a coping mechanism, but it was also a sad commentary on how judgmental people could be about skin color. Lexi had encountered it all her life like Noah certainly had.

She patted him on the leg before putting the car in drive. "No one judges there. Everyone is welcome."

16

Lexi turned onto McCallan Avenue, where the bright yellow neon lights of the Beebo Club lit the night sky, turning it into day. The homage to Ann Bannon's lesbian pulp fiction novels of the mid-twentieth century had been a Dallas landmark for two decades. It was the perfect venue for tonight's bachelorette party.

Lexi eased her car into a spot at the back of the parking lot, adding it to the sea of SUVs, pickups, and Subarus. She and Noah followed a group of women to the entrance. When a butch held the door open for him, he took it in stride without trying to switch roles, instead offering a polite thank-you. He clearly didn't conform tightly to gender norms.

Once through the secondary doors, lively country music thumped to a fast beat. Women dressed in a broad spectrum of outfits, from cocktail dresses to flannel and shit-kickers, filled the 1960s-themed club. Lexi scanned the dance floor, looking for her girlfriend, before turning her attention to the tables. She looked no further than the table with the woman dressed in white with a satin sash, laughing with four other women dressed in all black. All five looked as if they were several drinks in, but Lexi was confident Nita was merely caught up in the excitement.

"Over there." Lexi tapped Noah on the arm, gesturing toward the bachelorette and her crew. He replied with a tip of his broad-brimmed cap. "You fit right in with that thing."

"It was my uncle's. He passed away ten years ago, so I wear it to honor him."

"Well, it looks good on you."

Weaving their way through the retro-style low-back vinyl chairs, Lexi stopped behind Nita and whispered into her ear, "You're the sexiest one here."

"That's a damn good pickup line, whoever you are."

"I hope you don't have a girlfriend because I plan on taking you home tonight." Lexi used a low, raspy tone to relay that her sentiment was genuine, not merely playful banter.

"You are a bold one." Nita briefly cocked her head to show her coy smile.

"Only when I think my chances are pretty good."

"So, you think I'm an easy lay." Nita turned abruptly, facing Lexi, with her mouth agape.

"After yesterday, I think I'm a shoo-in." Lexi gave her a brief, passionate kiss. Nita acknowledged Noah with a wave. "He and I need to talk about the case, so I thought this was as good of a place as any."

"This is why I love you."

"Lexi! You made it." The bride-to-be slung her arms over Lexi's neck, giving her a sloppy kiss on the cheek before stepping back. "Nita said you were working."

"I am, but I couldn't let the night go by without wishing you good luck." Lexi gestured to her left. "This is Noah. I'm working on a case with him."

Jenny looked at him. "My, aren't you an exotic creature? I bet you're in high demand."

"Not where I'm from," Noah said.

"In this town, you'd never sleep alone." Jenny picked up her margarita glass.

"That would make a great billboard." He chuckled.

"If you plan on staying for a while"—Jenny sipped her cocktail, scanning Noah up and down as if he were the specialty on tonight's menu—"I know several men and women who would love to take you for a ride, including this one. She bats for both teams." Jenny jutted her chin toward her maid of honor. Zoe had violated the primary rule of a bachelorette party and had come more scantily dressed than the bride, with the apparent intent to command everyone's attention.

Noah tipped his hat to both women. "I appreciate the offer, but I have to return to Nogales tomorrow."

Jenny waved a server over, gesturing for two more chairs. The ladies shuffled seating positions, so Lexi sat between Nita and Noah at the end of the table. Jenny and her crew downed their drinks, shouted, and headed for the dance floor when Dierks Bentley started to play.

"Jenny seems like a handful," Noah said to Lexi over the music.

"You don't know the half of it." Lexi had known Nita's cousin for a month, but that was plenty of time to assess that she was high maintenance and the life of the party. She then leaned in to talk about more serious matters. "What about Grimes? Should we take another crack at him in the morning?"

"I think it's worth a shot. We know he's tied to the Red Spades, and the calling cards tell us they're behind the events at the border. In the meantime, we should find out if the Dallas PD got anything off the other suspects and their vehicle."

"Kaplan is already looking into it." Lexi's phone vibrated. The number meant that call came from someone in the Dallas Federal Building. "Speak of the devil. This might be her." She swiped the screen to answer the call and plugged her other ear with a finger to hear better. "This is Mills."

"Lexi, this is Kaplan. I found something interesting in the Dallas PD report from today's robbery. Is that music?"

"Yeah. Hold on. Let me get somewhere quiet." Lexi mouthed to Noah that she'd be right back and weaved her way through the few tables to the ladies' restroom. Every stall was occupied, and two women were washing up at the sinks. "Go ahead, Kaplan. What did you find?"

"Forensics analysis showed that the suspects' SUV contained traces of solid nitroglycerin."

Lexi considered how many people could hear her end of the conversation, so she moved to the back wall and kept her responses neutral. "That's the same substance I found at the border."

"It can't be a coincidence," Kaplan said, "so I did some digging. The EPA shows only two chemical companies in the region that manufacture solid nitro. I found another one, but it's a smaller operation that doesn't fall under EPA reporting standards. I'm texting you the addresses right now."

"Did they get any more intel from the vehicle? GPS history or registration?"

"A dead end. It was a stolen older model black SUV from Texas without GPS."

"Interesting. A witness from the church burning saw a black SUV with Texas plates near the church minutes before the fire started. I think we're onto something." Lexi's phone dinged to Kaplan's incoming text. "I got the addresses you sent. Thanks for the hard work, Kaplan. I'll let you know what we find." She finished her call, turned to walk out but stopped in her tracks.

"I'm glad you came." Zoe's slight slur and stumble on her heels suggested she was well past tipsy. She steadied herself by placing a hand high on Lexi's chest, but then she slowly slid that hand downward, grazing the swell of a breast.

"Whoa." Lexi tempered her response from nuclear—decking her with a right cross—to considerate. She attributed the inappropriateness to the tequila, eased Zoe's hand down, and took a step away to reclaim her personal space. "You better get back to the party."

"But I'd rather be here with you." Zoe stepped closer until she boxed Lexi against the stall door and the smell of her perfume tickled her nose.

"I'm flattered, Zoe, but I'm with Nita." Lexi slid across the metal door until she was clear of the potential disaster. When she turned, Nita was standing several feet away with her arms crossed over her chest, one hip cocked out in a fighting stance, and eyes screaming bloody murder.

"There you are. I was just coming out to find you." Lexi moved closer and kissed Nita, making a show of it for Zoe's sake. It had the added benefit of cooling down her girlfriend. Nita's expression turned from one of threatening to stuff Zoe's head down a toilet to wanting to take Lexi to bed. "I have to get back to work," Lexi added.

"You're lucky I don't want to get my dress wet." Nita glared at Zoe until she hightailed it out of the room. She then returned her attention to Lexi.

"You left poor Noah to fend for himself. Now half the women out there are trying to get him on the dance floor."

"I'm sure he's enjoying the attention, but I better rescue the man before Zoe gets her claws into him." Lexi moved toward the door, but Nita grabbed her by both lapels of her jacket, pulling their bodies together.

"I trust you," she said in a husky tone, "but I expect a proper apology when I get home."

"That goes without saying, but I'm not sure how long I'll be with this case."

"Based on how much Jenny's bridal party is drinking, I have a feeling you'll beat me back to our apartment. I'm going to be driving all over Dallas tonight getting them home."

"Let's rescue Noah." Lexi took Nita by the hand and led her back to their table. Nita was right. Four women surrounded Noah, none of whom Lexi had seen before. One offered him a shot glass, but he waved her off. Another whispered into his ear, but he shook his head with the vigor of taking a cold shower.

"Sorry, ladies, but the meat market is closed." Lexi snickered before winking at Noah. "We gotta go. Kaplan came through with some new leads."

Noah pushed himself up, looking unfazed after being labeled the prime cut for the night. In Lexi's younger days, she would have walked out of the club with an extra swagger, resembling a preening cock. But Noah wasn't, making Lexi wonder if he was merely focused on the case or if something else was bothering him.

17

After striking out at the first plant, Lexi and Noah waited for the night shift supervising engineer in the lobby of the second chemical manufacturer on Kaplan's list. Surprisingly, one name wasn't on it. Lone Star Chemical was the company that had shipped the powdered nitroglycerin to Kansas City fifteen months ago that the Gatekeepers had hijacked. Lexi assumed either it had stopped producing nitro or had gone out of business.

Scanning the paintings in the building lobby, Noah had dropped the long face he had leaving the Beebo Club. Lexi stepped up to him, shoulder to shoulder, eyeing the portrait of the company founder. "You were a big hit with the ladies."

"It would seem that way, but some women are only interested in the novelty of hooking up with someone with my condition."

"That might be true at a straight club, but the Beebo is home to lesbians, gays, bisexuals, trans folks, you name it. It's nothing but otherness. Yours is simply part of the mix."

Noah gave her a slight, playful shoulder shove. "Thanks."

"Agent Mills?" The deep male voice behind them had a noticeable drawl, reminiscent of a cheesy Western movie. Lexi and Noah turned to greet him.

"Yes." Lexi settled her badge dangling in front of her chest.

"I'm Brad Fisher, the night manager. How can I help you?" The curly ends of his handlebar mustache danced when he spoke. Lexi envisioned him with garters around the long sleeves of his shirt in a Wild West saloon, playing the piano. She introduced herself and Noah. "Well, what brings the ATF and a border fella out this time of night?"

"Nitroglycerin," Lexi said. "I understand you manufacture it here."

"Yes, that's one of many chemicals we produce. Our nitroglycerin is for pharmaceutical purposes. We crystallize the liquid into powder form."

"Is any missing?"

Fisher laughed. "Darlin', if some were missing, I'd be out of a job. We have strict controls for every chemical we produce because the EPA gives us a rectal exam every year. If we're one milligram off, heads roll."

"We'd still like to see your production and shipment records for the last two years." Lexi handed him a business card. "Can you email them to me?"

"I'll have to get the day shift on that. The support staff comes in at eight."

"That will be fine, thank you. Tell me, we've already been to BioTech, and we're on the way to TriStar Chemical. Do you know of any other manufacturers that produce nitroglycerin?"

"As far as I know, that's it, but Lone Star, I mean TriStar, is closed at night. They're too small to operate around the clock."

"Wait. You said Lone Star."

"Force of habit. They were Lone Star for twenty years until they got bought out two months ago. It's hard to call an old dog by a new name."

Lexi got her third wind of the night when the wheels churned in her head. The Gatekeepers had gone silent since Darby's death. Not a single law enforcement agency had heard a word about their organization. No one knew where Tony Belcher and his lieutenants had fled following the failed incursion into his compound. The only connection she could find was Belcher's brother, also known as Amadeus. According to an informant, he composed the grand revolution plan, but he was sitting in a windowless seven-by-eleven cell in the United States Penitentiary, Atwater, on federal weapons charges and wasn't talking. Looking into the Red Spades might be Lexi's chance to pick up the trail again.

Mr. Fisher assured Lexi he'd have the day shift send her the reports that showed they'd crossed every *t* and dotted every *i*, accounting for their nitro. She thanked him and returned to her SUV. Noah hopped in, yawning.

"I think we should call it a night," Lexi said. "The couch is still yours unless you want to find a hotel."

"I think I'll take the couch. We can get an early start tomorrow, and I can give Nita another cooking lesson at breakfast."

Once they returned to the apartment, Lexi set up Noah with a makeshift bed using a flat sheet, blanket, and pillow. "You'll be comfortable here. I've been falling asleep on this couch for years. I'll let Nita know to keep the light off when she comes home."

"I'll be fine. TriStar opens at nine. What time should we leave in the morning?"

"It's on the other side of town, so considering traffic, we should get out of here at eight."

"All right, then. Breakfast is at seven-thirty."

"Then it will probably just be you and me. I doubt Nita will be up by then. She's the designated driver tonight."

"Ahh. The last one home. Maybe another time."

"Good night, Noah. I'll set out a towel for you in the bathroom."

Lexi returned to her bedroom, where she started her limb care after removing her prosthetic. Having worn the artificial leg for eleven months, she thought she'd gotten used to it. However, these long days without giving her residual limb a chance to breathe had taken a toll on her. As expected, the nub was red. In addition, the surrounding skin had begun to chafe, making it extra sensitive.

Dating a physical therapist came in handy at times like this. On their first night in the apartment, after moving furniture and boxes for hours, Nita had given her a professional massage and reduced the soreness and swelling to virtually nothing. Lexi made a mental note to never plan a full day in the prosthetic without Nita being around at night.

Her phone chirped. The unique tone meant Nita had sent her a text. Lexi wiped the lotion from her hands with a towel before swiping the screen. The message read: *still going strong here. don't wait up. love u.*

Lexi hoped Nita could make it through the night without giving Zoe a well-deserved swirly. She texted back: *You're stronger than you realize. have fun. love u.* Resting her phone on the nightstand, Lexi slipped beneath the covers. She tried to clear her mind, but thoughts of the last few days roiled like a whirlwind. Sewer. Tunnel. Death. Fire. Church. Grimes. Torture. Nitro. They flew in, one after another, on a loop.

"Stop it," she told herself.

Whenever she encountered the periodic thoughtless homophobe or race-baiter, Lexi compartmentalized her emotion by chalking the experience up to idiots she'd never come across again. But work was a different story. Turning off the emotion switch at the end of the day always took time. The Beebo Club was a needed distraction, but seeing her girlfriend didn't help her lift the feeling that she had the weight of the world on her shoulders. Maybe Nita was right. Maybe Lexi hadn't healed emotionally from Darby's death.

Lexi rolled over and clutched her pillow, hoping she'd dream of Nita and that little black dress, but deep down, she knew what was in store—Darby and more guilt.

18

Nita's phone dinged as it rested on the tabletop. Reading it brought out a much-needed smile. Lexi intuitively knew the words she needed to hear... or read...tonight. Six years of sobriety still hadn't erased the craving Nita felt when she was around people who were drinking or doing recreational drugs. Her addiction was a slow creep that started with alcohol and weed to get her through college. Working her way through graduate school, though, she found escaping wasn't an option. She needed energy boosts to survive the sixteen-hour days. That meant cocaine. And when that didn't do the trick, she moved on to meth. It had given her the rush she needed, but the crash afterward was horrible. It had turned her into someone she didn't recognize. The morning of waking in her own vomit was the wake-up call she'd needed.

Apart from Jenny, Nita had burned every bridge with her family, which was why she put up with her cousin's crazy friends, including Zoe. However, her hitting on Lexi tonight, knowing they were girlfriends, made Nita rethink the patient approach.

A hand fell in Nita's field of vision at the table as she contemplated a sexy reply. Whoever it was, they nicked the cell phone from her grasp. "No phones tonight," Jenny slurred before plopping into the retro chair next to her.

"Can't a woman say goodnight to her girlfriend?" Nita snatched her phone back, tucking it into the hidden waist pocket at her back.

"Only if it's your hot butch, Lexi Mills," Jenny said as the others filled in the seats around the table. Each was dripping with sweat from bouncing around to the beat of Keith Urban and Tim McGraw.

"Is she coming back?" one asked. "We never got to dance."

"Yes, please tell me she's coming back," Zoe said, as if Lexi and Nita's relationship didn't exist. She'd laid out her chum in the water, baiting Nita to take it. But this was Jenny's night, and Nita wasn't about to stain it. Therefore, avoidance was the better option.

"I'll be right back, ladies. We should think about calling it a night." However, the groans Nita received suggested she was in for a long night still.

Nita went to the restroom for two reasons: the Coke she'd been drinking had kicked in, and so had her craving for a high. Though alcohol wasn't one of her addictions, she'd discovered early in her journey toward sobriety that drinking would lead her to them, so she avoided it. Tonight, though, with the constant bombardment of offers from strangers and watching her friends unwind until not a kink was left in their cords, was the closest Nita had come to giving in.

Nita finished and stood at the sink, washing her hands and giving herself a needed pep talk. "You got this." She pulled out her phone and texted: *Exactly what I needed to hear. C U soon to collect that apology.*

Zoe and another bridesmaid walked in on their three-inch heels, holding the other up from falling flat on their faces. Zoe bounced off the wall hard, sparking a giggle-fest between them. *I hope that leaves a bruise.* Nita plucked two paper towels from the holder at the far end of the counter, chuckling at her inappropriate thought.

"Did you see the Lexi lookalike come in?" the bridesmaid asked. "Swoon-worthy."

"You can have her," Zoe said. "I'm waiting for the real thing." Maid of honor or not, this girlfriend-steeling jezebel needed to learn boundaries. A swirly was rightfully deserved, but if Nita wanted to keep the peace through Sunday's wedding, she needed an equally shocking alternative.

Nita crumpled the paper towel and tossed it into the trashcan below the dispenser before holding up an index finger in front of Zoe. "Hold that thought." She exited the bathroom and went straight to the bartender. She was tall and thin, not necessarily her type, but attractive nonetheless in a black tie, white shirt, and shoulder-length hair razored on one side. "Hi, Sam. A pitcher of ice water."

"Coming right up, Nita." Sam fussed on her side of the bar below Nita's line of sight. "Is your crew slowing down? You're not even close to hitting your budget."

"Oh no, they're still going strong," Nita replied loudly over the music that had turned up a notch. "This is to teach someone boundaries."

Sam slid the full pitcher across the bar top. "Just no catfights. Anything broken goes on your bill."

"Gladly." Snatching the pitcher, Nita spun to return to the restroom, but Zoe and the bridesmaid had exited. They were staggering toward the bridal party table. That was Nita's target. She'd let Jenny and the others decide her fate. Instead of sitting, she stood behind her chair, ready to mete out whatever punishment the group chose. "Ladies, I have a question for everyone. What would you do to someone who was hot for your girlfriend and tried to steal her right in front of you?"

"Bitch-slap her," one shouted over the music.

"That might land her in jail," Jenny said. "Whoever she is, she needs to cool it."

"I thought you'd say that." Nita smiled, stepped behind Zoe, and dealt out her punishment. In two seconds, Zoe was a dripping mess from balayage to thong. She sat stunned, mouth agape. The others gasped before breaking out in laughter. "You better think twice before laying a hand on my girl-friend again, Zoe. If there's a next time, you'll get a mouth of toilet water."

Nita turned on her heel, letting a self-satisfied grin form. Message sent and received. She then retraced her steps to the bar and hailed Sam over. "Mission accomplished?" Sam asked.

"She might rethink her stance on girlfriend stealing." Nita slid the empty pitcher to her.

Sam laughed, grasping the plastic handle. "Just as convincing as a Louisville Slugger."

"I suppose so." Nita turned to go back to the table, but before she could leave, the woman standing next to her tipped her empty cocktail glass at her.

"That was an impressive show," the woman said. "Can I buy you a drink?" She must have been the Lexi lookalike the bridesmaid had mentioned. She had her girlfriend's collar-length brown hair, short stature, and a thin athletic frame. The woman was her type, but Lexi already had her heart.

"Thank you, but I don't drink." What that girlfriend-stealing brides-maid wouldn't give to be in Nita's position. She moved toward the tables, but the woman placed a hand on her arm—soft and seductive.

"A dance, then?" The rasp in her voice hinted that she had more than dancing in mind.

This one was persistent, attractive, and looked too confident to not be a player. Unfortunately, those qualities made her a triple dose of trouble to those who failed to read the lay of the land accurately. Harmless looking, though, she deserved to be let down gently. "Thank you, but my girlfriend has my dance card full tonight and every night."

The sound of party poppers rang from the other side of the nightclub near the entrance. Shouts from the dance floor got louder. Both were signs another celebration was underway.

"Perhaps another time, if your circumstances change."

The woman shifted as if to walk away but suddenly lunged forward into Nita. She slouched, and Nita braced her by both elbows, but she'd gone limp. Liquid trickled onto one of Nita's hands, making her grasp at the woman precariously. She then turned her head to ask Sam for help, but her torso lay slumped over the bar with her face turned on a cheek. Her eyes remained open but unblinking, unmoving.

The woman Nita had been propping up had become dead weight, and Nita could no longer hold on. The woman fell to the floor when shouts from the dance floor turned into terrifying screams. A wave of people rushed toward the back of the club, where the bathrooms and the bar were. Several fell and were trampled in the pandemonium.

Nita's pulse raced at an undeniable conclusion—a shooter was on the loose. Her breaths became shallow at the uncertainty of what she should do next.

The crackle of the party poppers had become louder and more decipherable, confirming her horrifying assumption. They were gunshots in rapid succession, and their source was coming closer. Nita frantically scanned the frenzied crowd for Jenny, but the chaos made it impossible to make out faces. She shouted her name. More people dropped to the floor in mid-stride. Some pushed past her, seeking refuge behind the bar.

Nita heard her name, but she couldn't tell where it had come from. She called out her cousin's name again, and then Jenny appeared, stumbling into her arms. Her dress was bloodstained, and her eyes bulged, unable to blink.

"Are you okay?" Nita asked, staring at the blood spatter on her face.

Jenny's hands and lips trembled. "Maria and Sophie were shot right in front of me."

"What about Zoe?"

"I don't know. She went to the bathroom to dry off."

"She should be okay. There's an exit at the end of the hallway. We need to get there."

The shooting continued, but the screams eerily slowed to isolated groans and cries. Finally, the shooting stopped. So did the music. But then the distinctive clang of an ammo magazine being slammed into the frame of a gun sounded. Nita had heard that same sound several times when Lexi had rearmed her service weapon in the morning before leaving for work.

If Nita and Jenny had any chance of getting out of there alive, they needed to go for the back exit while the shooter was reloading and other people were still moving. So, Nita tugged Jenny by the hand and dashed toward the restrooms. *Ten steps*, she thought, and they'd reach the hallway. Another twelve, and they'd be at the emergency exit.

Nita counted down in her head to keep herself focused as she rushed among a stream of people who seemed to have the same idea of escaping. Then, a gunshot rang out, followed by a scream. Then another. She reached the narrow corridor through which people funneled like blood flowing in veins.

A gunshot clanged, but this time it vibrated the walls in the confined area, and the smell of gunpowder clouded their path. Screams filled the hallway. The shooter had followed them. *Dear God.* They'd be trapped like fish in a barrel if the exit door clogged.

A butch pushed through, forcing Nita's and Jenny's hands apart. Nita was driven two steps farther down, but she forced herself against the wall to look for her cousin. She finally glimpsed Jenny behind a woman in flannel and reached out for her.

"Grab my hand." Nita's fingers stretched in desperation until they clutched Jenny's hand.

The flannel-shirted woman fell to the floor at the sound of another gunshot. Blood spattered on Nita's face, covering her eyes. She blinked to clear it. Panic filled the hallway, but Jenny froze in place, staring at the lifeless body at her feet.

"Move!" Nita yelled. She then yanked hard, pulling Jenny in front of her. They were only three steps from the door where others were escaping. She pushed her cousin forward two more steps, but then a sharp, burning pain enveloped her left shoulder at the sound of another gunshot. The force and agony made her stumble. On her way to the linoleum, she shoved Jenny out the door. "Go."

Nita looked back. The hallway was scattered with bodies and blood. The only one left standing was the masked man. She felt weak as he approached while pointing the gun directly at her head. Nita's surroundings grew darker. She was losing blood fast.

Another gunshot.

The man's posture stiffened, his eyes widening in the holes of his ski mask.

Everything went black.

19

Darby smiled in Lexi's direction, his white teeth glowing a neon green through her night vision goggles. His grin reassured her that everything would be all right. He then regripped his detector and turned to complete the mine sweep.

Bang. Bang. Bang.

The sudden noise distracted Darby, causing his foot to slip. A cylinder then sprang waist high from the ground, blowing him off his feet. As he flew through the air, a bright flash blinded Lexi.

Bang. Bang. Bang.

Lexi woke with a start, her heart pounding like a kettle drum.

"Lexi." Noah's muffled voice through her bedroom door contained a sense of urgency. "You should come out here."

"Hold on." It took her a moment to clear the fog of sleep from her head. Finally, she cast her gaze to the alarm clock on the dresser across the room. It read 6:38 a.m.—twenty-two minutes before she had set it to bray. "Give me a minute to get my leg on."

Lexi threw the covers off and hopped to the dresser, pulling out a fresh limb liner and two layers of socks to go over it. She returned to the bed to don her prosthetic leg correctly, wondering what had Noah up so early. Her money was on the coffee machine. It worked but not as advertised. The swing door that held the coffee basket in place needed a rubber band around it for the sensor to recognize it was closed. But other than their crudely fashioned solution, it was a perfectly good machine that Nita refused to replace.

Once dressed, Lexi entered the hallway to voices coming from the living room television. She recognized the tone of the local morning news reporter as she was going on about a shooting in the metro area last night. While all shootings were horrible, it didn't come as a surprise. Dallas was a center for narco-trafficking, and much of the city's gun violence involved the gangs peddling it.

Entering the room, Lexi stopped next to Noah, who was staring at the TV. She focused more on buttoning her shirt than on the screen. "Another gang shooting?" she asked.

"They're not sure yet." Noah faced her, gently gripping both upper arms. "Someone shot up the Beebo Club after we left."

Lexi went numb, fighting the rush of horrifying assumptions. Noah said something more, but his voice sounded muffled as if he were speaking under water, making his words indecipherable. She turned her head slowly toward the screen to read the graphics. The words and numbers paralyzed her chest. Breathing became an impossibility.

Thirteen dead. Twenty-eight wounded.

Video taken from inside the club played on the screen, but it was too wobbly to be security camera footage. Someone visiting the club must have taken it from a cell phone. It started with a familiar scene of the Beebo dance floor with dozens of women paired off swaying and bobbing to country music. It then focused on a particular couple, a femme dressed in heels and a tight red number and a Chapstick lesbian dressed in cargos, tennies, and a pullover golf shirt. A hookup was definitely on the night's agenda. Lexi scanned the other women in the frame, looking for Nita and Jenny, but didn't recognize any of the women's outfits.

A loud pop like a firecracker sounded in the video. A second. A third caused the couple to stop dancing and the camera to shake. All heads turned toward a single direction. A second later, a wave of people formed and retreated in the opposite direction. The camera view followed the wave, capturing the fear on people's faces with screams and loud music still in the background. The screen became jittery, but it was clear enough to make out that several people had fallen among the panic.

The video became clear again. The music had stopped. It appeared people had jammed into a narrow corridor. If memory served Lexi properly, the only hallway accessible to patrons led to the bathrooms and an emergency exit door. The wave of people thinned but continued to move with the camera view following behind a flannel-shirted woman. Then a woman in a white dress came briefly into view. Was that Jenny? The sash over her shoulder appeared stained with dark spots.

Lexi realized she'd been breathing too shallow when her rapid intakes of air made her dizzy. Then the crack of gunfire popped loudly onscreen. More screams. The woman in flannel fell. The video became jittery again before showing people running down an alleyway.

When the local reporter flashed on the TV again, Lexi steadied herself enough to turn on her good heel. "I'll be right back," she said to Noah in a slow, almost robotic voice. She needed to check her phone but refused to rush. If no unread messages filled her screen, that likely meant the worst had happened, and Nita was among the thirteen dead. Her plodding steps delayed the ghastly reality waiting for her. Its possible harshness had turned her legs into lead weights, making each step seem as if her feet were caught among the fallen and required extra-human strength to lift and move forward.

Lexi paused at the door. Her phone wasn't in its regular resting place atop the nightstand, so she'd hear it vibrate against the wood surface. She then remembered falling asleep shortly after reading Nita's sexy reply about collecting on her promised apology. Echoes of what she'd conjured up in her head last night came back. She'd planned to greet Nita with soft music playing when she came home, take her by the hand, and dance with her in the middle of their bedroom floor. And when Nita had become putty, Lexi would guide her to the bed. She'd then make love to her there until all thoughts of Zoe stroking her like a fur chinchilla had evaporated.

Lexi stepped to the bed. The covers were still near the foot where she had tossed them, exposing nothing but a wrinkled white fitted sheet. That left only one place where her phone might be hiding. She gripped the corner of the pillow that was askew on Nita's side and dragged it toward her.

The phone soon appeared right where Nita's head would have been most of the night if she'd made it home.

Lexi's heart thumped harder, making her chest flutter and cheeks flush with the heat of fear. Once she touched the phone, the screen would light up and show what notifications were waiting for her. She expected the breaking news alerts highlighting the horrifying events at the Beebo Club to be there and cautioned herself to not let their presence give her false hope.

Lexi lifted the phone. The screen lit. The top notification was a grouping of news alerts. The top one listed the wounded count at twenty-eight but had kept the fatalities steady at thirteen. She paused before touching the screen. Besides news alerts, she'd also set up her phone to display missed calls and text messages on the lock screen. If nothing was below the grim reports, she'd instantly know Nita's fate.

She thumbed down at an agonizingly slow crawl, reaching a blank section at the bottom of the news alert. The back of her throat grew thick, and she hoped she hadn't reached the bottom, but she continued. Finally, a green icon appeared with Nita's name listed to the left.

Three missed calls.

A rush of relief hit Lexi like a tidal wave. Her gut clenched, forcing her to hunch over. She placed her hands and the phone on her knees, gasping for air. Nita had called. That meant she was alive. Lexi slumped her bottom to the mattress, resting her elbows atop her legs. Her eyes welled with tears, lips trembling.

She turned her phone over again and scrolled further down the screen, where she found a text message alert. The preview said it was from Nita. She pressed to read it: *Shot highland park please come.*

Lexi gasped, covering her mouth with a hand. Though Nita never texted in complete sentences, she always used limited punctuation. Its absence meant Nita had likely used the voice function to draft and send the message. That meant she couldn't use her hands. Guilt then swallowed Lexi. The woman she loved had been shot and may be fighting for her life while Lexi slept.

"Focus," Lexi told herself. This was not the time to fall apart. Nita needed her, and Noah was in the other room, waiting to track down the next lead. Then, like cramming a bulky sleeping bag back into a small sack, she stuffed the emotion that nearly overwhelmed her into a virtual box, locked it, and hid the key.

Not knowing how long she might be at the hospital, Lexi gathered a few toiletries and extra sets of clothes. She added a limb liner and socks and tucked everything into her backpack. After securing her service weapon to her waistband, Lexi took a cleansing breath to clear the lingering emotion in her chest. She then returned to the living room, where Noah stood silent with a questioning expression.

Now in her professional mode, Lexi filled her voice with calm. "Nita has been shot and was taken to Highland Park ER. That's all I know. I have to go."

"Is there anyone I can call to meet you there? Family?" Noah asked.

"The only family still talking to Nita was Jenny, but I'm not sure if she's alive."

"I'll come with you then," Noah said.

"I don't know how long I'll be. You should follow up on our last lead."

"Are you sure? I know this can't be easy." At Lexi's hard no, he continued. "All right. I'll call for a ride and check out TriStar. I'll text if I find anything."

Lexi went to the entry table near the door, retrieved the spare key to the apartment from the ceramic bowl, and returned to Noah. "Leave your stuff here. Here's a key. If you still have to fly home tonight and I'm not back yet, lock up and leave the key with the super on the first floor."

Lexi stepped toward the door, but Noah grabbed her by the hand. He offered a sad smile and lightly rubbed her arms. "Let me know how she's doing, and please, call if you need anything."

20

Driving to the hospital was a novel experience in patience. According to her phone GPS, the commute traffic would nearly double the transit time. Listening to the local radio reports in the car threatened to unbolt the emotion she'd successfully locked away, but Lexi couldn't help herself. Like a rubbernecker passing a five-car pileup, she had to listen. The reports provided her with more information about the shooting, specifically that an off-duty San Francisco police officer had shot and killed the unnamed suspect. If not for the quick actions of the out-of-town hero, authorities surmised the death toll would have been much higher. Lexi also learned that, according to witnesses, the suspect was a white male in his thirties, with a bald head and tattoos, suggesting he had ties to the Aryan Brotherhood. That was no coincidence.

Lexi dialed her phone connected to her SUV's speakers via Bluetooth. Agent Carlson picked up on the fourth ring. "Boss, this is Mills."

"Mills?" He paused. The early hour must have found him still in bed or without his morning jolt of caffeine. "Why are you calling so early? Didn't you have a party to go to last night?"

"I went for an hour, but Detective Black and I left to follow up on another lead. Sir, have you seen the news about the nightclub shooting in Dallas last night?"

"I did. Shocking."

"That was the club I went to last night. I'm on my way to the hospital now because my girlfriend is among the wounded."

"Christ, Mills. I'm so sorry. Take all the time you need. I can assign someone else to assist on the Nogales investigation."

"Don't pull the trigger on that yet, sir. I heard a report that the shooter last night may have been associated with the Aryan Brotherhood, like the bank robbery suspect we interviewed yesterday."

"The Brotherhood has over twenty thousand members. It could be a coincidence."

"I don't believe in coincidences during investigations. Hours after I link the Aryan Brotherhood suspect to the Red Spades, someone from the same gang shoots up a club I'd just been in. I've stirred a hornet's nest, and that tells me that Detective Black and I are getting close."

"All right, Mills. I'll send Connors to look into it."

"What about Kaplan Shaw? She already knows the nuances about the case."

"Shaw isn't a field agent. Let me worry about assignments."

Lexi finished the call and pulled into the hospital parking lot, feeling uneasy about the tenor of the conversation. She made a mental note to never hit up her boss before he'd had his morning coffee.

The emergency department at the Highland Park Hospital was as packed as a subway station in Tokyo during rush hours. Yet, surprisingly, it wasn't chaotic. Gone was the traditional early-morning crowd of the uninsured seeking medical help for some ailment or minor injury that their primary physician could have addressed. But that assumed they had money to do so. Lexi surmised those people had been diverted elsewhere to accommodate the friends and family of the wounded brought in from the Beebo Club. She discarded the idea of using her badge to cut to the front of the three-person-deep line at the reception desk. In this instance, Lexi wasn't a cop. She was a concerned family member. Or as close to family as she could be without saying "I do."

Lexi stood in line and waited for the nurse behind the desk to call her up before flashing her badge and credentials. The man's droopy eyes made him look tired. It had been nearly six hours since the shooting, and he likely had been thrown into the role of keeping distraught loved ones calm since the first victim arrived.

"May I help you?" he asked.

"I'm Special Agent Lexi Mills. My girlfriend, Anita Flores, was wounded at the Beebo Club. Can you tell me how she is? Is she alive?" Worst-case scenarios suddenly ran through her head. All she knew was that Nita was shot but not how bad. Was it life-threatening? Did her condition take a turn for the worse since sending the text message to Lexi? Those unbearable thoughts brought back the anxiety she'd endured in her bedroom earlier, but thankfully it wasn't as debilitating.

The nurse entered something in the computer terminal. When he read the information on the screen, his expression was unreadable, adding to Lexi's frustration. Ten seconds passed. Then twenty before he responded. "I apologize for the delay. I had to check Miss Flores's HIPAA information." His expression softened. "She's alive, Agent Mills. Miss Flores had surgery to repair a gunshot wound to her left shoulder." He passed along her room number, which, thankfully, wasn't in the intensive care unit.

The shock of learning about the shooting and the ensuing half hour of worry had taken its toll. Lexi went limp, but she braced herself against the counter to prevent becoming another patient. "Thank you."

The last half hour would have reduced to ash any underlying doubt whether Lexi loved Nita, but she clearly had none. The emptiness she felt when she thought Nita might have been among the thirteen fallen blew that theory out of the water. Lexi had dated a dozen women and hooked up with a dozen more but had told only two that she loved them. But what she'd felt for Alyssa in college paled in comparison. Nita had peeled back the thick layers Lexi built to protect herself from the cruelness often encountered in a world where otherness was mocked and preyed upon. Nita was the only one with whom Lexi felt safe enough to reveal her true self. The only person to make her feel as if she wasn't alone.

The eighth-floor corridor was hopping with nurses, visitors, and patients waddling in gowns, pushing IV stands. Room 832, Nita's room, was nearly at the end of the hallway. Glancing into rooms as she passed, Lexi noted the patients. Everyone was female, some femme and some butch-looking, and of clubbing age. Lexi stopped and doubled back when she saw a familiar face sitting in bed, staring at the television mounted high on the wall. She entered.

"Zoe? Are you okay?" Lexi focused on the cast on Zoe's left lower leg.

Zoe, dressed in a hospital gown, ripped her gaze from the news channel playing video from last night's massacre on a loop. Her face was bruised, and her eyes were red and puffy, all signs of trauma. "My God, Lexi. It was horrible."

"What happened to you?"

"I got trampled when I came out of the bathroom and broke my ankle. Thankfully, someone helped me out."

"I've only heard about Nita. That's why I'm here. What about the rest of the ladies from the party last night?"

Zoe's eyes filled with tears. She shook her head with the vigor of untold grief. "Maria and Sophie are dead."

Lexi threw a hand to her mouth to mask her shock. "What about Jenny?"

"Unhurt. She was just here. I think she's in with Nita."

Lexi stepped closer and squeezed Zoe's hand, the one without the IV. "You're safe now."

Zoe shifted on the mattress and tapped the cast around her leg. "We'll be twinsies for a while." Her expression remained long, and her voice lacked the seductive tone it had at the club last night. In its place was a mix of fear and denial. Humor, Lexi supposed, was Zoe's way of coping.

"I guess we will. I'll have to give you some pointers on using crutches. Take care, Zoe." Lexi squeezed her hand again before leaving and continuing her trek down the corridor.

Lexi paused at the hospital room door. Until now, the worst she'd nursed Nita through was a paper cut. However, a gunshot wound was no minor skin slice. She needed a moment to gather herself before seeing her girlfriend this broken. Lexi stiffened her posture, put up a brave front, and stepped inside.

Jenny was sitting at the foot of the bed. She'd exchanged her white cocktail dress, bloody sash, and heels for a workout attire likely brought by her fiancée, who was standing sentinel several feet away. Her sweet Nita was propped up in bed at a reclined angle. She had a bulky bandage around her left shoulder and a loose-fitting hospital gown covering her upper body. Tubes and wires ran from her torso and wounded arm. The possibility that the shooter might have been associated with Lexi and Noah's case made her more emotional than she'd expected. It might have been Lexi's fault that her Nita was lying in a hospital bed.

Lexi cleared her throat to get their attention. Three heads snapped in her direction.

"It's about damn time." Jenny's curled lip smacked with disapproval, but Lexi couldn't blame her after sleeping through Nita's entire ordeal. However, that didn't seem to matter to Nita. She'd remained silent, but her eyes had become shimmery with moisture.

Lexi sat on the edge of the bed, opposite the side of the bandages and wires, and ran her fingertips gently down Nita's cheek. Her pupils were the size of pinheads, likely from the anesthesia or pain meds. "I love you."

Tears dropped from both eyes and trailed down Nita's cheeks. She then croaked the words, "I love you, too."

"Are you in pain?"

"Not right now." Nita clutched Lexi's hands. "They have me on pretty strong stuff, and that scares the hell out of me."

"I know it does." Lexi kissed Nita on the lips, making sure not to disturb the wires and tubes attached to her when she returned upright. "But you're stronger than you realize."

Nita squeezed Lexi's hand, and her lips trembled. "I hope so."

"I know you are because you're a fighter." Lexi cupped her other hand over their entwined ones. "I heard about Maria and Sophie. I'm so sorry."

Nita lasered her stare on Jenny still at the other end of the bed as a river of tears flowed from her eyes.

"They were shot right in front of me," Jenny said. "If Maria and Sophie hadn't blocked the bullets, I would have been shot too." Jenny rubbed Nita's leg through the thin hospital blanket. "And if not for this one shoving me out the door, I would have taken a bullet in the corridor. She saved my life."

"It doesn't surprise me." Lexi returned her attention to Nita, sending love in her voice and eyes. "My lady is the strongest, bravest person I know."

"Can you give us some time alone, Jenny?" Nita pressed a button on the side railing, raising it to a more upright position.

"Of course." Jenny kissed her cousin on the forehead before giving Lexi the side-eye. "You deserve better than an absentee girlfriend." She tapped the cell phone resting on the rolling bed tray a few feet away. "Call if you need anything. We'll bring you a milkshake for lunch."

When Jenny and her fiancée left, the temperature in the room rose several degrees. But Lexi wasn't about to let that tension linger. Instead, she closed the door behind them and returned to the bed. "Is there room for me?"

Nita grimaced while she scooted to one side of the vinyl mattress, clearing a section for Lexi. "There's always room for you."

Lexi sat next to her, side by side, so their bodies touched from shoulder to her prosthetic. Then, entwining their fingers, she brought Nita's hand to her lips and kissed the back of it. "I'm so sorry I wasn't here for you earlier. I didn't get your messages until I woke and saw the news."

"You're here now. That's all that matters."

"Can you tell me what happened?" Lexi asked, closing her eyes to let the images of last night form in her head.

Nita recounted the disturbing events, starting with talking to a Lexi lookalike at the bar. She concluded with, "When they put me in the ambulance, my first thought was of calling you."

Lexi weighed whether to tell her about the possible connection to her case but thought better of it. Doing so would only worry Nita when she needed to concentrate on healing. "I should have been there for you."

"You're here now." Nita snuggled her head into the crook of Lexi's neck.

"And I'm going to be *there* for you." Lexi gave Nita's hand an extra squeeze. "It's my turn to help you heal and make you whole again."

"You might be signing up for more than you realize. I'm not a good patient."

"As if I was a walk in the park." Lexi snorted at her own stubbornness and how it set her back more than once. And how those setbacks made her impossible to deal with for several days.

"You'd had a lot taken from you," Nita slurred.

"Do you know how extensive the damage is to your shoulder?"

"Not yet. I'm waiting for the surgeon to make his morning rounds."

"Then how about we get some sleep until he or she comes?" Lexi located the controls on the bed railing and pressed the down button for the head. "Tell me when."

Movement next to Lexi nudged her awake. "Lex, wake up," Nita said. "The doctor is here."

Lexi popped her eyes open, finding a male doctor in scrubs and a white lab coat standing near the foot of the bed. "I'm sorry to wake you two, but I need to examine Nita."

"Oh, sure, Doc." Lexi maneuvered from the bed, rubbing Nita's leg for extra assurance on her way up.

"I'm the surgeon who operated on you earlier this morning." The doctor raised the bed more before carefully examining beneath Nita's bandage.

"I'm glad it was you, Dr. Posten. My physical therapy patients rave about you."

"Well, then. It's wonderful to have another happy customer." He gently returned the dressing to its position. "The incision looks good. You're one lucky lady, Nita. The bullet missed your lung. It did, however, damage your scapula and deltoid and pectoral muscles. The damage was extensive, so I inserted a plate and four screws to stabilize the fragments. You'll be in a sling for a few weeks. Then we'll start you on physical therapy."

"I know all about PT, Dr. Posten. I'm a therapist."

"An excellent therapist," Lexi added.

"Then you know that you have a tough road ahead of you, but if we manage your pain effectively, I'm optimistic you can get back to a full range of motion in a matter of months."

"When can I take her home, Doc?" Lexi asked.

"She had some blood loss, so I want to keep her overnight. If her labs and numbers look good in the morning, there's no reason you can't take her home this time tomorrow." Then he turned his attention to Nita. "I'll send you home with a prescription for an antibiotic, an anti-inflammatory, and pain medication."

"I'd like to manage this without pain meds." Nita didn't explain further. Her addiction was a sensitive issue she rarely spoke of and never volunteered. And Lexi wasn't about to violate her trust by bringing it up.

"That's the physical therapist in you speaking," Dr. Posten said. "You've endured a severe trauma, followed by major surgery, so rest is critical early in your recovery. In addition, it will be important to manage the swelling and pain to avoid putting more stress on your body. The medication is the best way of doing that."

"I get that, but if it's all the same, I'll skip the opioids." The determination in Nita's voice made Lexi proud. Her girlfriend was stronger than even Lexi realized.

"We'll see how you feel when the morphine wears off." The doctor entered some information into a computer terminal in the corner of the room before promising to check on Nita first thing in the morning.

Lexi returned to her spot on the bed and snuggled next to Nita. "I'm very proud of you."

Nita clutched Lexi's hand again, squeezing it firmly. "I'm afraid I won't be strong enough."

"You can lean on me. We'll get you through this together." Lexi's phone vibrated in her coat pocket. She read the text from Noah Black saying he'd found a solid lead at TriStar Chemical before returning it to its proper place. If there was ever a moment when she wanted peace and quiet and to forget her job, it was right now. But everything she and Noah had dug up suggested that time was of the essence. She sighed at her dilemma.

"It's work, isn't it?" Nita asked.

"It's Noah. He said he has a solid lead."

"Then call him. I know this case is eating you up inside. The faster you find the people behind the bombing, the faster you'll come back to me."

How did Lexi get so lucky? How did she find a woman with enough patience to overlook her absence at a time like last night? Lexi smiled and pressed their lips together in a brief, passionate kiss. "I don't deserve you."

21

Walking out of the hospital, Lexi pushed back the guilt of leaving her girlfriend behind and digested the information Noah had passed along. This could be the lead they needed to catch up with the Red Spades and stop whatever was next on their target list. She then plugged in the address of TriStar Chemical on the western outskirts of Dallas and dialed Agent Shaw. "Kaplan, this is Lexi. I need you to run a background check."

"I'm so sorry, Lexi. News about last night's shooting and Nita is all everyone is talking about at the federal building."

"Bad news travels fast."

"How is she?" Kaplan's concerned tone sounded genuine, not like a social pleasantry.

"I saw her at the hospital. She was shot in the shoulder but should make a full recovery."

"Thank goodness." The relief in Kaplan's voice was palpable. "The few times I met Nita, I absolutely adored her. She's perfect for you."

"Thanks, Kaplan. I think she's perfect for me too."

"Now, whose name do you need me to run?" Kaplan asked.

Lexi reviewed the notes Noah had sent her. "David Lindsey. He's a former employee at TriStar Chemical, which used to be Lone Star Chemical."

"Is there anything specific I'm looking for?" Kaplan asked.

"Some solid nitroglycerine was stolen from a TriStar shipment two months ago. He might be involved. I'm texting you his last known address and the social security number he used there. You should also look up a previous case of stolen nitro from the same plant last year, but they went by Lone Star Chemical then. That shipment was stolen as it rolled into its destination facility in Wichita, Kansas."

"Got it. I'll call you with what I find. And Lexi..." Kaplan paused briefly. "If there's anything I can do to help with Nita, just ask."

"Thanks, Kaplan. I will."

Lexi soon pulled into the parking lot of a diner down the street from TriStar Chemical. She easily spotted Noah in a booth at the back of the restaurant by the unique complexion and white-striped hair that had become oddly comforting. It was another type of badge he and Lexi shared. They wore their otherness on the outside, and it followed them everywhere they went. There was no escaping it, and Noah was the perfect role model for embracing uniqueness.

She plopped down on the bench across from him, emotionally and physically drained. A server followed her to their booth. "Just coffee, please." Her stomach couldn't manage anything substantial. "I picked up your bags like you asked. They're in the back of my SUV."

"Thanks. You didn't say much on the phone." Noah's empty plate and half-filled coffee cup suggested she'd missed breakfast. "How is Nita?"

Lexi detailed the surgery and road of recovery ahead for her girlfriend but left out her concern about the pain killers she'd been given. Though her drug of choice had been stimulants, the addictive nature of opioids was troubling. "They're keeping her overnight, but I can take her home tomorrow."

"I'm relieved she'll be okay," he said.

"Thanks, Noah. I asked Kaplan to run a background check on David Lindsey. Until we hear from her, tell me about the missing nitro, because it was never reported through federal channels."

Noah pulled out a pocket-sized spiral notebook that flipped at the top and thumbed past several pages. "I interviewed the production manager and got a vibe of cooperation. The theft happened under the previous owners' watch. They had dropped the ball on many regulatory requirements around that time. This guy was brought in by the new owner to clean up what he described as a lax atmosphere harbored by the previous management."

"That doesn't surprise me. The company popped up in a case last year when a shipment of solid nitro going to Kansas City was stolen." But that wasn't merely any case. That investigation cost Darby his life and Lexi her lower left leg. And that connection lingered in the back of Lexi's mind. The Red Spades and the Gatekeepers now had two things in common: the nitro and charismatic leaders who could attract a fanatical army.

"The manager mentioned the previous theft. Both shipments were stolen in transit from their contract carrier as the truck entered the destination facility."

"Did Lone Star use the same carrier for both shipments?"

"They did. When the new manager came on board, he immediately changed carriers. What can you tell me about the previous theft?" Noah asked.

"That case cost me my leg and my partner his life."

"I'm sorry to hear that. Is it hard to talk about?"

"It's never easy, but I can tell you I won't rest until I put Tony Belcher behind bars or in a pine box."

"Tell me about Belcher." Noah leaned closer.

"He's a religious fanatic who we tracked to Wichita. He'd been building an army called the Gatekeepers, but it was more like a cult for the coming revolution. We connected the stolen nitro to him and got wind from a family member that he planned to steal a plane from an aerospace manufacturer there."

"Like 9/11?" Noah asked.

"My partner and I suspected he might load the plane with nitro and fly it into a high-value target, so we planned to raid his well-defended compound. We were tasked to clear a path to the fence line." Lexi swallowed the emotion bubbling in her throat as the memory of that night reared its head. "Then Darby tripped a mine."

Noah's expression turned soft. He let a few moments of silence honor Darby's memory. "Tell me more about the nitro. How did you connect the theft to Belcher?"

"The security guard at the chemical plant who was killed during the heist was Belcher's inside man. He was also a friend of mine. I got to his brother, who was also involved with Belcher, and convinced him to help us."

"That's good police work."

"Now it's my turn to ask," Lexi said. "Why does the manager think Lindsey was involved with the stolen nitro?"

"They had four employees who prepped and loaded containers for shipment. Lindsey was the one who loaded both shipments of nitro, plus a shipment of sulfuric acid that was stolen. The manager couldn't prove anything, but he suspected Lindsey of tipping off someone when the trucks were en route and giving that person the destination and approximate delivery time."

"We need to learn who he tipped off."

"Exactly." Noah pursed his lips, hiding the pink sections and forming a single oval of pale white skin. The change made him appear doll-like. "But what's more concerning is what the manager found on Lindsey's office computer. His web browser search history showed that he had researched the recipe to make acetone peroxide. I had to look it up."

Lexi let out a weighty sigh. She'd considered the nitro a public danger, but this changed the playing field. "It's also known as triacetone triperoxide, or TATP. It's the favorite explosive of terrorists and IED makers because it can be made by mixing commonly available ingredients. If they get the ratio right, the chemicals make a volatile explosive with eighty percent of the power of TNT. One of those chemicals is sulfuric acid."

Noah's cell dinged, alerting him to an incoming text. He swiped the screen and read the message. "I'm glad I called the state police for a search warrant of his last known address to save us time. They expedited the request and can have SWAT meet us there in two hours."

Things were moving fast, and Lexi had her attention divided. She was chasing an organization of militant extremists hell-bent on creating havoc to some unknown end who had proven themselves willing to kill innocents. At the same time, her girlfriend, shot and hospitalized, was traumatized and faced months of recovery ahead. The last few hours had thankfully set Lexi's priorities straight.

"You need to let them know this has turned into a possible bomb-disposal incident and that an ATF explosives specialist will be on scene. Let me make a call first. That will decide if that specialist is me or someone else."

Lexi pulled her cell phone from her jacket pocket and dialed. The call connected on the fourth ring. "How are you feeling, Nita?"

"Still woozy. The longer I'm on these pain meds, the more worried I am about getting off them. So I'm going to ask the nurse to lower my dose."

"That's a good idea, Nita. I'm glad you're staying on top of this. Hey, something has come up with the case, and I'll be out of town for the day. But if you need me to be there with you, I'll ask Carlson to send someone else."

"I know this is important to you, Lex. I'll be fine here. Jenny is coming back with lunch, and we plan to binge some shows on her phone."

"You're sure?"

"Positive. Go catch whoever killed those poor people in that tunnel."

"All right. I'll call when I'm heading back to town."

Lexi finished her call, hoping Nita wasn't putting on a brave front. She then turned her attention to Noah, who gave her a nod clearly filled with respect and appreciation. "I'll let Carlson know what's going on and that we're heading to Bowie, Texas."

22

After briefing Carlson and picking up equipment at the ATF field office, Lexi and Noah left for Bowie. Their route took them north on Interstate 35 and then west on Texas Highway 380, a short detour away from Lexi's hometown. The town she'd left in her rearview mirror when it had become abundantly clear her father would never accept her being gay. However, her family drama was a can of worms better left unopened today. Lexi then settled into the hour-long drive without mentioning the significance of the road sign to Ponder, Texas.

When she made the turn to go north on Highway 287, her phone rang through her SUV's Bluetooth. The console display read that the incoming call was from Kaplan. "Please tell me you found something on Lindsey. Detective Black and I are on our way to execute a search warrant of his place in Bowie."

"I'm sorry it took so long. Lindsey's adult record is clean, but I'm glad I continued to dig. His juvenile record showed he was arrested and convicted twice for grand theft auto. I ran the name of his accomplice, Robert Michaels, from Fort Worth."

"Bobby..." Lexi's voice trailed off. Her old friend had confessed to her about his troubles with the law when he was a teenager, but he'd made it sound as if he was arrested for taking cars out for a joy ride. And learning

Bobby had gotten mixed up with Tony Belcher was eye-opening. He was a lost soul back then. No wonder he blew her off when she'd offered to help him.

"You knew Michaels?" Noah asked.

Lexi gripped the steering wheel tighter, kicking herself for not doing more for Bobby when they were friends. "He was the security guard shot by one of the armed drivers in last year's nitro heist. He was also Belcher's inside man. Bobby and I were on rival pit crews when I worked for my father on the NASCAR circuit."

"You were on a NASCAR pit crew?" Kaplan shrilled. "Why am I just hearing about this? Talk about burying the lead, Lexi. That's the coolest job in the world."

"We can talk about it over a beer when this case is over. That's great legwork, Kaplan, but a childhood arrest doesn't necessarily connect Michaels and Lindsey as adults."

"Which is why I dug deeper into Michaels's and Lindsey's backgrounds. I pulled up the original nitro heist you mentioned and checked Michaels's financial records you'd assembled for the investigation. You did a very thorough job, by the way," Kaplan said.

"Thanks." Lexi shrugged off the compliment. "Continue."

"I compared Lindsey's bank records against Michaels's. They both made cash deposits of five thousand dollars the day before the theft. Lindsey made a similar deposit before the most recent theft. The payoffs tell me that both nitro heists are related."

"I'd say so." Lexi dug her fingers deeper into the leather steering wheel. This was her first solid lead into the Gatekeepers since Darby's death. She finally had a name and an address and might soon be back on the trail of Tony Belcher. "That means the Gatekeepers are connected to the Red Spades. Can you pass along your findings to Agent Carlson? Tell him we'll be at the rally point in a half hour."

"Will do, Lexi. Be careful."

Finishing the call, Lexi appreciated Kaplan's genuine-sounding concern, but it was unnecessary. She had every intention of being careful, for Trent Darby's sake and her own. This might be her only chance to keep the promise she'd made to Karla Darby—to catch the son of a bitch who'd made her a widow.

"I want this guy alive." Lexi glanced at Noah in the passenger seat. "I have a gut feeling that he can lead us to the kingpin of both extremist groups."

"Let's hope he cooperates when we roll in."

"Which is why I'll need your help." Lexi's mind drifted to a year ago. If this job went anything like her previous experience with the Gatekeepers, Lindsey would expect company and have that place wired, inside and out. She was good at her job, but she'd always done it with a partner who had her back.

"Name it," Noah said.

"I normally sweep for IEDs with a partner—one clears while the other provides overwatch, looking ahead with a scope. Can you be my extra eyes?"

"I'd be honored."

"Thanks, Noah. If this thing goes sideways and I have to go inside, I'll need someone on the outside with a cool head so we can take him in, not take him out."

"Then I'm your guy." Noah's confidence didn't come across as boasting, rather as poise and sureness in his ability. That was more comforting than he likely realized.

Soon, Lexi pulled into the parking lot of the Texas Highway Patrol Regional Office in Bowie—the designated rally point. Four tactical vehicles with *Texas DPS* printed on the sides were lined up in the official section, signifying their Special Operations team had arrived.

She held open the glass door at the main entrance, and Noah stepped through, removing his wide-brimmed hat. A flash of their badges got them past reception and to the threshold of a conference room. A dozen officers dressed in tactical uniforms were seated at eight-foot-long tables, facing the front whiteboard. They were drinking coffee or an energy drink, two were scrolling through something on their phones, and the rest were engaged in conversation. Some were white, some were Black, some were Hispanic, one was Asian, and two were women. Still, they all had one thing in common— Texas Rangers Special Operations patches in the shape of the Lone Star State on their sleeves.

Lexi had been around every famous racecar driver on the circuit but never had she felt the slightest bit giddy to meet them. However, standing among the Texas Rangers SWAT unit was special. Growing up in Texas, she'd seen them in action twice and idolized their bravery and skill. Today, she was about to work with them as a contemporary. This would be a treat.

Lexi and Noah stepped inside, but then her childlike bubble burst. All conversation in the room stopped when the Rangers set eyes on Noah. Their stares lingered beyond the point of social graces and crossed uncomfortably into the territory of bigotry. How disappointing. She'd built it up in her head that the men and women of the Rangers were above the petty reactions she'd encountered with Noah everywhere except the Beebo. The Rangers weren't superheroes. They were merely people.

"It's called vitiligo, people. It's not contagious." Lexi's voice dripped with disapproval. "Now, who's in charge?"

One man standing with a coffee cup in his hand wagged his thumb toward a small glassed-in office to the side of the whiteboards. "In there." Conversation in the room picked up again.

Lexi scanned the uniforms of the two people in the glassed-in area and spotted one person wearing a tactical uniform with lieutenant bars on the collar. To her surprise, that person was a tall, broad-shouldered Black woman with her dark hair pulled into a tight bun. So maybe the Rangers weren't as entrenched in intolerance as she'd assumed.

Lexi elbowed Noah in the side and approached the lieutenant reviewing documents on a clipboard while talking to an officer with sergeant stripes. Everything about the woman screamed professional, from the crispness of her uniform to the shined boots to her perfect posture.

Lexi waited in the doorway until the lieutenant looked in her direction.

"You must be Special Agent Mills from the ATF." She extended her right hand to Lexi. "I'm Sarah Briscoe. Glad you're here. Your SRT commander said you're his best explosives expert."

"I'm glad to be here." Lexi gestured toward Noah. "This is Detective

Noah Black from the Nogales PD. We were working the collapsed tunnel at the border there when our investigation brought us here. I'll need him as my oversight. His scope will be my extra eyes."

After greeting Noah, Briscoe said, "I want everyone out there not disarming bombs carrying a tactical weapon. What did you bring?"

"Just my service sidearm."

"We'll equip you with a rifle and scope." Briscoe then returned her attention to Lexi. "All right, then, let's not waste time and go through this only once in the briefing room." She led them to the next room, where conversations came to an abrupt halt. All faces turned forward. "Everyone, this is Special Agent Lexi Mills. She's our ATF explosives expert. With her is Detective Black from Nogales. Mills, why don't you get us started?"

Briscoe stepped aside, putting Lexi front and center. This wasn't a meeting with the ATF decision-makers dressed in suits. This was a tactical briefing for officers on the ground who were about to put themselves in danger, so it had to be concise and informative.

She tacked a blowup of a driver's license photo onto the whiteboard with a magnet. She took care not to cover a hand-drawn diagram there. "Our mission is to execute a search warrant and bring this man in for questioning, David Lindsey, a former warehouse worker at TriStar Chemical in Dallas. We've linked him to two stolen shipments of nitroglycerin and a stolen shipment of sulfuric acid. We believe he's trying to make acetone peroxide. Terrorists call it Mother of Satan. It's extremely unstable and nearly as powerful as TNT."

She paused to let the murmuring settle down. "We think Lindsey is connected to two militant supremacist groups, the Gatekeepers and the Red Spades. Those groups are fanatical and well-armed. We believe the Red Spades are behind the border tunnel bombing and are on the precipice of something big. That is why we need to bring in Lindsey alive. He's our only lead to stopping whatever they have planned.

"This will be a dangerous operation. Consider everything a booby trap. I'll clear a path to the trailer door. After you breach, if you find anything out of the ordinary, back off. That's when I'll come in. Detective Black will provide my direct cover." Lexi then took a step back, gauging the officers' responses. She saw no hint of dissention.

Briscoe moved forward again, only this time glancing at the sergeant who was in the smaller room with her earlier. "Sergeant Mosley, give us a recon report."

Mosley approached the whiteboard, pointing at the various rectangles, squares, and circles drawn there as he spoke. "The target's home is in a remote corner of a trailer park. His is this one, a fifteen-by-seventy-two-foot single-wide. It sits in a grove of trees and shrubs on three sides, with a clearance of twenty-five feet on each side. On that perimeter is a chain-link fence all the way around with only one vehicle gate that is padlocked. The closest trailer is seven hundred feet."

Mosley pointed to a rectangle at the top of one row. That meant the rectangles represented the trailers and that there were six units. "There is one door with three-foot-wide straight-on metal stairs leading up to it." Next, he pointed to a smaller rectangle on the same long side of the trailer. "And six windows. The trailer is on a pier foundation thirty inches off the ground. The crawl space was skirted, so there's no telling what surprises might be underneath." He glanced at the paper in his hand. "And the power line is aboveground."

Wow! Lexi thought. That was a thorough assessment.

Briscoe turned her head toward the center of the room. "Dunbar, is the city ready to cut the power?"

"Yes, ma'am. They'll have a crew set up at the transformer by the top of the hour."

"All right, then." Briscoe turned to Lexi. "Mills, what do you need from us?"

"The amount of explosives is unknown, but I'd like a standoff cordon of two hundred feet and the perimeter set at a minimum of five hundred. I'd still clear up to eight hundred to be on the safe side."

Mosley circled two rectangles on the whiteboard. "Then we'll need to evacuate these two trailers."

"Detective Black? What do you need from us?" Briscoe asked.

"Nothing yet."

"Okay," Briscoe said. "We'll set up shooters on the three sides with windows. Black, you can float into position as Mills directs. Once Mills clears a path to the door, I'll announce the search warrant. If the target doesn't come out willingly, we'll cut the power and breach through the door softly, two by two. Sergeant Mosley will make the assignments. Questions?"

"Whose turn is it to buy?" one asked.

"Watson's," three or four sang in chorus while the others laughed.

"Hope you brought your Amex," another said.

"Settle down." Mosley wagged his hands at the rowdy crew.

"Take your pisses now," Briscoe ordered. "We saddle up and roll in fifteen. Hopefully, we'll be back before dark." She then pulled Lexi and Noah into the smaller room for privacy, exuding an air of confidence. "I know you're concerned about bringing Mr. Lindsey in alive. My team is well trained, and not one member is trigger-happy. I guarantee my shooters will only fire on my order. Unless the breaching teams face imminent danger or Mr. Lindsey has surprises waiting for us, I'm certain we can put him in your excellent hands."

"I have every confidence regarding your team, Lieutenant." From what little Lexi had seen, these Rangers were as well trained and skilled as any federal agent she'd worked with. And their lively banter in the briefing room highlighted their cohesiveness. "Like you, I'm concerned about what Lindsey might have done with those stolen chemicals."

"Well, it's our job to help you get to the bottom of it," Briscoe said.

"Thanks, Lieutenant. I better prep my gear." Lexi shook her hand. "I'll see you on the other side."

23

The Texas Rangers Special Operations team quietly set up their sharpshooters and evacuated the nearby trailers. A mother with a terrified expression clutched her toddler's hand while carrying a baby in the other and scurried down the trailer park's gravel road. The toddler dropped her stuffed animal and tattered baby blanket. The mother tried to pick them up, but the Ranger pulled them along, forcing her to leave the items behind.

Noah swooped in behind, picked up the precious belongings, and caught up with the mother and sobbing child. "Here, darlin'." Noah bent and handed the items to the little girl.

With her tiny fingers, the girl touched Noah's face where the vitiligo had affected him. "Does it hurt?"

"No, but you're tickling me." She giggled. Noah stood straight. "Now, follow the officer. Everything will be okay."

That man has a good heart, Lexi thought. Any person would be lucky to have him as a partner on the job and in life.

Lexi pulled out her blast-proof bodysuit from the back of her SUV. The Gatekeepers had taught her a hard lesson—never put the mission above safety. She'd never recon an area without the protection of her suit, even if it meant losing precious hours.

Lexi had put it on several times in training since the explosion that had taken her leg, but this marked the first time she would don it for a real-world field operation while wearing a prosthetic. The mechanics worked the same, but she first doubled the layers of socks in her residual limb, bringing the number to four, to pad it from the inevitable pressure from the weight of the eighty-four-pound suit.

Sliding the pants over her legs, Lexi felt her stomach flutter. It had every time she'd put the suit on for an operation, but this time the sensation was especially intense. If she fell hard or something knocked her prosthetic socket out of place, she wouldn't be able to fix it. But that was a remote possibility, so she brushed off her worry, secured the trousers around her waist, and programmed the suit's communication unit to the Rangers' tactical channel.

After Noah field-checked the rifle Sergeant Mosley had issued him, he helped Lexi. They first put on her heavy jacket, secured each fastener of the suit down to the boot covers, and connected her communication system. When he was done, he patted her shoulder pads with both hands like a football player winding up a teammate for the big game. "You got this, Mills. This is what you've trained for."

Those were the words she needed to hear. "Thanks, Noah."

"Where do you need me?"

Lexi scanned the area between Lindsey's trailer and the Rangers' outer perimeter. Their vehicles lay a few feet inside at such angles so their sides could absorb fragments from a blast and ensure that ingress and egress remained unabated. In addition, one car was ideally located to provide Noah an unobstructed view of the path leading to the trailer door.

"Set up on the hood of the lieutenant's SUV." She handed him a high-power scope, an earpiece, and a tactical radio she'd programmed to the correct channel. "Use whichever scope gives you the best field of vision in this light. Stay ahead of the area I'm sweeping. Look for tripwires or anything uneven on the ground, like a rock at an odd angle."

"Got it. The JTTF training course I took walked me through this scenario." Noah helped Lexi put on the helmet and fragmentation gloves. "Do your thing, Mills."

Lexi gave him a thumbs-up to not trigger the voice-activated microphone that kept her in contact with the rest of the team. Her final image of Darby flashed in her head when he'd given her a similar gesture moments before making the mistake that took his life. She swore to herself to not make the same mistake and to place her foot down firmly with each step.

Lexi then flipped on the demister switch of her helmet. The faint mechanical hum it created was a good tradeoff to keep her face shield from fogging up. Taking one last deep, cleansing breath, Lexi announced, "SR One. This is BT One. I'm going in."

"Copy, BT One," Lieutenant Briscoe said. "Godspeed."

Stepping through the section of the fence the Rangers had cut out, Lexi whispered to herself, "This is for you, Trent." She then swept her detector in a five-foot-wide path toward the trailer door. She staggered white flags in the ground on both sides every five feet, delineating the way for the Rangers. The weedy and dry grass-covered route she'd picked was void of objects, requiring only one minor curve to avoid a suspicious rock grouping about eight feet to her left.

"Lexi, stop," Noah barked in a firm tone. She froze. "Those rocks to your left."

"Yes, I see it," Lexi replied. "I'm shifting right to give it a wide berth."

"No, stop," he repeated. "I'm not sure with this light, but I think I saw a shimmer of fishing line or thread running across your path to a garden stake."

The soft golden hour light was magical for photographers, but the shadows it created were wreaking havoc on Lexi's central vision. She kneeled and lowered her head to the ground level to get a better angle. Shifting several times, allowing for the shadows, she saw something. There it was—a run of fishing line about three inches off the ground.

"Great eyes, Noah." Lexi followed the line visually, first to the rock grouping. Then she doubled back to the side with the garden stake. Next, she expanded her visual search to the poor excuse for a garden about five feet from the trailer. Four stakes marked the corners of the dirt patch. Careful examination revealed that the fishing line ran from each stake in multiple directions. Her heart thudded fast and hard when she realized she had entered an active minefield.

"SR One, I've got multiple hits. Keep everyone back until I identify the devices."

"Copy, Mills," Briscoe said. "All teams stand fast."

Lexi rose to her feet and scanned the path to the rock grouping with her detector. She slowly circled it and followed the fishing line, discovering the distinctive round shape of the M67 fragmentation grenade. One false move and she'd pull a pin, release the lever, and trigger the delayed fuze. She'd have only four seconds to clear the kill radius. "Shit."

"That didn't sound good, Mills," Briscoe said. "What do we have?"

"Military fragmentation grenade. It's fatal up to fifteen feet and can injure up to fifty." Lexi glanced at the stakes in the minefield again. "And it looks like we might have eight, maybe twelve."

"Do you need assistance?" Briscoe asked. "Should I call in the state bomb squad and get more specialists here?"

"Hold that thought. Let me disarm this one."

"Copy," Briscoe said. "Standing by."

Lexi slid a rock covering half the grenade, exposing the safety lever. The safety clip that held it in place if the pin accidentally dislodged had been removed. The end of the fishing line was attached to the ring of the safety pin. It was a crude but effective booby trap for anyone not looking for it. Thankfully, she could quickly disarm it.

Lexi reached into a pouch Velcroed to the outside of the blast jacket and retrieved her scissors. They were razor-sharp, and the finger holes were large enough to accommodate her fragmentation gloves. A single snip would cut the line and render the trap ineffective, but her hand shook, which it never had before. She paused, debating whether she still had what it took to do this job. Wondering if the explosion that killed her partner had rendered her ineffective.

Then Noah's calm voice broke the nerve-wracking silence. "You've got this, Lexi." Those words came at the right time. They punched holes in the doubt that had threatened to paralyze her.

"I got this," she whispered to herself, and in a single snip, she cut the line. She then retrieved a roll of two-inch duct tape from her pouch, cut off a foot-long section, and taped the pin and safety lever in place.

"Got it, Lieutenant." Lexi blinked away the beads of sweat that had rolled down her brow. "Let me secure the remaining devices before I clear the way to the door."

"You have nerves of steel, Mills," Briscoe said. "I'll leave you to your work."

Lexi ignored the genuine-sounding compliment and went on to cut the fishing lines meticulously coming from the garden patch, making ineffective the eight M67 grenades she'd located. When she finished securing one grenade, she moved directly to the next, not giving her self-doubt time to resurface. Once she'd disabled the final device, the sun had gone down, and she'd sweated so much that her blast suit felt like multiple layers of wet blankets. She was soaked through and through and cringed at how the liner on her residual limb must have smelled. She'd have to change it out as soon as this operation concluded to avoid developing a skin fungus.

Without pausing, Lexi continued her sweep of the path to the base of the metal stairs at the door. She easily cleared the skeleton-looking stairs before inspecting the door from her position at their bottom. Again, nothing appeared out of the ordinary, suggesting it wasn't rigged, at least from this side.

Then Lexi's breath hitched. She saw movement through the narrow, six-inch-wide window on the left side of the door. The torn, soiled curtain covering most of the glass fluttered as if someone had walked past it in a rush.

"We have movement at the door." Lexi didn't bother taking cover. Thankfully, her blast suit not only protected her from fragments and shrapnel, but the Kevlar plates all around her also made it bulletproof. "It went to my right toward the back of the trailer."

"Mills, are we clear yet?" Briscoe asked.

"Affirmative. All clear." Lexi stepped to the side nearest to the window to watch for further movement from inside the trailer.

"Copy. All clear. It's our turn in the batter's box, Mills," Briscoe said. Then over a loudspeaker, she announced, "David Lindsey, this is the state police. We have a warrant to search the premises. We have disabled your explosive devices. Open the door and hold your hands over your head." She waited for a ten count. "This is your final warning. Open the door now, or we will force our way in."

Even through her helmet and the trailer's tin siding, Lexi smelled Lindsey's fear. Every nut who laid out IEDs and landmines on their property to keep out trespassers had one thing in common—they were paranoid. Fearful and obsessed that the government would come for them. Today, Lindsey's fears had come to fruition. She'd taken out his outer defenses, and now he was exposed and ripe for the taking.

"All right, people. We're breaching," Briscoe said through the radio. "Let's sound off. Spotters, are we a go?"

"Spotter One, go."

"Spotter Two, go."

"Spotter Three, go."

"Teams One and Two, prepare to breach on my mark."

"Team One, ready."

"Team Two, ready."

"All right, Rangers," Briscoe said, "let's earn our paychecks today. Cut the power." When the faint glow in the trailer went dark, she ordered, "Go. Go. Go."

Four special operators in camouflage uniforms, helmets, and armored vests with *Police* emblazoned across the front jogged down the path Lexi had cleared for them. Each carried short, tactical rifles, and one had theirs slung over his shoulder and was gripping a battering ram in both hands. Pebbles crunched under their boots, and the gear attached to their vests and web belts swayed in a cacophony of rhythmic swooshing.

The four reached the bottom of the metal stairs. The first in line was the brawniest, carrying the battering ram. He quickstepped to the top while the rest remained at the bottom. The second glanced at Lexi, issuing her a thumbs-up for a job well done. She returned the gesture, showing her respect for those forming the tip of the spear. Unfortunately, they were going in blind, and the danger couldn't be greater. The two other operators placed a hand on the shoulder of the one next in line, ready to move in an instant.

The one at the top settled into a wide stance and heaved the battering ram in a robust and clean motion. Clearly, it was well practiced. The heavy metal impacted the door in a loud thump, followed by the cracking of splintering wood as the door swung right. He then tossed the ram over the side of the stairs, thudding it against the sun-hardened dirt, and slung his weapon into the ready position.

Going in soft as the lieutenant had directed meant not leading with flash-bang grenades. The resulting concussion might trigger an explosion or unleash a lethal chemical. Unfortunately, the officers wouldn't have the upper hand without disorienting whoever was inside. Unfamiliar with the layout, they'd be at a clear disadvantage. Their night vision goggles, now that the power had been cut, would be their only benefit.

The first Ranger stepped through, aiming his rifle left and then right. He turned right. The next filed in, aiming their weapon right and then left, turning left to the shorter end of the trailer. The third went right, and the fourth went left, forming their two-person teams. Lights mounted atop the upper receivers of the rifles cast beams that danced erratically from wall to wall.

All four disappeared into the bowels of the trailer. Seconds later, the two who had gone left reappeared and went right toward the longer end with their lights dancing again on the walls.

One calmly called through the radio, "One subject detained on the bed." A moment later, the same voice yelled, "Bomb! He's rigged to blow! Backing out!"

"Take pictures," Lexi directed. Realizing that her work wasn't done yet, her breathing shallowed in the seconds waiting for the Rangers' retreat.

24

Jogging back to the outer perimeter with Teams One and Two, Lexi sensed their tension. It was an emotion Lexi understood from personal experience. Years of training and familiarity with explosives had tempered her fear. Still, the anxiety over the risks remained close to the surface every time she put on that suit.

Those three men and one woman had stumbled upon a powder keg without the benefit of Lexi's protective gear. Their bulletproof vests and helmets provided some defense, but their faces, necks, and limbs had been vulnerable. They were likely jumping out of their skin at the moment.

The group reached the line of SUVs and armored vehicles lit by their headlights and flashing red-and-blue overheads. All four Rangers bent over with their hands on their knees. One said, "Holy shit. That was close."

Lexi removed her helmet and cradled it in her left arm. She then thought back to her first week as an explosives specialist and how her hands shook so hard, she'd thought she'd knock her gloves off. The Rangers' reactions were much like her own, so she rested a hand on one of their backs. "You did great. I threw up my first time."

"How do you do this every day?" one asked, straightening his posture.

"Training and repetition. You can get used to nearly anything if you do it enough times."

"That explains how Fisher survives her wife's cooking." He gave her a playful shove.

"And how your wife didn't divorce you years ago." Fisher nudged him back.

"Did any of you get pictures of the device?"

"I did," one said. "They automatically uploaded to our cloud. The LT will have them on her tablet."

Lexi read the name tag on his vest. "Thanks, Watson." She took one step toward the command vehicle but stopped to give one last piece of advice. "Don't sit down yet. Walk off that extra energy until you can focus again."

Lexi headed toward the SUV, where Lieutenant Briscoe, Sergeant Mosley, and Noah had huddled. The white glow lighting up Briscoe's face suggested she had Watson's pictures on the screen.

Briscoe looked up when Lexi approached and handed her the tablet. "What do you think?"

The first thing that caught Lexi's eye was how much Lindsey had changed from his driver's license photo. He'd shaved his head and added a plethora of tattoos to his arms and neck—a sign he'd radicalized since that picture was taken six years ago. His time with whatever extremist group he'd hitched his wagon to had clearly hardened his exterior. And the number of explosives in his yard suggested he was hardened on the inside, too. The track marks on both arms had undoubtedly hastened his downslide.

The dead-man switch Lindsey had in his right hand and the syringe in his left bolstered Lexi's assessment. He was an addict on edge. He had his thumb smashed on the red aircraft safety cover protecting the toggle switch from a premature detonation. He'd connected a long electrical wire to the bottom of it. That line ran to the floor in front of the bed Lindsey was sitting on and had formed several bunched loops. The amount suggested it might be long enough to stretch the length of a bedroom. The other end of the wire disappeared under the bed.

But the detonator wasn't the most concerning thing in the photo, and neither were the beads of sweat on Lindsey's brow. If he'd had a relaxed look, Lexi would have leaned toward the possibility that the bomb was fake. If Lindsey had had a harried expression, the device was likely real, and he was high or having second thoughts. His distant look, though, was worrisome. In Lexi's experience, that suggested he'd resolved himself to an inevitable outcome and was making his peace with whatever held his faith.

Lexi flipped to the next picture, which captured what was beneath the bed from the vantage point of the floor. Dust bunnies and crumpled fast food wrappers littered the decades-old worn carpet and surrounded a cluster of five metal pipes. They'd been bound in a pyramid shape, perhaps by duct tape. The ends of the devices set off alarm bells in Lexi's head. Instead of the traditional metal pipe caps, Lindsey had used what looked like automotive body filler. That meant he'd gone to great lengths to not attract attention. And that suggested a white supremacist group was likely behind this.

Nearly every manual distributed by those extremist groups contained detailed instructions on constructing an IED without raising attention. That started with cutting lengths of metal pipe to one foot instead of buying them precut with grooves at the end along with two endcaps. That combination at a register would set off alarm bells even in the most inattentive cashier.

Lindsey must have bought a three-foot or six-foot length of iron pipe and cut it into shorter sections. The body filler he'd used was an excellent substitute for the screw-on endcaps because it could contain the pressure inside the pipe long enough to cause maximum fragmentation.

The line connected to Lindsey's dead-man switch had been split into five shorter wires beneath the bed. Each led to the center on the long side of the iron casing on each device. This meticulous configuration of simultaneous ignition ensured it would generate maximum damage. Lindsey had been taught well, and from the appearance of the IED, he'd executed the blueprint flawlessly. That realization convinced Lexi that he'd successfully mixed TATP. Considering the number of pipes and estimating the standard length of one foot for pipe bombs, Lexi calculated Lindsey had nearly two kilograms of TATP beneath his bed. That equaled a kill radius of thirty feet and a chance of serious injury within sixty feet. It was a mother of a bomb, even with her blast suit.

"Mills?" Briscoe repeated her question. "What do you think?"

"That your team was wise to pull back. I've seen this configuration before. If it's what I think it is, this thing is powerful enough to level a trailer twice the size of Lindsey's."

"I'm calling in the bomb squad." Briscoe dialed her phone and explained the situation in concise detail. "We already are... ATF Agent Mills saw to it... What is your ETA...? Copy." Hanging up, she returned her attention to Lexi. "They're an hour out. Our orders are to pull back to five hundred feet, evacuate a quarter-mile, and not engage the subject."

"I don't think we have an hour." Lexi flipped back to the first picture on the tablet. "See this face? That's the look of a man ready to die. I need him to tell me what he knows about the Gatekeepers and the Red Spades."

"I can't let you go in," Briscoe said.

"I respect and appreciate what you and your team have done here, Lieutenant, but this is an ATF investigation. It's not your call."

"Even with your suit, going in is a suicide mission, Lexi," Noah said. "There has to be another way."

"You just need to talk to him, right?" Briscoe asked, gesturing for the tablet again. She thumbed to a wide shot of the bedroom where Lindsey was holed up. Near the foot of the bed was a window covered with rickety metal blinds. Several slats were bent, providing a partial view inside from their position. "There's a window in the room. You can talk to him through the glass there." Briscoe pointed toward one end of the trailer. "If you can lure him to it, we can end this with one shot."

"Direct your team to hold fast until I get what I need from him. Do I have your word?" Lexi asked.

"You have it."

25

Noah raised Lexi's helmet over her head, putting it in place, and then tightened the neck guard to provide her optimum protection. "I don't have to follow Briscoe's orders, so I plan to keep the promise I made to Nita."

"What promise is that?"

"To keep you safe. If I think Lindsey is about to press that trigger, I'm taking the shot if he steps in front of that window."

Lexi narrowed her eyes at him. She could almost taste the juicy leads Lindsey might give her about Belcher, and she wasn't about to let this opportunity slip through her fingers. "Dammit, Noah. Give me a chance to talk to him. He's our only link to the Red Spades."

"And the Gatekeepers." Noah matched Lexi's narrowed eyes. "Don't let your thirst for vengeance cloud your thinking. No case is worth your life, even the one into your partner's death." In three, albeit long, days, Noah had unpeeled Lexi's layers and gotten to her core, but this wasn't the time to debate the wisdom of her motivation.

"I have no intention of dying today," she said.

Lexi patted Noah on the shoulder and took off down her white-flagged path. She veered off to the minefield area she'd cleared earlier, stopping even with the bedroom window but five feet from the trailer. She considered how to get Lindsey talking and quickly ruled out appealing to a sense of right and wrong. Anyone who turned his yard into a killing field couldn't distinguish between the two. Vengeance was the solution. It was an emotion Lexi had experienced firsthand.

She flipped up her face shield, accepting the risk doing so would put her in. If she didn't expose herself to fragmentation, her voice wouldn't carry through the glass pane.

"David, I'm Lexi."

"Go away, or I'll blow myself up and take you with me." Lindsey's unwavering voice was loud and clear through the window. His warning was a positive sign—he wasn't ready to die. That wedge could open dialogue before the meth he'd injected took over.

"I know you don't want to do this, David. How can we end this without bloodshed?"

"I want to be left alone."

"I can't do that," Lexi said, "because I need your help."

"Help? I won't help a damn cop."

"Not even if it's for Bobby Michaels?"

"What do you know about Bobby?" Lindsey's question was a good sign. Getting him talking was the first step before getting him to back down.

"I know he was a friend. He was my friend too. I knew him after you two were pinched for boosting cars."

"That was a long time ago."

"Nineteen years ago was another lifetime for you and me," Lexi said. "You and Bobby were buds in the Big D, about to get arrested for the first time, and I was working in my father's garage, about to get my NASCAR cert."

"That's how you knew Bobby?"

"Yeah. He was a confused young man back then. We both were confused." Lindsey's breathy chuckle meant Lexi was onto something. If he'd spent as much time around Bobby as she suspected, then maybe Lindsey was equally confused. She could use that to her advantage. "That was what drew me to him. Bobby had an edgy, tough exterior, but he was kind and considerate on the inside. He helped me figure out who I was. Did he help you, too?"

"I don't want to talk about that." Lindsey's tone turned tight, suggesting that the nerve Lexi had hit was still raw. Then shadows floated in and out of the window frame several times, implying Lindsey was pacing.

"It's all right, David. We all have our crosses to bear. Mine was not staying in touch with Bobby after I left the circuit. If I had, he might be alive today."

"He was lost long before you knew him." Lindsey's voice had softened a fraction, inferring Lexi was making headway. Now was the time to get to the heart of what she needed from him.

"That might be true, but he didn't deserve to be shot by the Gatekeepers."

"That never happened. He got caught in a crossfire and was shot by another guard."

"Maybe that's what Belcher told you, but he lied. The ballistics didn't match the guard's gun."

"You lie," Lindsey grunted, proving that Lexi had pushed too hard. "Tony is the hand of God. He will save the true believers."

"I'm telling the truth, David. Belcher is not your savior. He's a killer. That's why I need your help to find him. He needs to account for what he did to our friend. If you cooperate, I can get you the help you need."

"And what help do you think I need?"

"The marks on your arms tell me you've been escaping for some time and that you're in a vicious cycle. It doesn't have to be that way."

"Meth and Belcher aren't the problems. You are, Lexi. You and all the other puppets of the government. By killing the one man who can hold back the tide of evil, you will condemn the believers to damnation. Without his protection, we won't survive the tribulation when God reveals himself."

"Belcher is a false prophet, David. Belcher is the evil he seeks to keep at bay. He's killed two people I cared about deeply, and he needs to account for sins according to man's law. Where is he?"

"You're not a believer and don't understand. There must be sacrifices. Some will have to die to hold back the tide until the Lord returns."

"But not innocents. Belcher has amassed too much nitro to only protect the believers. We know he planned to steal a plane last year and fly it into a building before he disappeared. We just don't know to what end."

"For the war."

"What war?"

"Of the unbelievers. Don't you see?" Lindsey's voice faltered. Until now, the conversation had a constant back-and-forth flow, and Lexi had thought she was wearing him down, but she wasn't. Instead, her mention of Belcher had the opposite effect and had wound him up tighter. Maybe it was the meth working its way through his veins, but she needed to reverse course before she pushed him over the edge.

"I don't see, David. Can you open my eyes?"

"If the unbelievers all die in the war, God will know who to come for."

"So, it's a process of elimination," Lexi said.

"Exactly. The war has already begun. When it is over, the Rapture will begin."

"If that's true, does it make sense to kill yourself when you're so close to seeing the fruits of your labor? Don't you want to be here to see the Rapture?"

"Alive or dead, I will see it because I am a believer. God will take those who have sacrificed first."

"And who taught you this?"

"The hand of God."

"But how can you be sure that Belcher is the hand of God? What if he is a false believer? God won't come for you when he returns because you followed the wrong prophet. You will be left behind with all the other unbelievers. Ask yourself if Tony Belcher is worth that risk."

Lindsey grunted again, signaling that Lexi had found his weak point—doubt. This was her last chance to break him.

"Dying for a false prophet is the wrong way to prove your worthiness to God."

"Shut up! Shut up! Shut up!" Lindsey rushed his words. He was on the precipice of either falling off the cliff or into Lexi's arms. One last push would begin that descent.

"How can you be sure that Belcher is a prophet and not a political puppet? A true prophet should speak with righteous anger, not hate. He must have compassion for sinners and unbelievers and speak with love in his voice. Tony Belcher doesn't do that. He pits the unbelievers against one another to make room for those he deems salvageable. He sounds more like a bigot than a prophet."

"You don't know what the hell you're talking about. He *is* the hand of God."

"Then tell me where he is so I can see for myself."

"All you want is revenge, not truth. That makes you a government puppet, and my orders are to never be taken alive by your kind. You're so curious about whether I believe, well, here is my answer."

Lindsey suddenly appeared at the window, shoving the blinds to the side and pressing himself against the glass. The dead-man switch was still in his hand, and fire was in his eyes.

"Lexi," Noah said over the radio, "I don't have a shot. I'm repositioning."

"Standfast. Hold fire," she whispered into the helmet microphone.

Lindsey's gaze darted toward the trees behind Lexi. "I see them. The puppets are coming for me. It's over." His stare then shifted, focusing on Lexi. A look of recognition enveloped Lindsey's face when their eyes locked. "I remember you. You were at the compound." Lindsey flipped the red safety cover up, the fury in his eyes instantly changing into pure ecstasy. He'd committed to putting his trust in the hand of God, and Lexi was in the kill zone. She'd failed.

"Nooooo!" Lexi yelled.

"It's time to finish what we started."

Time slowed to a fraction of its normal speed as if the laws of physics didn't exist outside the trailer. She had only seconds—two for him to position his thumb and two for the signal to ignite the TATP. She counted in her head as a rush of adrenaline filled her veins.

One.

Lexi lowered her blast shield and turned in the opposite direction.

Two.

Eighty-four pounds of bulky Nomex and Kevlar restrained her legs from stretching to their fullest, but those legs were strong. Stronger than they were before the amputation. Lexi pushed against the layers of thick fabric and hurled herself toward the minefield she'd disarmed earlier.

Three.

She needed eight long strides to clear herself from the kill zone, but she didn't have enough remaining seconds. So she stretched further, grateful she'd pushed herself on the treadmill the past few months. She'd learned the technique of pushing down and backward in a scooping motion on her prosthetic to get the most power and balance.

Four.

Lexi launched forward in the air in a desperate attempt to put a few more feet between her and the coming blast wave. Her suit would protect her from flames, fragments, and shrapnel but not from the crushing pressure created by the explosion. She was still in the danger zone and braced herself for the wave that would over-pressurize her lungs, eardrums, eyes, and intestinal tract and rupture them.

Five.

Lexi landed with a thud, using her body to cover the only vulnerable parts to fragmentation—her hands. Her heart pumped wildly out of control, waiting for the explosion to rip her organs apart. Images of the people who had been influential in her life flashed in her head—Nita, her mother, her father, Darby, crew chief Gavin, and the first girl she'd kissed. Each molded Lexi into the person she was today by giving her life, love, friendship, and clarity.

Then.

Nothing.

What changed? Did Lindsey's thumb slip? Did he change his mind? Whatever was behind the delay, Lexi had to get to safety.

"Go! Go! Go!" Briscoe ordered.

Getting up with her prosthetic in the suit became awkward. Lexi first kneeled on all fours, pushed her good knee up, and rose, using her hands to steady herself upright on her prosthetic leg.

Lexi then resumed her run toward the safety zone but stopped when she spotted Briscoe's team charging toward her. She turned toward the trailer. A spotlight from a Ranger vehicle was aimed at the window Lexi had run from moments earlier. A single bullet hole had pierced the glass pane.

"Nooooo!" Lexi yelled before taking off toward the trailer door.

"Mills, stop," Briscoe ordered. "Subject is down. Repeat. The subject is down."

But Lexi didn't stop. "If he's alive, he might tell me where Belcher is."

"Stand down, Mills." Briscoe repeated the order, but Lexi refused to stop. This was her last chance to get what she needed from Lindsey.

"I'll secure the bomb. Call back your team and turn the lights back on."

"Team Four, retreat. Lights on. Lights on." Briscoe's voice was tight. "Talk to me every step of the way, Mills."

The footsteps that had been gaining on Lexi stopped. She glanced in their direction to confirm they were on their way to the outer perimeter and outside of the fragment ring. Then, pounding her boots up the metal steps, Lexi turned right and called out, "David, I'm coming in."

Her bulky suit forced her to slow down in the dark, narrow hallway. Light from the back bedroom suddenly appeared and spilled through the open door. Lexi paused several feet short of the threshold, waiting for her heart to settle to a non-dizzying beat. "I'm at the bedroom door," she said softly into her mic.

"All right, Mills," Briscoe said. "Confirm the subject is down, disarm the device, and get the hell out of there."

"Copy." Lexi inched her way farther down until a corner of the bed came into view. Lindsey wasn't there. "David? It's Lexi. I'm coming in."

Lexi stepped inside. The electrical line leading to the explosive beneath the bed was still on the floor, but the loops were gone. The cable had stretched toward the broken window with the metal blinds askew. Farther inside, she glanced beneath the bed to assess the condition of the bomb. It appeared undisturbed from when Watson had taken the photos.

Following the line, she continued around the bed, where Lindsey lay motionless on the floor. A small pool of blood had gathered near his head, a sign that whoever took that shot was deadly accurate.

"Subject is motionless. Securing the detonator."

"Copy," Briscoe said.

The wired switch lay on the carpet next to him with the red safety cover still in the up position. It was nothing short of a miracle that it didn't hit something on the way down and trigger an explosion.

Lexi straddled Lindsey's cockeyed legs with one foot between them. Reaching for the dead-man switch, she let her fingers first scrape the soiled carpet. Next, she gently cupped the device, taking care to not put pressure on the toggle. Once Lexi stood upright and stabilized her stance, she slowly closed the safety cover, eliminating the chance of accidental contact. She then fished the scissors she'd used earlier and cut the switch from the wire. Finally, she taped off the end to eliminate the possibility of a stray spark and tossed the wire out of Lindsey's reach.

"Trigger secured."

"Copy. Trigger secured," Briscoe said.

With the immediate danger neutralized, Lexi removed her glove and pressed two fingers against Lindsey's neck, checking for a sign of life. However, the bullet hole at his right temple gave her little promise. Fifteen seconds later, her last hope of getting back on the trail of Tony Belcher was gone.

"Subject is dead." Lexi couldn't hold back the breathy sigh of frustration. "The bomb squad should handle the disposal."

"Copy, Mills. You've done heroes' work. It's time to get out of harm's way."

"Coming out."

Lexi plodded out of the trailer with the weight of disappointment, making her legs feel like lead. She sensed that disappointment transform into anger, step by step toward the outer perimeter and the command vehicle. She had Lindsey talking. She'd heard the doubt in his voice. And before Noah had shifted position, she'd had him pausing at the risk he was taking. If she'd had another few minutes with him, she might have flipped him. But someone took that opportunity from her.

She removed and cradled her helmet under one arm. By the time she marched up to Lieutenant Briscoe and Sergeant Mosley, her anger had turned into a belly-burning fury. "Who in the hell took that shot?"

"I didn't give the order." Briscoe's reassuring voice was firm, defusing Lexi's verbal joust without a harsh word in return. Sarah had proven her grace under pressure, and so had her entire team. Except for making a spectacle out of Noah when they first arrived, the Rangers had lived up to the legend of being the best-trained law enforcement agency in the state.

"I took the shot, Lexi." Noah joined the group, tipping back his fedora and slinging the sniper rifle that had taken Lindsey's life. "And given the same circumstances, I'd do it again."

Lexi stood toe to toe with him, letting the stress and emotion that had built over the last few days dictate her response. "Dammit, Noah. I almost had him."

"He almost had you, Lexi. I couldn't let that happen."

"You're pretty cocky for someone way outside their jurisdiction." Lexi regretted those words the instant they left her mouth because Noah had been nothing but professional and kind.

Noah stared at Lexi for several beats with soft eyes, letting the tension recede. "I know you're hurting. Maybe it's time to take a break."

"Maybe you're right."

26

Lexi disappeared to the back of her SUV to peel off her blast suit. She then removed her prosthetic, exposing the socks protecting her residual limb. They smelled like unwashed gym clothes at the bottom of the hamper that had fermented for two weeks. The rest of her reeked as bad, but her first long day in the suit years ago had thankfully taught her to pack disposable bath towelettes and an extra set of clothes.

She freshened up and redressed except for her leg, taking the time to put the day into perspective. She had woken to the news that Nita had been shot. After rushing to her side, Lexi realized her life meant nothing without her in it. She'd concluded in the last hour that Nita was the woman she was meant to grow old with.

However, that realization hadn't taken away her single-mindedness to find justice for Darby. On the contrary, she pushed herself beyond the boundaries of common sense. She'd put herself in unnecessary mortal danger at the window on the off chance she could reason with an irrational man. Lexi asked herself if she'd do it again, and surprisingly, the answer was yes.

"That was one hell of a job back there, Mills." Lieutenant Briscoe had circled her SUV. Several strands of her hair had escaped the tightly formed bun at the back of her head, likely a flaw Lexi had created by going back in before the bomb squad had arrived. "You'd make an excellent hostage negotiator."

"Thanks, Lieutenant, but I think I'm more suited for blood-pumping work."

Her father had been a NASCAR-driver thrill seeker. He'd taught her by example that a Mills never shied away from danger. He'd pushed the envelope on the track week after week, searching for the ultimate prize. Her father never stopped until the accident that wasn't really an accident had crippled him. Even then, he continued to push, but from the executive chair instead of the driver's seat. And despite his intolerance of her sexuality, she'd grown up just like him. Lexi considered stepping away from the danger, but that wasn't how she was built. She was born to step into the flames. Though, massaging her residual limb reminded her of the heavy price tag she'd already paid for that mindset.

Briscoe gestured toward Lexi's partial leg. "Is that how you lost your foot?" Lexi nodded her response. "If you ever hang up your ATF shield, come see me. The Texas Rangers would be lucky to have you on board."

"I'll keep that in mind."

"I thought you'd like to know that the bomb squad has cleared the trailer. Their sergeant asked if you'd like the honor of ordering the detonation."

"I would, actually." Lexi rushed, donning her prosthetic in record time and closing her cargo pants with the hidden zipper on the left inseam for easy on and off. She lowered herself from the open back end of her SUV, wiggling her stump into place in the socket and closing the tailgate with a push of a button.

Walking side by side with Lieutenant Briscoe toward the bomb squad van, mutual respect flowed between them. They were both darker-skinned women who had risen in a white man's world, and the synergy that they created was powerful. They were proof that being damn good at your job should be the only thing that counted when rising through the ranks.

Briscoe pounded on the back of the bomb squad command vehicle. The door swung open, and an officer dressed in black fatigues and chevrons on his collar invited them inside. The interior was modern, filled with wall-mounted flat screens on one side and racks of equipment and gear on the other. The narrow walkway in the middle led to an electronics alcove where another officer sat with headphones on, overseeing the communications.

"We're almost set for controlled detonation." The sergeant turned his attention to Lexi. "Great call on the TATP. We estimated about two kilograms."

"Sounds about right. Where did you take the containment vessel?" Lexi asked.

"To an open field a mile from here. That's nasty stuff, so we couldn't chance triggering it by taking it any farther." The sergeant pointed to a monitor. The screen showed a container that resembled the mixing drum of a small cement truck sitting in the middle of a weed-ladened field. The camera's night vision capability was incredibly crisp, showing every detail. "The nearest structure is a half-mile away."

"And your team?"

"One thousand feet." He handed Lexi a tactical radio. "On your order."

Lexi had the honor of detonation only four times before tonight. In their circles, when explosives couldn't be rendered inert, the privilege of conducting a controlled detonation fell upon the specialist who risked their life to disarm the trigger. With the Texas Rangers taking over the disposal, Lexi was pleased the commander had extended the courtesy of issuing the order.

"Who is on the trigger?"

"Voight."

"Thank you. This is an honor, Sergeant."

"You earned it."

Lexi raised the radio to her mouth, thinking of those she might have left behind if Lindsey's bomb had gone off with her still in the kill zone. Her mom and dad would have lost their only child, and Nita would have been left alone when she was already struggling. But Lexi had avoided those needless heartaches through training and steel-like nerves. So yes, she had earned the right to destroy the thing that could have destroyed her.

Lexi pressed the radio mic. "Texas Ranger Voight. This is ATF Special Agent Mills. Status report."

"Loaded and secured. Blast zone cleared, Agent Mills. We're a go for detonation."

"On my mark." Lexi paused and whispered to herself, "I'm coming home, Nita." Then, she pressed the mic again. "Go."

"Fire in the hole," Voight announced. The screen showed the containment vessel shake and throttle up and down on the shock absorbers a second later. A loud boom echoed in the night, negating the damage Lindsey could have caused. Unfortunately, when the smoke from the vent holes cleared onscreen, that didn't mean the end of the danger. The detonation didn't end the Gatekeepers or the Red Spades. That meant Lexi and Noah still had more work to do.

"Well done, Voight." Lexi returned the radio to the sergeant. "Thanks. That felt good."

"It always does," he replied.

Exiting the trailer, Briscoe agreed to collapse the perimeter to fifty feet and have her Rangers continue guarding the crime scene until their forensics team arrived in an hour.

Lexi replied, "Until then, Detective Black and I will comb through the place. Something in there might tell us where to find Belcher or the Red Spades."

Donning latex gloves, Lexi and Noah entered the trailer, where the bomb squad had done an excellent job during their sweep to clear the rest of the trailer for explosives. As promised, they'd left anything that might be of evidentiary value undisturbed where possible. They'd found no further explosives but had encountered a treasure trove of iron pipe, automotive Bondo, electrical wire, switches, and timers. Lindsey was clearly a bomb maker.

"I'll start in the bedroom," Lexi said. "You take the living room."

Noah scanned the filth and collections of moldy food and drug paraphernalia. "Thanks."

"Trust me. The back isn't much better."

Lexi stepped down the narrow hallway, less encumbered this time without her bulky blast suit. When she crossed the threshold to the bedroom, the havoc created when the bomb squad extracted the device came into view. The mattress and frame had been cut into pieces and stacked in the corner of the room. Lexi smiled at their work. She would have done the same thing.

Her room search began with taking photos from her cell phone to document its condition before tearing it apart. Then, focusing on the window and perfectly shaped bullet hole with the telltale spiderweb cracks, Lexi gritted her teeth. Noah did what he'd thought was right, and she couldn't fault him for that. Still, if he hadn't moved his position, a part of her felt she could have talked Lindsey down.

Lexi shook off her frustrations and began looking for clues. The pressed wood dresser drawers were open and partially filled with shirts, pants, and underwear. She inspected each drawer, even removing them to look for items that might have been taped underneath, but she found nothing. A search of the closet and nightstand yielded the same results.

Lexi turned her attention to the mattress sections, feeling for anything suspicious. Squeezing one piece, she sensed something hard. She cut a slit through the fabric, using her pocketknife, and pulled out the object—a manila folder. Opening it, she discovered a collection of papers secured together by brass-plated fasteners. The title page read, *Rise of the Red Spades*.

Below the words appeared a triangle with three images in the corners. A red spade was at the top. In the lower left corner was a shield with a sword lying over a swastika—the symbol of the Texas Aryan Brotherhood. In the lower right corner was an image of a red fist—the sign of the Gate-keepers. It was a symbol Lexi would never forget. But this one was more sophisticated than the crudely hand-drawn one she'd come across in crime scene photos from the Wichita compound. This one was computer-generated.

She thumbed through a few pages, keying on certain words—*borders*, *panic*, *Red Spades*, and *revolution*. This was it. The taste of revenge sweetened her mouth. This document was what she'd been looking for since last year. It was the plan she and Darby had been searching for when he lost his life.

"Noah!" Lexi yelled. "I found something." Giddy with anticipation, she felt her chest tighten as she absorbed more of what was written on the pages.

Noah appeared seconds later. "Good, because I'm going to need a course of antibiotics after sifting through that crap."

Lexi handed him the collection of paper. "This could be it. This could tell us what the Red Spades' next move is." She pointed to the red fist. "That's the symbol of the Gatekeepers. This could also tell us where to find Belcher."

Noah read several pages, rubbing the back of his neck. "This reads like a manifesto, not an attack plan."

"I've seen documents like these from the Gatekeepers' compound. They spouted nonsense about the betrayal of our government leaders and how a revolution was needed to return the country to what the founding fathers had intended. Those who took part in the revolution would be true believers and would be saved by the hand of God. Check out the mention of the border."

Noah scanned the page. "They blame the leader of the betrayers for erasing the border through unfettered immigration."

"Farther down." Lexi pointed at a certain passage.

"The Gatekeepers will close the borders and start the clock." His eyes darted up to meet Lexi's. His excitement was palpable. "The tunnel explosion."

"Exactly."

Noah flipped another page. "What's the birthplace?" He showed Lexi the page, pointing to the second paragraph. "It says that the revolution will begin by killing the leader of the betrayers and by taking over the seat of government at the birthplace of the true leader."

"The Red Spades leader is General Calhoun." Lexi pulled out her cellphone, searched the Internet for Major General William Calhoun, and found a biography on a military history website. "It says he was born in Evergreen, Missouri."

"It makes little sense," Noah said. "There's no seat of government there."

"Maybe Kaplan can help."

27

Lexi put Kaplan on the hunt, hoping the documents found at the Gatekeepers' compound in Wichita might hold the key to deciphering more of the manifesto found in Lindsey's trailer. Kaplan sounded neither optimistic nor pessimistic, which gave Lexi hope. Kaplan Shaw was like a bloodhound. When she caught the faintest scent, she could follow it to its source.

In the meantime, Lexi and Noah headed back toward Dallas with Noah in the driver's seat. Hours in that blast suit had taken its toll, and Lexi needed an hour or two to turn the volume down and not stay alert.

Once on the main highway, Lexi reclined the passenger seat a few inches and pulled out her cell phone. "I need to call my boss."

"Good luck with yours. I'm officially off the case and am on administrative leave, pending a shooting board. On the positive side, I don't have to turn in my badge and weapon until Monday."

"I never know what to expect with Carlson. He runs hot and cold, which makes him hard to read." Lexi dialed her phone. After her boss answered, she explained about Lindsey.

"Dammit, Mills. Lindsey was our best lead. We don't need a trigger-happy detective on what has become an ATF case."

"Black is a good detective, sir. He made a decision in a fraction of a second to save my life. All things considered, Noah did the right thing."

"I disagree. He needs to get his ass back to Arizona, and I want you to get back here tomorrow, so I can assign you a partner."

"Give us one more day, sir." Lexi explained further about the manifesto and that Kaplan was on the job of cracking the code. "Black plans to go home if Agent Shaw doesn't come up with anything."

"One more day, Mills. That's all he gets." Carlson's stern, unwavering voice left no room for negotiation.

Noah glanced at her briefly when she finished her call, keeping both hands on the wheel. "Hot or cold?"

"All hot under the collar."

"Sounds like he's getting easier to predict," Noah snickered.

"Maybe." Lexi returned her phone to her pocket, feeling like she was battling Carlson and the clock. Both were making it harder to catch up with these extremist groups before they made their next moves.

Lexi settled back into her seat and watched approaching headlights wobble closer and then zoom past. Road markers ticked down the miles to Dallas, and then she saw the first road sign to Ponder.

"Hmph," she whispered to herself. Lexi hadn't bothered returning to her hometown since Christmas months ago, preferring to keep that part of her life in her rearview. But the harrowing events from earlier in the evening had her regretting that choice.

The second sign to Ponder tugged harder at her conscience. Her mother shouldn't have to suffer because her father refused to change. "Noah, I know I said we should head back to my apartment to wait for Kaplan's call, but would you mind if we swing by my parents' place? I'd like to see them after what we went through tonight."

"Say no more," Noah replied. "Just give me directions."

Lexi brought up her mother's home address on the car's GPS and then sat quietly while Noah followed the highlighted route until he passed Crazy Red's Mobile Home Park. "Unless you can afford a ticket, you better cut your speed in half. Like now."

At the city limits, he slowed for the reduced speed limit sign—one of the bigger revenue-makers for the town. Dropping from sixty to thirty had surprised nearly every out-of-towner and half of the locals several times a year. Lexi almost had her license suspended at eighteen because of that damn speed trap.

Lexi marveled at how big Ponder had gotten. The town had grown five times its size since Lexi had gone to high school here. She cringed at the ultimate sign of progress—a Starbucks where the Ponder Coffeehouse had once stood. Deeper into town, Valero had taken over Seth's Gas Station, and Subway had moved into the building next door. It was sad, really. In most parts, people viewed growth as a good thing, but for Ponder, it meant losing its micro-town, mid-century appeal. Most of the newcomers were tradition-alists, escaping the urban blight of central Dallas, who also wanted to remain close enough to use their Cowboys season tickets. Unfortunately, that migration brought tract homes and fast food.

Heading toward the western outskirts of town, Lexi smiled at the familiar sign of her childhood—Old Man Robbins's place. His son had since taken over the land after the old man passed and taken down the dilapidated barn, but the pond and mesquite tree with the rope swing remained intact. She'd spent countless summer days at that pond with friends, and that tree witnessed her first kiss with a girl.

"At least some things never change," Lexi mumbled.

"What was that?" Noah asked.

"Just reminiscing. Take the next gravel road on your left. It's the only house. Park around back."

"Got it."

The car tires crunched pebbles when Noah made the turn. He slowed to a crawl when the main house came into view. It was still the largest home in this stretch of Ponder, but that was because her father had built on a new wing during his money-making years with NASCAR. Until recent years, no one else in town had that kind of money. Other than a fresh coat of paint on the main house and the now-missing tree in the front that had fallen during a windstorm last year, the home hadn't changed since the day she moved out.

Unsurprisingly, both doors to the detached four-car garage were open, and light spilled out to the gravel surface. When Noah came to a stop close to the back porch, her father emerged from the garage with his recogniz-able limp in greasy coveralls, wiping his hands with a well-worn rag.

Lexi exited from the passenger side, feeling years of heartache and disappointment manifest in the back of her throat. Then, hearing the driver's door shut, she stepped toward her father. "Hi, Dad."

"Hi, Lexi. What brings you here?" His blank expression was heartbreaking. When she was little, she would come running into his garage after school and jump into his strong, welcoming arms. His smile, though, was the best part of his warm greetings. His signature handlebar mustache would stretch to his dimples. But he hadn't smiled like that for her since the day she told him she was gay, and she missed it.

"I had a rough day and wanted to see you two." Footsteps behind Lexi told her that Noah had caught up with her. She gestured toward him. "Dad, this is Noah Black. We've been working together the last few days."

"If you've been working with my daughter, that must make you an ATF agent."

"Police detective, actually. I'm from Nogales."

"It's good to meet you, Noah." Her father gave Noah a curious look before shaking his hand. "Vitiligo, right?"

"It's a pleasure, Mr. Mills, and you're correct."

"I had an uncle who had it. He was the toughest son of a bitch in Knox County. My hat goes off to you for landing on the right side of the law. Unfortunately, my uncle wasn't so lucky."

"If it wasn't for *my* uncle, aunt, and a kindhearted nun, I'd likely be behind bars, not wearing a badge."

Lexi's father returned his attention to her. "I'm sure you came to see your mother. You best get inside before she heads off to bed."

"I'd like to ask you something first, Dad," Lexi said. He nodded. With Noah there, this might be her only chance to get an honest reply without the conversation turning into an ugly scene. "How did you know Mom was the one before you asked her to marry you?"

His narrowed eyes looked as if he was angry that Lexi had cornered him. She was sure he would have much preferred to walk away rather than give her love-life advice. "It was the day her mother said they'd rushed her to the hospital for appendicitis. I thought about how my life would be without her in it, and it felt like a knife in the gut. I went to the hospital and fell asleep, waiting for her to wake up. When I finally opened my eyes, seeing her staring into them was the most beautiful feeling I'd ever experienced. That's when I knew I had to wake up next to her every day."

"Thanks, Dad."

That was the most heartfelt conversation they'd had in fifteen years, and though it required an outsider to referee, it still felt good. Yet she remained realistic that this didn't change their tenuous relationship. She was, though, hopeful that one day he would smile for her when she walked through the door.

She turned around, taking Noah and her foolhardy optimism toward the house. Stepping onto the back porch, she pulled the screen door open, squeaking the hinges to a familiar tune. The kitchen smelled like baked apples and cinnamon, her mother's favorite dessert to make. The thirteen pies sitting on the counter meant her mother had prepared for the Saturday rodeo in Denton. Lexi recalled her mother once saying that she'd missed only one church fundraiser, and that was because she was giving birth. But that was before her father's accident. After that, her mother had missed more events than she'd cared to count.

"Mom!" Lexi shouted. She then grabbed three forks, plates, and a pie from the refrigerator and invited Noah to join her at the breakfast table. "Single or double slice?"

"I'm starved," Noah said. "Better make it a double."

Lexi plated two large slices of pie and nearly moaned with her first bite. Her mother's pies were a slice of heaven. Footsteps on the stairs deeper inside the house meant the creator of that pie was coming.

Lexi's mother appeared through the doorway that led to the central part of the house. "That better be from the fridge, or you're going to spend the next hour baking." She held out her arms with a smile as wide as the Lone Star State.

Lexi placed her fork down before melting into her mother's arms. The hug started like their last embrace, firm but tight. But when her mother relaxed to pull back, Lexi squeezed harder, holding her tighter than the day she'd fallen from her bike and had the wind knocked out of her. She'd thought then, like she'd thought earlier tonight, that she'd come close to dying. That she'd never see her mother and father again. "I love you, Mom."

Her mother didn't question. Instead, she cradled her daughter with the same love and affection as she did that day on the gravel road by her broken bike. "Everything will be all right, Peanut." Her soft words convinced her it would be true. That once she recharged her batteries, she and Noah would resume their hunt and get their man.

When Lexi finally released her hold, her mother eyed Noah. "Who do we have here?"

"Mom, this is Noah Black. He's a detective from Arizona. We've been working on a case together." Lexi turned her head toward the table. "Noah, this is my mother, Jessie."

Her mother held out her arms. "Well, come here. Anyone who can put up with my daughter needs a hug."

"Don't I know it." Noah gave her mother a brief, warm embrace. "Your pie is delicious, Mrs. Mills. Can I get you a slice?"

"As you can tell, I've had far too many slices of my own pies." Her mother sat in the chair next to Lexi. Her waist had grown several inches over the years but so had her good nature. The less she cared about looking good on camera at her husband's NASCAR races, the happier she'd become at dinner time. She indulged in her own treats whenever it struck her fancy.

"You look beautiful, just like your daughter," Noah said.

"In that case, I'll take a small slice." Other than their eyes, hair color, and height, Lexi and her mom looked nothing alike. Dark brown skin versus tanned. Frizzy hair versus straight. A prominent nose versus a rounded one. "What brings you two out here this time of night?"

"We were working a case in Bowie." Lexi casually took another bite of pie, trying to pass off the last few hours like they were just another day at the office. But they weren't. Disarming the minefield was Lexi's final test, and she passed. She still had what it took to do this job.

"That was you?" Her mother clutched her chest with a gasp. "It was on the news. They said the man had a bomb and nearly blew up a trailer park."

"It's over now." Lexi left emotion out of her voice to downplay the harrowing experience. To do otherwise would be like throwing gasoline on a fire.

"That's why you're here. It scared you." Her mother's wrinkled nose meant a lecture was coming. "I wish you would find a less dangerous job, Peanut. I understand wanting to catch bad guys, but disarming bombs is an unnecessary level of danger."

"I don't need this tonight, Mom. I wanted to let you know Nita will be okay, but she was hurt last night."

"What happened?"

"Did you hear about the shooting at the Beebo Club last night?" Lexi asked.

Her mother gasped and clutched her chest again. "She was there? The news is calling it a hate crime."

"She was there for her cousin's bachelorette party. Then, when all hell broke loose, she was shot in the shoulder."

"And you're here? Why aren't you home?"

"I *was* there. Then Noah and I got another lead on the case we've been working on, and Nita told me to go."

"For a lesbian, you sure don't understand women." Her mother shook her head. "Nita told you to go because she knows what makes you tick, not because that was what she wanted."

"If you're so smart, what did she want?"

"For you to be there."

"She's never liked me doting over her."

"You hung around your father too much growing up. Doting and being there are two different things, Lexi. Answer me this. When you lost your leg, did you prefer being alone at night or having Nita around to snuggle up to?"

"But she's staying the night in the hospital and won't be released until lunchtime."

"Is she in a private room?"

"Yes, why?"

"That makes it even worse. Hospitals allow spouses and partners to stay in private rooms overnight. A sore back squeezing into the same bed or sleeping on those uncomfortable chairs is a small price to show Nita how much you love her."

"I did that, and she still told me to go. I think we each gave what the other needed." Lexi played in her head the words Nita had said this morning before taking off to Bowie. *"I know this case is eating you up inside. The faster you find the people behind the bombing, the faster you'll come back to me."* Those words told Lexi everything she needed to know about the woman she hoped might be her wife one day. They said that both of their needs mattered.

"I'll be darned." Her mother smiled. "You did learn a thing or two from me."

"I saw how you took care of Dad after his accident, but I also saw how he guilted you into missing church to make him breakfast during the races on TV. He took advantage of you, but Nita and I don't do that to each other. She knows if this case wasn't eating me up, I wouldn't leave her side."

"I can't believe some nut from Bowie is more important than the woman you're living with. I raised you better than that."

"Not Bowie, Mom. Nogales."

Her mother snapped her head in Noah's direction. "The border bombing? That was horrible. So many women and children were killed."

"Which is why Nita told me to go. We thought the man in Bowie could lead us to whoever was behind the bombing, but it didn't work out." Lexi glanced at Noah, reconciled that he'd done the right thing. "Noah took the shot before he could trigger the bomb."

Her mother reached across the table, taking one of Noah's hands into hers with tears welling in her eyes. "You saved my daughter's life, Noah. I can't thank you enough. You're family now, so that means you're welcome here any time."

"Thank you, Mrs. Mills." Noah squeezed her mother's hand before letting go. "I was just keeping a promise I made to Nita to keep Lexi safe."

"Hogwash. You're a hero in my book. And you better start calling me Jessie, or I'll have you feeding the chickens in the morning."

"Jessie it is," Noah said. "If we weren't heading back to Dallas tonight, I'd be happy to help you with the chickens. I tossed feed for years as a kid before heading off to school."

"Don't be silly. You two look exhausted. We have plenty of room. I'm not taking no for an answer." Lexi's mother pushed herself from the table. "I'll put fresh sheets on the guest beds and towels in the bathrooms."

28

Lexi stood at the foot of Noah's bed for the night and snatched the sheets from her mother's hands. "We got this, Mom. I know it's way past your bedtime."

"It will only take—"

"Go to bed, Mom. We're getting up early too. Would you like some help loading the pies into your SUV in the morning?"

"That would be great. I need to pick up Shirley Beamer before sunrise."

"I remember. You two haven't missed a rodeo since Dad's accident."

"Cut your father some slack, Peanut. He's a different man now. Much more attentive."

"He's not different enough." If he were, the exchange he and Lexi shared outside tonight would have started and ended with his signature bear hugs.

"I still think he'll come around." Her mother's eyes went dull with sadness.

"It's been fifteen years, Mom. He's not coming around."

"Let's not let your father ruin your impromptu visit." Lexi's mother kissed her on the cheek. "I'm so glad you came." She then hugged Noah again. "Sleep well, you two. I'll see you in the morning."

Lexi handed Noah his sheets, keeping one set for herself. "I'll be in my old room across the hall. I'll knock on your door if Kaplan calls. If she doesn't, I'll see you around six."

"Six it is."

Lexi entered her childhood bedroom. The bedding and wall paint had changed, but her mother had left the furniture and wall decorations untouched. She made the bed, unpacked her nightclothes, and slung her backpack over the chair of her old desk.

Her gaze drifted to the lower left desktop corner. Lexi then ran her fingertip over the hand-carved initials *AH* there. She'd put them there with her pocketknife the day she returned from the pond at Old Man Robbins's place, still high from her first kiss with a girl. That experience was so confirming that it deserved commemoration. She then ran her fingers across her lips, feeling them tingle with the echoes of that magical kiss.

A knock on the door drew Lexi from her reverie. "Come in." She turned.

The door opened, and Noah stuck his head around it. "Sorry to bother you, but my toothbrush broke." He held up both ends. "I checked the drawers in the bathroom, but I couldn't find any."

"I have some in my bathroom." Lexi entered her private bathroom and sifted through the vanity drawer until she found a toothbrush still in the package. She returned to the room and found Noah inspecting the framed pictures and news clippings hanging on the walls. Finally, he stopped at her favorite.

"That's from my first race as a certified pit crew member. It was Bobby's too."

"But you two are wearing different uniforms."

Lexi removed the picture from the wall, focusing on her much-younger self. In the photo, she was leaning against the pit wall with a very special eighteen-year-old boy next to her. "He and I met in pit crew training class. I worked on my father's team, and he got picked up by another crew."

"Did either of you win?"

"No, but our cars both finished in the top ten."

"Not bad for a first day."

"That was also the day I lost my virginity."

"But I thought—"

"It confirmed my sexuality, and his, too."

"Ahh." Noah tore his stare from the picture to look Lexi in the eye. "He was the security guard who was killed in Belcher's nitro heist?" He paused at Lexi's nod. "No wonder this is personal." When Lexi returned the picture to its proper place, Noah continued, "I got the impression that your dad doesn't like the notion of you being gay."

"That's putting it politely."

"That's a shame. He seems like a nice man."

"He's nice but not accepting." Lexi's phone rang. She recognized the caller and put the phone on speaker. "Hi, Kaplan. I have you on speaker with Noah."

"Hi, Noah. I owe you a drink for saving our girl."

Noah smiled wide again, making his vitiligo patch around his mouth the shape of a football. "Just keeping a promise."

"I hate to break this up, kids, but it's late." Lexi gave Noah a playful shove. "What did you find, Kaplan?"

"I think I may have pieced something together. Turn to the third page of the manifesto."

"Hold on. Let me dig it out." Lexi fished the folder from her backpack and laid out the document on her childhood desk, taking care to not cover the cherished memory there. "Got it."

"So, we all agree," Kaplan began, "that the line about the revolution beginning by killing the betrayer and by taking over the government at the birthplace of the true leader is key to figuring out where the Red Spades might strike next, and that Calhoun is the true leader, right?"

"Right," Lexi said, "but he was born in a small town in Missouri."

"Calhoun was born in Evergreen, but he's a Baptist. He was baptized later in life and reborn in Spicewood, Texas."

"How does that help?" Lexi asked.

"Look at the picture on the next page in the manifesto."

Lexi turned the page to the now-familiar painting of a giant grizzly under attack by a pack of hounds. Each dog had red spades for eyes. "I took the picture to be symbolic of the Red Spades toppling the government."

"It's more specific," Kaplan said. "That picture represents Governor Ken Macalister."

"Bear hugs." Lexi remembered thinking about the big hugs her father used to give her. Bear hugs were also the signature move of Governor Macalister when he was on the campaign trail two years ago. "Everyone calls him Bear. But the governor's mansion is in Austin. This would only make sense if Calhoun were born in Austin."

"I thought the same thing at first, but then I did more digging. Macalister spends the weekends at his private mansion on Lake Travis in—"

"Spicewood." Lexi's heart fluttered as she put it together. "The Red Spades intend to kill the governor to start the revolution, but when?"

"Everything about the manifesto is in threes. The Red Spades, the Gatekeepers, and the Aryan Brotherhood form the triad of righteousness. The plan to set the country on the right path is three-pronged: seal the border, create widespread panic, and launch the revolution. The manifesto also says that the clock will start when the Gatekeepers seal the borders. If the pattern holds, that could mean the revolution would start in three days, weeks, months, or years."

Lexi did the math. "If it's three days, the attack could be tomorrow. The governor could be in grave danger."

"That's my take." Kaplan's tone had turned from serious to ominous, which bolstered Lexi's fear. This top-notch intel analyst never jumped to wild conclusions. Instead, she followed the information and connected the dots. "Nothing in the document leads me to believe the Red Spades intend to draw this out. They talk about striking fast while the iron is hot."

"Thanks, Kaplan. You're the best at this. I'll call Carlson." Lexi finished the call and locked eyes with Noah. "Did you catch all of that?"

He nodded. "I'm with you one hundred percent. We need to up-channel this."

Lexi checked the time on her phone. Midnight was late but not late enough to require more than an upfront apology for the time.

Carlson picked up on the fourth ring. His voice was groggy. "Yeah?"

"This is Agent Mills. Sorry for waking you, sir, but this can't wait until morning."

"Hold on," Carlson said, rustling following in the background. "All right. Go ahead."

"I had Agent Shaw pore over the manifesto we found. Everything points to the Red Spades making an attack on the governor of Texas tomorrow at his private mansion on Lake Travis."

"I read what you sent over, Mills. Nowhere does that thing specify their target nor when they plan to attack." Lexi explained about the symbolism of three and their take on the meaning of the birthplace of the one true leader. "That's quite a leap."

"But we've already connected the Red Spades to the tunnel explosion, the church burning, the bank robbery, and the nitro and weapons heist. They're well-armed and have already executed the first two prongs of their plan for revolution. The final step is coming."

"I appreciate your enthusiasm, Mills, but I can't send this up as a confirmed threat. The most I can do is alert the FBI of an unsubstantiated one. Once I do that, this becomes their case."

"I get that, sir. I can liaison with the FBI like I did with Nogales PD, but we have to act now."

"I'll pass along your name, but they rarely ask for help. Until then, I need you to check into the office tomorrow and turn in your gear."

"About that." Lexi had no plan of giving this up, but she had the perfect excuse. "My partner is coming home from the hospital tomorrow. I need to get her settled. So I'll secure everything until Monday."

"Of course," Carlson said. "Take all the time you need."

Finishing her call, Lexi turned to Noah. "You got that?"

"All cold."

"He expects us to hand everything over to the FBI, but by the time they get up to speed, it will be too late."

"What do you want to do?" Noah asked.

"Warn the governor, but first, I need to talk to Nita."

"I'll give you some privacy. How far of a drive is it to Spicewood?"

"Four hours. I'd like to get going by four."

"What about your mother?"

Lexi's shoulders slumped from the weight of everything she was juggling. "We'll pack her up and leave a note."

Noah closed the distance between them. He wasn't a tall man, but compared to Lexi, he was. He then kissed her on the forehead. "I'm glad I took that shot. I'll see you at four."

Before Noah stepped out the door, Lexi replied, "I'm glad you did too. Sleep well, Noah."

Lexi had met Noah only two days ago, yet he'd already weaved his way into every facet of her life. Even into her dysfunctional relationship with her parents. And the most incredible thing was that everyone who had met him, even her judgmental father, instantly liked him. No matter what happened tomorrow, when this case was over, Lexi sensed he'd always be a part of her life.

Before stepping to the bed, Lexi grabbed her nightclothes and lotion. She then plopped atop the downturned covers and doffed her prosthetic. Removing it felt good after the day she'd had in that blast suit. Her residual limb was red but had only minor swelling, which boded well for her continuing as a member of the Special Response Team.

Once Lexi changed into her night shorts and tank top, she texted Nita, *Still up? I'm in Ponder.* Waiting for a response, she started her limb-care routine. By the time Lexi had finished with the lotion and massage, she still hadn't received a return text. So she assumed Nita was asleep and planned to call her from the road.

Lexi turned off the light on her nightstand and slid under the covers, wishing Nita were there beside her. Perhaps her mother was right. She should have been in her girlfriend's hospital room. If she had, Lexi would have Nita to snuggle next to, not her childhood memories.

Then her phone vibrated on the nightstand. She swiped at the screen, thinking it must be telepathy. "You're awake. I was just thinking about you."

"The nurse came in to change out my IV, so I checked my phone. Then I saw a message from my handsome butch."

"You wouldn't think me so handsome if you saw me right now."

"You sound tired," Nita said. "What has you worn out more, work or your father?"

"Work. Dad was indifferent tonight." Lexi sighed, already lamenting her next words. "Nita, I feel horrible about this, but I can't be there to pick you up from the hospital tomorrow."

"Is it the same case?" Nita's momentary pause signaled her disappointment, rubbing in the grime of regret. But Lexi had to go. If she didn't, the state and country would be in turmoil.

"Yes, and it's bigger than we thought. I can't tell you the specifics, but the life of someone very important in the state is in jeopardy. Noah and I have to head it off. Can Jenny and her fiancée take you home?"

"I don't think they can. They're visiting Maria's and Sophie's parents tomorrow."

"I've been so worried about you and this case that I hadn't considered what their parents must be going through. How are they holding up?"

"They're devastated." Nita paused. "Jenny feels guilty because they were there for her party."

"I'm so sorry they're going through this." Lexi swallowed past the thickness in her throat. "I wish I could be there for you."

"I know you do, Lex."

"Don't worry about a thing. I'll arrange for my mother to pick you up. She'll stay with you until I can get home."

"Okay." Nita sniffled. Her voice trembled.

"I love you, Nita. When this is over, I'm going to take a week off to take care of you."

"I love you, too."

Lexi ended the call with her heart feeling like it had been through a meat grinder. The woman she loved was lying in a hospital bed with a gunshot wound. Yet Lexi was fifty miles away, unable to hold her and reassure her that everything would be all right. But if she couldn't be there for Nita, she could send the next best thing.

She quickly donned her prosthetic, went down the hallway to her parents' bedroom, and peeked in through the open double doors. Her mother was lying on her side, but her father had yet to come to bed. Lexi then sat on the edge of the mattress in the dark, placing a hand on her mother's shoulder. "Mom."

Her mother slowly opened her eyes. She then croaked, "What?"

"I need to ask a big favor."

Her mother shook the sleep from her head and pushed her upper torso upright, turning on the nightstand light. "What do you need, Peanut?"

"Something broke on the case, and Noah and I have to go south toward Lake Travis before dawn. So I need you to pick up Nita from the hospital tomorrow and stay with her until I get back."

"Does she know to expect me?" Her mother furrowed her brow.

"Yes, and please don't give me another lecture. I'm feeling guilty enough as is."

"I can see it on your face. Of course I'll go."

Lexi hugged the one person she could always count on to help, especially when she needed it the most. Having her mother to lean on was a gift. It was proof that requesting reassignment to the Dallas office was the right decision. Reconnecting with the woman who would drop everything and fly to the moon and back to help her pick up the pieces was long overdue.

As women of color, they shared a bond that her father could never understand. He could never walk in their shoes and experience the world as they did. Never appreciate how assumptions based on skin color wear down the soul.

Despite their closeness, her mother could never understand the level of otherness Lexi faced every day. Walking through this part of the world as a gay woman of color was a category of otherness that Lexi couldn't change, and frankly, wouldn't, if given the opportunity. It was what made her unique. However, having only one leg was a curveball that Lexi wasn't prepared for. If she could change one thing about herself, that would be it. Though she couldn't get her leg back, she could prevent it from making a difference in how she walked in the world. Lexi Mills was a lot of things, but a quitter wasn't one of them.

"Thank you, Mom. When this is over, I'm going to ask Nita to marry me."

"Peanut." Her mother pulled her into a tight embrace. "I'm so happy for you. Nita is perfect for you."

"I think so. Though, I have no idea what to give her for an engagement ring."

"I have the perfect solution." Her mother flipped the covers back, padded to her dresser beneath the window, and opened the stone jewelry box sitting on top. She then rummaged through the right side. "Here it is." Returning to the bed, she sat on the edge next to Lexi. "This was my mother's engagement ring."

The ring was a simple single diamond mounted on a thin gold band. It wasn't elaborate, but it had history. Lexi remembered the story of her grandfather proposing to her grandmother on her eighteenth birthday over the objections of both sets of parents. They were both too young, supposedly, but that marriage ended up producing three children and lasted fifty-eight years before death took her grandfather.

"This is perfect, Mom. I love you." Lexi stuffed the ring into her front pants pocket, hoping it would launch her and Nita on the same long, loving path.

29

Lexi figured her mother could drop off the pies at the Beamer place on her way into the city, so the least she could do was prep them before she took off for Spicewood. Therefore, at 3:50, she and Noah met in the kitchen. They individually boxed twelve of her mother's pies like a well-oiled team, loaded them into two old Amazon boxes, and left them on the kitchen table. Then, while Noah took their bags to the car, Lexi stayed behind to pen a brief note to her mother.

Using the pen and magnetic notepad tacked to the refrigerator door, she wrote, *Mom, pies are all ready to go. Thanks for helping today. It means more than you realize. Give Dad a kiss for me. Love you both. Lexi.*

Lexi then walked out of her childhood home, wishing for one more thing she could change: her father. She longed for the symbiotic relationship they once shared over cars and racing. They were once of one mind in the garage and at the track, building the fastest and most reliable machine for the race. "One day," she told herself.

Hopping in the driver's seat of her SUV, Lexi glanced at Noah in the passenger side. "Ready to save the governor?"

"And possibly get my ass fired if this proves to be nothing? You bet."

After three hours behind the wheel, Lexi dialed the last number she'd saved to her contacts list, hoping the synergy she'd felt last night wasn't an illusion. The line connected to a groggy hello. "Lieutenant, this is Lexi Mills."

"Lexi." Briscoe's voice became clearer. "I hope this means you've changed your mind and want to become a Texas Ranger."

"I'm afraid not, but I have a favor to ask."

"Name it."

Lexi explained about the intelligence Kaplan had gleaned from the manifesto and about her fears the FBI wouldn't get up to speed in time to make a difference. "Noah and I are an hour out from Spicewood. We need to brief the governor."

"Say no more. Stay on the line while I call the governor's security detail at the mansion." Briscoe put Lexi on hold and returned several minutes later. "Lexi, I got you a meeting with the governor's head of security at the mansion at eight-thirty. Ask for Simon Winslow. He's a reasonable man and will listen."

"Thanks, Lieutenant. I hope to repay the favor one day." Without Briscoe's help, Lexi doubted she would have gotten past the front gate. However, the governor's security chief was only the first step. Her biggest obstacle was convincing the governor that the threat was real.

"You can start by calling me Sarah."

"Thank you, Sarah."

"Keep in touch, Lexi. Godspeed."

Lexi spent the final hour to Spicewood in silence, weighing the consequences if the governor refused to take her and Noah seriously. Besides costing him his life, Texas and the country could devolve into chaos. She'd have to choose every word wisely and appeal to his common sense.

Rolling down her window at the guarded gate at the outer edge of the Lake Travis upscale community, Lexi smirked at the level of security it provided. A single rent-a-cop with a handgun and a flimsy traffic arm wouldn't stop a redneck in an F-150, let alone an extremist group hell-bent on revolution.

Coming to a stop, she flashed her badge at the guard dressed in shiny shoes and a uniform pressed perfectly like an honor guard presenting the colors at Arlington Cemetery. If not effective, the man looked professional.

"Good morning, ma'am. May I help you?"

"I'm Special Agent Mills." Lexi gestured toward Noah in the passenger seat. "This is Detective Black. We have an appointment at the governor's mansion."

"Yes, ma'am. We've been expecting you. You'll have to show your credentials at the secondary gate." He provided directions to the mansion and raised the traffic arm. "Enjoy your visit to Lakecliff."

Lexi rolled up her window, chuckling to herself. *All show.*

Approaching the governor's Mediterranean-style mansion, Lexi was impressed with the security precautions. The ten-foot-tall wrought iron fence topped with spires didn't look easily scalable. The double gate and the Texas Rangers stationed on either side with automatic weapons slung over their chests would stop any passenger vehicle. The only missing things were retractable bollards to stop a car approaching at ramming speed.

Lexi greeted one guard and presented him with her and Noah's badges and credentials. At the same time, the other searched the undercarriage of her SUV with a mirror. In her experience, a visual inspection was inferior to bomb-sniffing dogs. They could detect anything under or inside a vehicle.

The guard returned their credentials and directed them up the driveway paved in stone that split near the house, making the shape of a lollipop. "Drive through the breezeway. You'll see parking spots on the other side."

Lexi parked as directed. Before exiting her car, she dug her grandmother's engagement ring from her pocket. She tossed it in the center console cup holder among her change collection. A gut feeling had her thinking that it would be safer here than with her chasing down the governor.

Following more greetings, the door guard invited her and Noah inside. The impressive grand entry, replete with Greek columns and a curved marble staircase, branched off to an equally ornate hallway. The guard knocked on the partially closed door at the end of the hallway marked *Security*.

A man inside said, "Come in."

The guard retreated.

Lexi entered with Noah steps behind. A tall, broad-shouldered African American man was circling a wood desk near the wall of windows at the rear of the office-sized room. He shook Lexi's hand. "I'm Simon. You must be Lexi Mills. Sarah Briscoe has nothing but good things to say about you. And that's saying something."

"Thank you. It's a pleasure," Lexi replied.

Winslow turned to Noah and shook his hand. "You must be Noah Black. I hear you made one hell of a shot last night and brought the standoff to a safe conclusion for Lexi and my fellow Rangers."

"Thank you, Simon. I was just keeping a promise"—Noah gestured his chin toward Lexi—"to keep this one safe."

"No matter the case, you have my gratitude." Winslow invited them to sit in the guest chairs while he returned to the chair behind the desk. "Sarah said you have evidence of a credible threat against the governor. Can you walk me through it?"

"Of course." Lexi explained how her and Noah's investigation of the church burning and tunnel crossing explosion led them to David Lindsey in Bowie. She made special note of the Gatekeepers, the Aryan Brotherhood, and the Red Spades. "We found a reference in the manifesto stating the revolution would begin by killing the leader of the betrayers at the birthplace of the true leader. We believe Governor Macalister is the target and General Calhoun is the true leader."

"What makes you think the governor is the target?"

Lexi showed him the photo she'd taken of the painting from the manifesto, where a pack of hounds was attacking a giant grizzly. "The governor is known as the Big Bear in Texas. We believe this image represents the Red Spades, the Gatekeepers, and the Aryan Brotherhood killing Governor 'Bear' Macalister."

"That's possible, but I did some initial research." Winslow cocked his head in apparent skepticism. "Calhoun is from Missouri, not Texas."

"But he was baptized right here in Spicewood."

Winslow rubbed his smoothly shaved chin. "With the religious undertones of the manifesto, the place of Calhoun's rebirth makes sense." His soft nod suggested Lexi had won him over. "But what makes you think the attack might be today?"

Lexi explained about the symbolism of threes. "The manifesto specifies the closing of the border starts the clock. That was three days ago."

Winslow picked up the receiver of his desk phone and speed-dialed a number. "Tom, I've received a credible threat from the ATF. So I'm elevating to THREATCON CHARLIE at the Bear Den... Redirect SWAT to the Spicewood to escort Papa Bear to the cave... I don't care if they're tired. Send them." Finishing the call, he snatched a portable tactical radio sitting on a charger atop the desk and keyed the mic. "Attention, all teams. This is not a drill. Implement THREATCON CHARLIE. I repeat. This is not a drill. Implement THREATCON CHARLIE. Tango Four, this is Tango One. Delay Papa Bear until I get to the dock."

"Copy, Tango One. He won't be happy."

"Sit on him if you have to," Winslow barked.

"What is THREATCON CHARLIE?" Noah asked.

"It means a threat is imminent. All off-duty guards report to their posts and arm up to the teeth. They'll move two SUVs into position to block the front gate. And no one comes in or out of the mansion until we get an armed escort."

"Thanks for believing us, Simon." Lexi exhaled a deep breath of relief.

"Just don't make a fool out of me." Winslow opened the lower desk drawer and removed his holstered sidearm. He then stood, clipped it to his belt, and gripped the radio tight. "Let's go talk to the governor. We need to catch him before he takes off fishing."

30

Winslow exited to the backyard through the office's double French doors, leading Lexi and Noah into the warm spring air. They walked past a dual-level pool, where the cloudless sky reflected a tropical-like blue, and down several steps to an immaculately manicured expansive green. Once at the edge, he led them down a set of aged stone steps and past a private chapel. Next, they followed a long wooden boardwalk along the rocky shore of Lake Travis until reaching steep metal stairs that would take them to the water. Lexi estimated eighty stairs, which in her prosthetic might pinch the skin surrounding her residual limb if she took them too fast.

She whispered to Noah, knocking once on her plastic socket. "I'll go last in case I'm a little slow." He responded with a firm, silent nod.

Three-quarters of the way down, Lexi felt her stump slide deeper in the socket, causing the pressure against it to build with each additional step. Maneuvering challenges like these were stark reminders that she wasn't whole. But by the time Winslow and Noah had reached the bottom, she lagged by only four steps. Her hard work paid off.

The thirty-foot-long gangway from the shore's edge ending at a covered two-slip dock was thankfully level. Lexi recognized the man loading a Boston Whaler fishing boat the length of two SUVs. Anyone who'd spent a day in Texas recently would know the fresh face of the

Lone Star State. Since his election nearly two years ago, Ken Macalister's image had been plastered on billboards and television commercials everywhere, promoting his progressive approach. He intended to make Texas into a kinder, gentler state that put the needs of those less fortunate first.

Winslow placed a hand on the shoulder of a second man helping the governor with tackle boxes and ice chests. Presumably, he was Tango Four.

"I'll finish, Theo," Winslow said. "Why don't you take a position at the end of the gangway?"

"Sure, boss." Theo handed the governor the box he'd hoisted before assuming his new station.

"Something must be up if Windy is taking fishing duties." Macalister chuckled.

"It's important, Governor. We've received a credible threat that I believe we should heed and get you back to the capital."

"Is anyone rolling down Haynie Flat Road in tanks?"

"No, sir."

"Then it can wait until I reel in a few. I haven't been on the river all month." Macalister pointed at the last item on the dock. "Hand me my rod. I'm not missing out on my only free morning while the bass are biting."

Winslow handed the governor his fishing rod but refused to let it go. He then turned his tone soft but firm. "Ken, you need to listen this time. We've been friends for twenty years. If you value our friendship, you'll hear what the agents have to say."

Macalister narrowed his eyes at Winslow. They suggested a rich history between the two men. "They can have one hour aboard with me. If I'm not satisfied, they're swimming back."

Lexi froze at the alternative Macalister had laid out. If she failed to make her case, she'd have to jettison her prosthetic on the boat and hop on one foot up those stairs to her car. Once submerged, that thing was useless. She kicked herself for not packing a spare—another lesson learned for future SRT assignments.

"I'll have Theo follow in the twelve-footer in case you try to give them the heave-ho." Winslow winked before raising the radio to his mouth. "Tango Four, follow us in *Goldie Locks*."

"On my way." Theo retraced his steps down the gangway toward the dock.

"Grab a line, you two." Macalister gestured for Lexi and Noah to retrieve the bow and stern lines. "And toss in the fenders. We don't want to look like weekend amateurs."

After Winslow stepped onto the boat, Lexi stalled at her end, allowing Noah to finish first. Then, unsure about her prosthetic footing, she let him pull her on board. "Thanks, Noah."

"Just keeping my promise."

"Will you stop it with the promise thing?"

"I will when the case is over." Noah's lopsided grin was clearly his signal that he meant what he'd said. And if Lexi were honest with him, she'd tell him that his steadfastness was comforting. That it was what she needed to get through her first case as an amputee.

"Find a seat." Macalister took a position at the helm. Lexi and Noah took a seat aft of the governor while Winslow sat forward, scanning up and down the river for threats. "I'm throttling in three, two, one, go."

While the whaler lumbered out of its slip, Winslow radioed, "Papa Bear taking *Mama Bear* for a spin."

Once Macalister had put twenty feet between it and the dock, he turned upriver. He then opened the throttle enough to cut against the current and send a healthy spray of water into the aft area. A glance past the stern confirmed Theo was following in the smaller Boston Whaler at such a distance to avoid absorbing the rise of Macalister's wake.

Lexi scooted closer to the governor across the cushioned bench. He had one hand on the wheel, one on the throttle, and a grin as wide as the river he was navigating. "Governor, I'm Special Agent Lexi Mills of the ATF. My partner is Detective Noah Black of the Nogales Police Department. We've been working the tunnel bombing at the border, and our investigation led us here."

"You have my attention." Macalister kept his gaze forward. "Make good use of your time, Agent Mills. I plan to drop anchor up a piece at the bend."

Lexi glanced up. His destination was about a mile from the mansion and a half-mile from their current location. "Yes, sir." Lexi stepped the governor through the highlights of her and Noah's investigation, including the church burning, the stolen arms at the bank robbery, and how the stolen nitro led them to Bowie and the manifesto. "The Triad of Right-eousness blames our governments for unfettered immigration and intends to set the country on the right path." She then showed him the photo that had convinced Winslow of the threat. "We found this in the manifesto. You're the bear in this painting, and the three hounds are the Red Spades, the Gatekeepers, and the Aryan Brotherhood. They intend to start the revo-lution today by taking out the leader of the betrayers in the birthplace of the true leader. That's you, right here in Spicewood."

"Darlin'..." Macalister throttled down, slowing the boat to a crawl. "There's been a threat on my life since the day I took office. Every politician flaps their gums a mile a minute, spewing promises. I'm one of them, but what sets me apart from my predecessors is that I intend to keep every damn one of mine."

The boat came to a stop, and Macalister killed the engine and dropped anchor. A glance back confirmed Theo did the same about twenty-five yards behind. "I firmly believe we can make Texas a better state, and that starts by doing better for those who cross the border into Texas in search of a new life. This country was forged on the backs of hardworking immi-grants. Until federal laws change, I intend to welcome anyone without a criminal record or on some damn watch list with open arms."

Macalister opened his tackle box and Texas-rigged a plastic crawfish lure on a worm hook. "The border shouldn't be a barrier to seeking a better life. With Mexico's help, it should be a way station. I know these policies aren't popular with the boys at the bar or the hardcore militants in compounds, but I won't let them slow me down." He made his way to the bow and cast his line upstream close to the rocky shoreline. He then slowly reeled it back in. "They'll have to roll through downtown Austin with tanks and break down the damn gate before I let them deter me from keeping the promises I made to every Texan."

"I'm not asking you to claw back on your promises, Governor," Lexi said. "I'm asking you to take precautions now. The tunnel explosion started the clock to revolution, and our three days are up. We believe they intend to strike today with a force as well armed as your National Guard."

Macalister recast his line into the rocks and reeled it back in again. This time the rod bowed, and a bass the length of Lexi's father's old Stanley thermos bottle flew out of the water, swinging from a nearly invisible line. "Hot damn, Simon. Get the net."

Winslow broke from his constant watch of the avenues of approach long enough to net the rascally fish and throw it into a waiting ice chest. He then looked the governor in the eye. "I believe them, Ken. I've raised the threat level to Charlie and asked for a SWAT escort back to Austin."

"Holy hell, Simon. Nothing like jumping the gun. You're a Texan, not an Okie," Macalister said.

"You know me better than that." Winslow appeared hurt by his friend's accusation.

Macalister patted Winslow on the shoulder. "Then get me home, my friend." He turned to secure his rod on the hooks below the port railing when the sound of approaching helicopters shattered the calm.

Seconds later, two helos emerged around a bend upriver, flying low between the river's shores. They were so low that a semi would have trouble passing beneath their skids. At first glance, they appeared to be from a military unit at Fort Hood conducting training. But as they flew closer, their older shape became clear. They were Vietnam-era gunships.

Lexi instinctively placed her hand on the grip of her service weapon, fearing the worst. "I don't like this, Simon."

"I don't either." Winslow also gripped his weapon. He yelled over his shoulder loud enough for Theo to hear. "Anchor up."

The governor pressed a button on the helm console, retracting the anchor.

A second later, the Hueys lifted a fraction and flew overhead. Each had a heavy caliber machine gun hanging out one side and a red spade painted on the nose and tail. Several men dressed for combat were inside, but they weren't United States soldiers. They were like the men Lexi had tracked to Belcher's compound in Wichita. This meant one thing:

They were too late.

31

In a pageant of seven armored vehicles, the midmorning rumble of steel-belted tires rolling down Haynie Flat Road in Spicewood, Texas, turned several heads on the golf course lining the north side of the street. It was a brief spectacle necessary to spark the Red Spades' revolution.

Jamie Porter and five other men occupied the command vehicle in the rear. This was what he'd prepared for all his adult life. Every engagement he'd encountered in the sandbox was a dress rehearsal for this moment. Screw the Army promotion board. Fifty Calhoun had seen fit to place Jamie in a position typically performed by bird colonels, and he had no intention of letting him down. He would lead the primary attack on the mansion with precision and distinction.

Since the first team through the gate would have to absorb the defending gunfire from the Texas Rangers guarding the traitor's mansion, Jamie had assigned the Red Spades' most fearless men to the lead vehicle. Most likely, they wouldn't make it out of the car alive, but that probable fate wouldn't deter the Kader Teufel. The team of six had earned the nickname that roughly translated to the Devil Squad because they left a path of hell wherever they attacked. Even Jamie knew to give that team a wide berth when they'd had a drink or two too many.

The other thirty men in the middle five vehicles were well trained and well-armed but didn't have the same soullessness as the Devil Squad. They would, however, serve as a formidable show of force while defending the nineteen-thousand-square-foot mansion and wooded three-and-a-half-acre waterfront property.

The caravan was a half-mile out from the outer gate of the snotty, exclusive community of multimillion-dollar homes. Jamie picked up the microphone attached to the dashboard-mounted tactical radio. "Red Spades, this is Sparrow. This is what we've trained for, and if we each do our jobs, the next few minutes will bring us what we've hoped for. Kader Teufel, give 'em hell."

The lead vehicle turned onto the main road leading into the fenced-in community. The gate lay fifty yards straight ahead. A uniformed man stepped out of the guard shack, dutifully waiting to greet the people in the approaching vehicle. However, the devils had something else in mind. The driver gunned the engine, bringing it to ramming speed. If the man in the seat directly behind the driver was doing his job, he should be rolling down the window, preparing to take out the unsuspecting guard.

Pop. Pop. Pop.

The guard jerked before falling to the pavement. They'd defeated their first obstacle. The lead vehicle broke through the traffic arm the next second, sending shards of splintered wood and plastic into the air. Obstacle two cleared.

The caravan tore past the guard shack, each vehicle rising and falling several inches on the driver's side twice as it rolled over the dead guard on the ground. The seven cars kept in tight formation down the straight half-mile stretch of Cliff Point Road. Then, the lead vehicle pulled ahead once it hit the sweeping left curve and the last section of pavement that ended at the gate of Macalister's mansion. If the attack force had the element of surprise, the wrought iron gate would be closed with only two armed guards standing street-side. Otherwise, two SUVs would be there, blockading the only entrance. Either way, they'd planned for both contingencies.

Once the lead vehicle rounded the turn, a voice came over their radio channel. "Bravo. Plan Bravo." That meant the blockade was in place, and the attack group would have to blast their way through.

The last cars slowed, including Jamie's command SUV. At the same time, the first two armored vehicles sped to the T-intersection forty yards shy of the gate. One spun left and the other right until both had their tail ends—the most fortified end—facing the mansion. The four Texas Rangers at the entrance let loose multiple volleys of gunfire, peppering both armor-plated attack vehicles but creating no damage.

Each vehicle came to a stop, and their rooftop access door flew open. A man popped up from each hatch, holding a rocket-propelled grenade launcher—the most effective infantry weapon in their arsenal. In two seconds, each man steadied the launcher on his shoulder. Then they fired, sending two high-explosive warheads in a trail of smoke and vapor. Each explosive, powerful enough to take out an Abrams tank at two hundred yards, was hurtling toward a blockading SUV.

The four Rangers dove for safety, but they weren't quick enough. In two seconds, both grenades hit their targets. Then two loud, fiery explosions launched the SUVs off the ground several feet and dispatched metal and debris in every direction. Two Rangers lay motionless. The other two were a bloody mess, spending their last bits of energy to low crawl a few extra feet. Unfortunately, the effort only took them closer to death.

"Second wave. Go. Go. Go," Jamie Porter announced over the radio. That was the cue for the driver of the third vehicle to plow through the burning wreckage and ram the weakened gate. Cars four, five, and six would follow. They would either stay on the tail of number three or push it through if the wheels snagged on rubble.

Number three gunned it, wedging through the SUVs perfectly and knocking the gate open. Both panels bent and settled at cockeyed angles. The rest of the caravan followed with numbers one and two swinging around as the tail.

In the meantime, number two gunship had arrived and sprayed a hail of .50-caliber bullets into the compound, taking out at least two Rangers near the portico.

As three and four split to take either side of the circular driveway, two rocket-propelled grenades launched in their direction from the mansion rooftop. Those munitions were faster than bullet trains traveling in trails of smoke. That was an unexpected twist. Jamie's intelligence gathering didn't unearth that level of armament at the private mansion, only at the public one in Austin.

Both warheads speared their targets, bringing the vehicles to a lurching halt. They landed such that both sides of the driveway were blocked. Inside were twelve men, but Jamie couldn't remember if those were ex-Army or Aryan Brotherhood recruits in the chaos. If they were the latter, he wouldn't mourn their deaths. Most of those barbarians were unnecessarily brutal. Jamie was more concerned about the impact that losing 30 percent of his force would have on his attack plan. Their loss presented a giant gap in their defenses once they secured the compound.

He glanced at Sergeant Major Sanders behind the wheel of the command vehicle. "Shit."

"Agreed."

"Eagle Two, take out that rooftop," Jamie ordered into the mic.

Five and six came to a stop shy of the burning vehicles, using them as defensive shields while flames danced inside, engulfing what was left of the corpses. At the same time, the gunship had swung around and leveled its .50 cal at the rooftop embankments. Terra-cotta tiles, wood, and other debris went flying, knocking out both guard nests and likely most of the top floor.

The Rangers losing the high ground put the battle on even footing, though it was by no means an even match. If Jamie's intel was correct, the Rangers were down to no more than eight people, compared to the Red Spades' remaining thirty-eight in the vehicles and helicopters. It wasn't a fair fight, but that was by design. Shock and awe by overwhelming force.

Jamie keyed the mic again. "Breaching formation."

The devils took a position near vehicle five, and team two reinforced team six on either side of the portico. The command vehicle remained back, and the four other men jumped out the rear to secure the entrance where the gate once stood. The battle for the mansion was about to begin. Only two-thirds of the force remained, but the attack plan was still sound. Jamie would, however, have difficulty holding the line once the National Guard arrived.

"Go. Go. Go!" Jamie yelled into the mic.

Six men fanned out on the structure's south side, and another six went around to the north. Three would secure the entrances on each side while the other three from each team would continue around to the back. That left two teams in the front to breach the main entrance. One group would wait in reserve. But if the Devil Squad did the job Jamie knew them capable of, he would need the reserved team for only mop-up.

Jamie raised the mic for what should be his last command to take over the compound. "Give 'em hell, devils. Go. Go. Go."

32

Simon Winslow snagged his tactical radio and pressed the mic. "Attention all teams, THREATCON DELTA. I repeat. THREATCON DELTA. Aerial attack on the river." He then shoved the radio into his back pocket and retrieved his cell phone, thumbing the screen twice. "Tom, we're under attack. Papa Bear and the den compromised. Roll all units."

The heavy anchor was taking too many precious seconds, and until it fully retracted, the governor's Boston Whaler was a sitting duck in the water. In the meantime, Theo had the manual anchor in the smaller whaler up in a fraction of the time and motored beside the governor's boat. He'd drawn his sidearm, as had Lexi, Noah, and Simon.

Chest heaving with adrenaline, Theo spun his head in every direction. "We're out of position, boss. What's the plan?"

A double explosion in rapid succession rocked the area, but it was hard to tell where it originated. Though, common sense dictated that it likely came from the governor's mansion. Escaping was imperative.

Someone said over the radio, "Bear Den under attack."

Lexi hadn't fished this river, but if it was anything like the others she'd been on in Texas, the surrounding terrain and vegetation offered little overhead camouflage. They couldn't outrun the Huey, so their only option was to dock and make a run for it on foot, hoping to find a tree grove to hide beneath. "We need cover."

Winslow glanced at the governor, gripping his SIG Sauer tight. "Ken, take us to Blue Cove."

"But it's dried out."

"Exactly. Beach it on the rocks," Simon said in a calm voice. "We'll run for the trees at the Dell spread." He then gestured for Theo to swing *Goldie Locks* around and follow.

Once Theo cleared, the governor yelled, "Hold on."

Everyone grabbed a railing with one hand while holding their weapons in the other. The engines roared with the dual propellers cutting deep into the water and churning up bubbles like a submerged volcano threatening to erupt. The boat lurched hard, nearly ripping Lexi's grip and sending her overboard. A glance past the stern confirmed Theo was following close behind in *Goldie Locks*, fighting against the wake *Mama Bear* created.

Simon kept his stare forward while Lexi and Noah split their attention between port, starboard, and aft, watching for threats. Then a single heli-copter reappeared from around the bend behind them, flying low against the water with the .50 cal hanging out like a Vietnam soldier, preparing to strafe Vietcong strongholds along the Mekong Delta.

A barrage of gunfire peppered the water close to *Mama Bear*. Theo slumped at the wheel, *Goldie Locks* instantly veering starboard. As bullets splashed around them, the smaller boat hurtled toward the shoreline at top speed. *Mama Bear* continued to race upstream, putting distance between the two boats. Then, *Goldie Locks* smashed against the rocky shore, exploding in a fireball and shattering into a hundred pieces.

Lexi gasped. Theo was dead.

More explosions sounded from downriver, convincing Lexi the mansion was undergoing a full-on ground attack.

The radio squawked again. "They're everywhere."

The helicopter swung around above the treetops, making a tight turn and settling over the river. It headed straight for *Mama Bear* with the bright red spade on the nose leading the charge. The .50 cal had been fixed forward and fired in a straight line. The spray of bullets was coming for the boat in a rhythm of loud pops. Water sprang up as each bullet pierced the surface two yards apart.

Lexi's heart pounded. She estimated those rounds would reach *Mama Bear's* bow in five seconds. She, Simon, and Noah fired at the approaching helo, aiming at the reinforced glass windshield. However, their barrage created only a cluster of opaque circles where the bullets had failed to penetrate.

The trail of oncoming bullets then veered several feet to their port, seemingly on purpose. They missed *Mama Bear* by inches, making Lexi think that the chopper's mission was to capture, not kill.

The Huey zoomed past them, less than fifty feet above their heads, sending Lexi's shallow breathing into overdrive. She was a bomb expert, not an ATF agent on the search warrant squad. Those brave men and women trained and mentally prepared for receiving gunfire every time they broke down a door. However, the danger Lexi regularly faced on the job was dramatically different. She didn't have to dodge IEDs vaulting in her direction, nor did she have to concern herself with moving targets. Instead, bombs remained politely still while she did her job.

Lexi made a mental note: *If I get out of this alive, I will never needle the warrant team again for not having to suit up like I do.*

"We're almost there," the governor yelled. "Prepare for a sharp starboard turn." Seconds later, he spun the wheel, angling the bow toward a river outlet as wide as two school buses parked bumper to bumper. The water level on either side of the shoreline appeared low, exposing rocks and riverbed gunk. As they darted farther into the cove, the marshy gunk grew wider, narrowing the water width to a single bus length.

The end of the water was in sight, two hundred yards down. Once they ran aground, they'd have to jump out into the muck and make their way to the tree line up the steep slope of the riverbed. If the foot of Lexi's prosthetic sank too deep into the mud, she wasn't sure if the socket could maintain its suction on her residual limb long enough to free it.

Lexi gulped at the thought that Noah might stay behind to help her instead of running for cover. She then tugged on his coat sleeve. "If I get stuck, I want you to run. Save the governor. Do you hear me?"

Noah visibly swallowed before resting a hand on her shoulder. "You'll do fine. Aim for the rocks."

Lexi replied with a short, firm nod. It would be like navigating a mine-field, zigzagging a safe path until she cleared the danger. That she could do on one leg like playing hopscotch.

"Prepare for a hard stop," the governor yelled.

The next second, the Huey appeared over the roof of the Dell mansion on the port side and dove, positioning itself at the river's end and coming to an abrupt midair stop. It hovered ten feet off the surface, pointing the .50 cal at *Mama Bear*.

With little maneuvering room, the governor had no choice. He throttled down hard, causing the ice chests and tackle boxes to fling forward. One hit Lexi square on the prosthetic. If it had hit her natural leg, the force might have snapped the fibula. The titanium, however, absorbed the energy, causing the shoe attached at the bottom to slip on the deck. For the first time, she was relieved to have that damn thing.

The boat swung to port, coming to a stop and sending a wave toward the marshy river end. The motion was more intense and nauseating than any Disney thrill ride. *Mama Bear* rocked port to starboard several times as it settled in the water. The two outboards idled, making the sound of the chopper blades whirling in the air that much more ominous. They were in the gunship's crosshairs, but the combatants inside had yet to fire.

Lexi, Noah, and Winslow leveled their sidearms at the Huey in a final stand.

A voice came over the helicopter's external speaker. "There is no use in resisting. We have your mansion. Lower your weapons now or die."

Winslow positioned himself between the governor and the .50 cal, ready to take the first bullet. However, at that range, the round would rip through his body like a knife through bread and riddle the man he'd sworn to protect.

The governor placed a hand on Winslow's back. "It's over, Simon. Let's see what these yahoos want."

"Your head on a pike, I'm afraid." Winslow refused to budge from his protective position.

"You've done your job well, my friend. Lower your weapon." The governor shifted his stare to Lexi and Noah. "You too. It's hard to get blood out of the cushions." He winked.

His humor was disarming and had the added benefit of being practical. There was no sense in making a stand with only one ammo clip each. Lexi remembered a FLETC instructor's advice during a hostage training seminar. *"There might be a time when you'll find yourself the hostage. Don't be a hero. Be smart. Find the weakness in your surroundings or the hostage-taker and exploit it."* The smart thing in this situation was to buy them time.

Lexi looked at Noah. "He's right. We're out of options."

"For now," Winslow said. The three lowered their weapons but kept them at the ready.

The voice from the helicopter announced, "Return to your dock at half throttle. If you vary your course, I'll open fire."

Macalister waved at the helicopter and engaged the throttle, steering toward the cove's mouth. The Red Spades followed overhead. "Sorry, people, but the party's over."

Winslow retrieved his cell phone again and dialed. "Bear Den overrun. Papa Bear taken hostage... What's the SWAT or National Guard ETA...? This will probably be my last communiqué. Tell my wife that I love her."

Noah took out his phone and typed out a text message. Lexi had an inkling it was to his aunt. She was the only family he had, or at least the only family worthy of his love and attention, as far as she could tell.

Lexi then pulled out her phone, taking Noah and Simon's lead. Talking to loved ones at a time like this would be overly emotional, so a text would have to convey her last thoughts. She then scrolled through her message strings until she found her mother's name and typed: *You've always been my role model. Your example of strength and love made me who I am. I love you.* She swallowed past the lump of emotion in the back of her throat and hit send.

Lexi then scrolled to the text string she used most often. Without enough time to think carefully through what words she wanted Nita to remember her by, she typed out the first thing that came to mind. *You make me whole. No matter where I go, I'm thinking of you. I love you, now and always.* Hand shaking, Lexi pressed send.

Lexi then sent one more text to Kaplan. *Me Noah hostage by red spades w gov in Spicewood.*

Repocketing the phone, Lexi looked up, discovering the governor had navigated them out of the cove and was nearing the covered dock at the foot of the mansion. Six mercenary-type men, carrying automatic weapons, likely from the stash stolen from Fort Hood nine days ago, were standing beneath the covered slip. Each had tattoos on their arms and necks, and one had plastered a cocky grin on his face that would piss off Mother Teresa.

When *Mama Bear's* bow eased into the slip, the six ruffians leveled their guns at the people on the boat. One with a devil emblazoned on his forearm yelled, "Throw your weapons in the water."

Noah was the first to comply. Then Lexi. Winslow narrowed his eyes at the devil man as if targeting him for special attention if the opportunity presented itself. He then flung his weapon as close to the rocks as possible while still hitting the water.

"Come with us." The devil man wagged the muzzle of his automatic rifle at the group.

Noah went first, offering Lexi a hand to steady her footing onto the dock. Winslow followed next, offering his hand to the governor. He then whispered something into Macalister's ear, receiving a slight nod and a palm on the back in return.

One man patted down each person from the boat, confiscating cell phones, watches, knives, wallets, lighters, keys, and anything else they deemed threatening. Why they snatched Noah's large-brimmed fedora was a mystery. After each was searched, another man followed along, zip-tying their hands behind their backs.

When the man searching patted Lexi's left leg, he stopped. "What the hell is that?"

"Prosthetic," Lexi replied. "I need it to walk, so if you plan to take it, you better be prepared to carry me up those stairs."

"Just shoot her," the other man said.

"Calhoun said no shooting down here. He wants them alive." The first directed his attention to Lexi. "If you try anything, screw orders, I'll put a bullet in your head."

Lexi acknowledged with a nod. Cooperating was the safest route until she assessed her circumstances.

Three attackers then led the way down the gangway. The other three brought up the rear in an eerie prisoner march as if leading the four from the boat to their execution. Lexi had a feeling that was exactly what they had in mind for Governor Macalister, and she feared the rest would meet the same fate by association.

Once up the eighty steep metal stairs, the gaggle traipsed across the wooden walkway paralleling the shoreline past the private stone chapel and ascended the stone stairs. With each step, Lexi's socket pinched the skin of her already tender residual limb. By the time they were halfway up, the helicopter that had cornered them on the river had landed on the grassy expanse at the top of the hill. The higher the group climbed, the slower the chopper blades whirled. Once Lexi reached the top, she shook her left leg, hoping the socket would shift a fraction to relieve the pressure and chafing.

The right helicopter door swung open. A man dressed in a perfectly pressed camouflage military uniform stepped out, crouching a fraction to protect his head from the slowing blades above him. When he turned toward the group, the emblem on his black beret came into view—a red spade. The collar insignia reflected two stars. One of the men Lexi and Noah had been chasing finally made his appearance.

The general walked toward the group that had now stopped on the walkway pavers. He looked exactly like he did in his official US Army photograph, only without all the medals and insignia badges. If he hadn't already submitted his retirement papers, Lexi suspected that today's action was his official resignation.

The man returned the salute from the devil man who had given the orders at the dock, shook his hand, and whispered something in his ear, earning a beaming smile in return. He then approached the governor.

"Ken Macalister, I hereby relieve you as governor and now control the great state of Texas. You have committed high treason against the United States. Therefore, I sentence you to death. Your execution will commence at noon for the entire country to witness."

"Who the hell are you?" Macalister smirked.

"I am Major General Bill Calhoun, one of the many patriots you betrayed by erasing our borders and flooding the country with foreigners who have no right being here."

"Well, if that doesn't take the cake. You accuse me of treason because you disagree with my policies. Yet here you are, committing insurrection, the highest form of it. If you don't like how I run things, run against me, and we'll have it out on the campaign trail like gentlemen."

"It's too late for speeches," Calhoun said. "We are here to reverse the damage you created. Within a month, we will have rounded up and executed every invader you let through the front door." He then turned to the devil man. "Take them inside. Anyone who defended a traitor shall die as one." The man saluted.

Lexi's breath hitched. Not only did Calhoun intend on the revolution laid out in the manifesto, but he also planned to commit widespread murder, beginning with the governor, Simon, Noah, and her. This man had to be stopped.

The devil man and his team marched the group past the pools and inside the mansion's main sitting room. The smell of spilled booze mixed with sweat was strong. A half-dozen tattooed attackers were there, making a game of destroying the room's contents. They were using a fire poker like a baseball bat to swing at the cocktail glasses thrown at them like fastballs.

A throw. A swing and a miss.

A throw. A swing and hit. Glass shards flew in every direction.

Others were filleting couch cushions and curtains, knocking books and knickknacks off shelves, and spray-painting crude symbols of their organizations. Swastikas were the most prevalent.

The devil leader took them toward the sweeping staircase. Instead of going up, he turned down an ornate hallway wide enough for Lexi to drive her SUV through. He then stopped at the second to the last door on the backside of the house. It had two armed men standing in front. One swung the door open, allowing them inside. The space was a media room with a large-screen television tacked to the wall, two rows of four theater chairs, and dark furnishings. The one window on the wall opposite the half bath was covered with blackout curtains.

"Don't get too comfortable," the devil man said. "Your execution is in two hours."

He left. The door closed, and so did Lexi's hope of getting out of this alive.

33

Nita closed her eyes and tried to meditate while the nurse activated the pump connected to the blood pressure cup around her arm, hoping to bring her numbers down. She might not go home today if they were anything like the last few overnight readings. Nita had insisted on going without pain medication, hoping the mind-over-matter technique she'd learned in drug rehab would work in this case. But the bullet had done extensive damage to her shoulder, and the three-hour surgery to repair the muscles and tendons had left her with extensive swelling. Unfortunately, ice, elevation, and an anti-inflammatory hadn't been enough to relieve the stress on her body. As a result, her blood pressure elevated to dangerous levels.

The cup tightened around her upper arm and squeezed until her fingertips tingled. Once the cup deflated, the nurse annotated the numbers on her virtual chart at the computer terminal in the corner. Her stony face meant one thing—the reading wasn't good. If it were, she'd smile, give Nita a wink, and make some comment about going home.

"The doctor is down the hall. He'll be in to see you in a few minutes. Can I get you anything?"

"A ticket out of here is the only thing I need."

The nurse tidied Nita's bed tray and refilled her water pitcher before leaving, a sign she didn't expect Nita to go home if she remained stubborn.

Nita considered checking her phone, but she knew herself. If Lexi hadn't sent a message, she'd worry and conjure up a myriad of worst-case scenarios as to why. Working herself up into a tizzy was the last thing she needed before the doctor came. The television seemed like a safe option. She could turn on a game show or a morning talk show and learn how to cook a three-course meal out of leftovers.

Nita reached for the corded remote attached to the mechanical bed to power up the wall-mounted set in the corner near the ceiling, but then her surgeon appeared around the privacy curtain near the door. "Good morning, Nita. I hear you had a hard time sleeping last night."

"The incision was hurting pretty bad."

"I think declining the pain medication overnight had a lot to do with it." Dr. Posten walked to her injured side and inspected under the surgical bandage. "How is your pain level this morning?"

"About the same."

"The incision looks clean, but that's not what I'm concerned about. I looked at your medical records, and you show no history of high blood pressure. In fact, you're typically on the low side. But last night and this morning, you were sky high. If we don't get that under control, you could be at risk of stroke. Is there a reason you don't want the pain medication?"

Nita considered telling him the reason, but she had to work with dozens of his patients. Despite HIPAA restrictions, she couldn't risk word getting back to them about her addiction. Other than her best friend, Samuel, no one else at the clinic knew of her challenging past.

"I always tell my patients that opioids are a last resort. I'd be a hypocrite if I took them every time I felt pain."

"That's sound advice, Nita, but you're one day post-op. Your body is under tremendous stress. You need rest, and the medication will help you do that. I highly recommend it to every surgical patient for the first three days."

"I don't know, Doc." Nita's resolve was cracking. Even now, her shoulder was throbbing, making it difficult to concentrate on anything else.

"Then I can't in good conscience send you home until we control your blood pressure. I'll need to put you on an ACE inhibitor at a minimum."

Nita felt like she'd been backed into a corner. Lexi loved her enough to arrange for her mother to pick her up this morning, but that wasn't the problem. Jessie was already en route. She was giving up her entire Saturday, forgoing a church event to drive an hour into the city and settle Nita into bed until Lexi could come home. That left Nita little choice but to do whatever was necessary to get Dr. Posten to release her. But she had two crappy choices—an opioid that might resurface her addiction or a heart medication that could cause kidney damage.

I can handle this, Nita told herself. "What's the lowest dose of pain meds you can put me on?"

"Three hundred milligrams should be enough to let you get some rest," the doctor persisted. "And if your numbers are down in an hour or two, I'll sign your release."

"Fine. I'll take it." Nita hoped those four words wouldn't erase six years of sobriety. When she got home and had a few minutes to herself, she'd have to call her NA sponsor for guidance and support.

Minutes after the doctor left, her day-shift nurse entered, carrying the dreaded small cup. Then, using a handheld scanner, she confirmed the medication and Nita's identity. Once satisfied, she offered the pill that would likely relieve the stress on Nita's body enough so she could go home.

Nita accepted the container, leery of this single pill kick-starting the cravings she battled every day. "For only three days. Mind over matter," she muttered to herself before swallowing it with some water.

The nurse squeezed Nita's hand. "Before your partner left yesterday, she asked me to pass along a message if you agreed to pain medication. She told me to remind you that you're stronger than you realize."

The back of Nita's throat tightened as moisture pooled at the bottom rims of her eyes. Miles apart, she felt Lexi's love and support. That wouldn't be all Nita would need to fight the demons deep within her, but without it, she'd crumble.

"Get some rest. I'll come back in an hour to check your vitals," the nurse said.

Nita returned the squeeze. "Thank you."

She closed her eyes to the sound of the curtain drawing closed against the ceiling track. Nita's thoughts drifted to home. She conjured up Lexi curled next to her in bed, enveloping her in a warm embrace and whispering into her ear, "You're stronger than you realize." A calm overtook Nita, instilling confidence that she would make it home this afternoon and have Lexi holding her by tonight.

Nita woke to someone fiddling with her uninjured arm. Opening her eyes, she discovered the kind nurse preparing to take her blood pressure. The pain was gone, but when she shifted on the bed, the familiar lightheadedness she'd avoided for many years welcomed her back like an old lover. A lover who was disastrous for her but one she couldn't resist. It had the power to draw her in with a single taste. The pull was more potent than she'd remembered and would require more strength than she'd ever mustered to overcome it.

"I'm sorry to wake you, Nita, but I let you sleep a little longer than I should have." The nurse gestured her chin toward the other side of the bed. "Your ride arrived a bit ago. Let's see if we can get you out of here before noon."

Nita craned her neck toward the window side of the room. Beyond the bed table and the food tray, Jessie was seated in the guest chair with her reading glasses on and a paperback folded in her lap. "Good morning, sleepyhead. I'm so glad you're doing well."

"Thanks for coming, Jessie. I really appreciate you rearranging your day."

The cup around Nita's arm inflated, tightening until the machine beeped.

"You're like another daughter to me." Jessie removed her glasses, placing them and the book she was holding into her oversized handbag on the floor next to her feet. "There's nothing more important than taking care of you today." She glanced at the nurse. "How is it looking?"

The pressure cup deflated into a wide grin from the nurse. "Much better. It's nearly at her normal low. I'll message the doctor your vitals. He should give the okay to send you home and into Jessie's good hands."

"I see my girlfriend's mother has already made a good impression," Nita said.

"Free pie will do that around here." The nurse winked.

Nita shifted her stare to Jessie. "Apple or cherry?"

"Apple."

"No wonder. It's a slice of heaven."

"You get that from my daughter."

"I'd have to agree, Jessie. It's heavenly." The nurse patted Nita's lower leg before heading out the door.

Nita pressed the button on the hospital bed, raising the head to a comfortable position. Jessie bounced to her feet, adjusting the two thin pillows—one for her head and the other to cushion her injured shoulder.

"Thanks, Jessie. That's much better." Nita made final adjustments, crossing her legs at the ankles. "Have you heard from Lexi? I don't even know where she was going. All she said was that the life of someone very important in the state was in danger."

"I didn't know that piece. She and Noah headed to Lake Travis before sunrise. I'm afraid that's all I know. She did send me a sweet, sentimental text message when I pulled into the parking lot earlier but said nothing more about the case."

"Maybe she sent me one too." Nita looked for her cell phone. It should have been sitting on the bedside rolling table. Instead, a breakfast tray was there. She then shifted to rummage through the cubby holes, but Jessie stood.

"What do you need, dear? I'll get it."

"My phone. I thought I'd left it on top."

"You did. I moved it when the attendant brought your meal that's gone cold." Jessie reached underneath a shelf. "Here you go, dear. I heard it beep a few times."

Nita grabbed the phone, facial recognition unlocking it. Several alerts were on the lock screen, but those would have to wait. She swiped the glass quickly to see if Lexi had sent her a message. The message icon showed four unread texts, but only one mattered.

She thumbed Lexi's picture. The message at the bottom read: *You make me whole. No matter where I go, I'm thinking of you. I love you, now and always.* Nita clutched her chest. The love she felt for Lexi poured through her smile.

"I never pictured my daughter a romantic," Jessie said, "but the look on your face tells me otherwise."

"She's all aces in that department these days."

"It's good to know that she's treating you right." Jessie scooted her chair closer and lowered her voice. "I rarely talk out of school about my daughter, but none of the women she dated had the effect on her that you have. I couldn't be happier that you two are together."

Nita reached for Jessie's hand, debating how much of her past to reveal. It wasn't something she readily discussed, but this sweet woman deserved to know the truth before she placed full faith in an addict in recovery. "I don't know how much Lexi told you about my past, but—"

Jessie took Nita's hand. "We all have pasts, dear, some more sordid than others. All I need to know is that you love my daughter and won't break her heart."

"I love her with every fiber. The last thing I want is to see her hurt."

"Then that's good enough for me." Jessie patted their clasped hands with her free one before letting go. "The rest doesn't matter."

They chatted more about Lexi, pies, work, and life in Ponder until the nurse returned with the good news that she could go home. She then prepped Nita for release by removing the IV lead from the back of her hand. Despite the pain meds still coursing through her veins, peeling off the see-through barrier keeping it in place hurt like the dickens.

"Now for wound care and use of a sling," the nurse said.

"No need. I'm a physical therapist. I lecture patients on those things every day of the week."

"This makes my job much easier. The only things left are for you to get dressed and for me to get you a wheelchair so you can blow this popsicle stand." The nurse left with an extra pep in her step.

"Would you mind grabbing my things?" Nita asked Jessie. "They should be in a plastic bag in the closet."

"Sure." Jessie retrieved the bag and placed the contents on the bed.

Thankfully, Nita's cousin had dropped off some clothes yesterday, including a lacy thong, of all things. Not the item Nita wanted Lexi's mother to see. At least she wouldn't have to go home in a bloodstained cocktail dress the emergency department staff likely had to cut from her torso the night of the shooting.

"Interesting combination." Jessie's observation forced Nita to hide an incessant grin. A sports bra and date-night thong definitely didn't go together.

"My cousin's selections."

"Ah. That explains things," Jessie said. "Lexi tells me she's quite a handful."

"She did, huh? What else did she say about Jenny?"

"I've said too much already." Jessie cleared her throat. "Do you need help getting dressed?"

"I teach getting dressed with one hand, but your help would make it go a lot faster."

After Nita explained that she'd have to forgo the sports bra, Jessie helped with the rest, including a button-down blouse. Once they secured the sling again, Nita slipped into the flip-flops Jenny had picked out for her.

Jessie then dug a brush and mirror from her handbag. "Let's get you looking like you're ready for a night on the town."

Nita took one look in the mirror and realized that Jessie was a saint for not mentioning the bird's nest she'd been sporting all morning. After several brushstrokes, Nita had made her hair appear windblown, not like she'd survived a massacre two nights ago.

Minutes later, the nurse came in with the wheelchair. "Sorry for the delay, ladies. I was distracted by the news."

"What news?" Jessie asked.

"At the governor's estate on Lake Travis. Some lunatics blew up the place and took the governor hostage." The crease between the nurse's brow became more prominent. "They're going to execute him and his security team in an hour."

Nita's chest tightened. Her empty belly churned the bile in her stomach as she pieced the information together. Finally, her hand shaking, she reached for the corded television remote and pressed the power button.

Before seeing a single headline on screen, she already feared that Lexi had been ensnared in the cataclysmic event.

She channeled up until she reached the first station with live coverage. A video played on the left side of the screen, showing the front of the governor's private mansion and the burned-out SUVs and demolished gate. Two armored vehicles were blocking the entrance where the mangled metal gate once stood. The video then zoomed to a grassy area in the center of the circular driveway. The tall flagpole touted a banner with a giant red spade in the center. Several militia-type men with automatic weapons were guarding the gate and front entrance of the mansion.

Nita was so focused on the visual horror that she barely deciphered what the news anchor was saying. Instead, she read the text below the images. It detailed that several Texas Rangers were killed in the initial attack. In addition, the governor and members of his security team were taken hostage, including a visiting ATF agent and an Arizona police detective.

Nita gasped, reaching for Jessie's hand. "Lexi."

34

Nita, I'll make it back to you, Lexi thought, watching the media coverage on the big screen. Surely, Nita and her parents had seen the news by now and pieced together that Lexi had been taken hostage.

If those goons hadn't taken the television remotes, she could have used the smart TV to hop on the Internet or Facebook to send a message and get word they were still alive. But the men had stripped the room of everything the captives could use to cut themselves loose or club someone over the head. They even took the hex key Lexi carried to adjust her prosthetic ankle and foot, which left her feeling vulnerable if something happened to her leg. Thankfully, though, the power and channel buttons were on the lower edge, accessible with their hands tied at their backs.

The live newsfeed showed the Texas Ranger SWAT squad outside the compound. It then switched to an armored unit of the Texas National Guard rolling through the ineffective community gate. The commentary said that the Red Spades were moments away from being over-matched in firepower and personnel. A corner of the screen displayed the time. They had forty-nine minutes until their live-streamed execution, with no sign that negotiations were underway.

With a publicly announced execution deadline looming, that meant the friendly forces outside the compound would likely launch a counter-offensive before then. Unless they had a plan to take out the guards outside the media room door first, the hostages would be in great danger. That left Lexi and the others with only one option: free themselves and fight their way out. But even that was a longshot. They were unarmed and outnumbered and would be dead before they made it out the door.

"They weren't kidding about a live-streamed execution." Winslow looked out the window. "They've cleared an area on the back patio and are setting up a camera stand." He returned to the center of the room, tugging mightily on his restraints without making progress. "If only I could get out of these damn things, we might have a chance of making it to the safe room."

"What safe room?" Lexi asked.

"I had a virtually impenetrable room built and equipped with communications, food, water, and first aid in the governor's suite. The hidden door is in his walk-in closet."

"Is it big enough for all of us?"

"Yes, but it would be a tight fit. It was designed for the governor and his wife before the divorce."

"Where is his bedroom?"

"On the next floor up, on the other wing of the mansion," Winslow said. "If by some chance we overpower the guards, the elevator and main stairs are out of the question, but we could use the servants' stairs. They are three rooms down the hallway. My guess is that we'd attract a lot of attention, but with two weapons, we might make it."

"Put me on a gun," Noah said. "I'm an excellent shot, and I never miss."

"You're hired." Macalister angled his bound hands so the others could see. "But we need to get out of these things first."

"I have an idea. We can use my foot." Lexi plopped on a chair and raised her prosthetic leg off the floor. "I'll walk you through pulling off the shoe, Noah."

"Great idea." Noah positioned himself on Lexi's left side near her knee.

"How did you earn that, Agent Mills?" Macalister cocked his head to one side.

Lexi knocked twice on her plastic socket. "Courtesy of the Gatekeepers last year. They're in bed with the Red Spades, and there's nothing I'd like more than to pay them back."

The governor briefly bowed his head. "If I weren't handcuffed, I'd shake your hand, young lady. My hat goes off to you."

"Thank you, sir." Lexi then directed her attention to Noah. "The shoe is designed to not fall off, so after you untie it, you'll have to apply a lot of force to wrench it off. But if you don't twist, you won't hurt me."

"Thanks for the tip." Noah first fumbled the laces loose with his fingertips.

"Good," Lexi said. "Now stretch the sides of the shoe outward to loosen the laces more." Once Noah completed that task, exposing the lower structure of her prosthetic, Lexi continued. "The foot is made of carbon fiber. The edges of the struts leading to the ankle should be sharp enough to cut into the flex cuff. I'll lay on the floor belly-down and prop my leg against the wall with the heel outward. Then you'll need to straddle me."

"Got it," Noah said. Once they were both in position, he located the struts blindly using his fingers. He then worked his lower arms up and down rapidly. Lexi struggled to keep her leg in place, losing her strength only once. After Noah repositioned, he worked so fast that Lexi swore she smelled smoke caused by the friction. Within a few minutes, he'd weakened the plastic binding enough to break free of it.

"Your turn, Simon." Lexi braced herself for another round of pressure. She sensed the socket had shifted minutely several times against her limb and feared the lower part of her prosthetic was moving similarly. Without her hex tool to make the corrections, her leg might be unstable. But that was a risk she had to take to give everyone a chance of survival.

A few minutes later, Simon was free, leaving only the governor. He went to work, but it became apparent he wasn't putting in enough effort. "You're going to have to press harder and move faster, Governor, if you want to get out of here," Lexi said.

"I have a few years on these two, young lady. Give an old man a second to get it into gear."

"So that bit about you being fit as a fiddle and working out regularly was all campaign hype." Lexi hoped to shame him into kicking it into high gear.

Simon snickered.

"You certainly know how to get a man to do what you want," Macalister said. "I'm sure you have to beat them off with a stick."

"My girlfriend does a fine job of it. Now hit it, sir. My back is hurting with my hands this way."

Once the governor was free, Lexi rolled to her bottom. "Can one of you give me a hand up?"

Macalister instantly eased her up by the elbow. "How do you propose we get your hands free?"

"Someone will have to take my leg off and hold it while I try to cut myself free," Lexi replied.

"Wait," Simon said. "Now that my hands are free, I have a better idea." He walked behind a theater chair, quietly flipped up the Velcro on it, and manipulated both sides' hidden mechanism to release the back. He then lifted it off the seat portion, exposing the metal rods that had kept it in place. "I cut my hand on this damn thing once, repairing it. It should be sharp enough to cut through."

Simon was right. Lexi had her hands free and shoe back on within a few minutes. "Now we need a diversion." She flexed the soreness out of her wrists and eyed the contents of the room, finding two of the ingredients.

"What do you have in mind?" Noah asked.

"What else?" Lexi grinned.

"A bomb," he said.

"If the bathroom is well stocked, we're in business." Lexi lumbered to the half bath, working out the kinks from her back muscles with each step. She opened the cabinet beneath the vanity and instantly smiled. "Bingo." She grabbed what she needed and returned to the media room. "Noah, I need you to empty two water bottles from the wine fridge. Simon. Governor. I need you to unwrap those Hershey kisses from the counter and roll the foil into balls the size of a peanut M&M."

While the men worked on their tasks, Lexi glanced at the television, looking for the time. Their execution would be in thirty minutes, which meant their captors would likely come for them soon. She then closed her eyes, gripping the bottle of drain cleaner and remembering the lesson she had on homemade bombs. "What was the damn ratio?" she mumbled to herself.

"Done, Agent Mills," the governor said. "We made a dozen. I don't get it. How does foil make a bomb?"

Lexi turned around. "The aluminum reacts with the acid in the drain cleaner to create hydrogen gas. If the gas isn't vented, pressure will build in the bottle until it explodes. It should make one hell of a bang and send plastic shards everywhere."

"Should?" the governor asked.

"If I don't use the correct ratio of sulfuric acid to aluminum, my so-called distraction will only fizzle at the bottom of the bottle."

"Well, then," the governor said, "let's hope you have an excellent memory."

"What's the plan, Lexi?" Noah asked.

"If we set off one device near the door, that should entice the guards to open it. The second one should disorient them long enough for us to over-power them and get their weapons."

"You and Noah should be on the rifles," Winslow said. "I'll shield the governor in the middle and bark out commands to the safe room."

"Noah is the better shot." Lexi gathered her bomb-making materials. "He should take the lead. I'll protect our rear. Simon, you and the governor should shield yourselves behind the chairs closest to the TV screen. Noah and I will set up behind the row closest to the door." Once the others were in a safe position, Lexi walked toward the door, unscrewing the bottle caps. "Get ready."

35

Shoving six wadded foil balls through the neck of each water bottle, Lexi estimated the level to which she needed to fill the drain cleaner to achieve the correct ratio of sulfuric acid to aluminum. *Just enough to float the foil should do it*, she thought.

Lexi placed both bottles on the floor, one a foot from the door and the other five feet from the first to ensure both didn't explode in the initial blast. She then poured an inch or so of liquid drain cleaner into each bottle, replaced the cap on the one near the door, and began a count in her head. A ten-second delay should be about right.

Lexi rushed to the second bottle. On the count of ten, she tightened the cap. Lexi then tipped the bottle on its side against a chair pillow to minimize rolling after the first explosion and camouflage it from their captors when they came in. She then circled the first row of theater chairs and crouched next to Noah. "Everyone, first blast in less than a minute. The second will be ten seconds later. Hold position until I give the all-clear. Oh, and you might want to plug your ears."

Lexi then looked Noah in the eye. Their plan was risky and had a high probability of failure, but waiting to be taken to slaughter wasn't an option. She, like the others, preferred to go down fighting. A sense that the end was coming struck Lexi hard. Every time she walked up to disarm a bomb, she knew there was a good chance she wouldn't get out of the situation alive. She had the same feeling now, only ten times as strong.

"It's been an honor, Noah Black."

"It's been an honor, Lexi Mills." Noah squeezed her hand before plugging his ears.

Silence.

Waiting. Lexi lowered her head and silently whispered, "I love you, Nita."

Bang!

The force shook the chairs Lexi and Noah were crouched behind. It created pressure powerful enough to force the air from her position momentarily. However, the blast that took her leg was much stronger. She remembered being unable to take a breath before passing out. This was nothing.

Lexi then counted down in her head. The next ten seconds would decide their fate.

Six. Five. Four.

The door flew open. "What the hell?"

Two. One.

Bang!

The second wave shook the chairs, but this time Lexi was ready for the pressure and relaxed her shoulders to exhale completely. The next intake of breath was seamless, signaling the danger from the explosion had passed.

Lexi's heart pumped faster before she straightened her back to look over the couch. If anyone was going to risk putting their head up first after detonating her makeshift bomb, it was her. Popping her head up, she discovered both guards lying on the floor, stunned by the explosion, and bloody from the plastic shards peppering their arms and faces.

"Clear."

Lexi and Noah were the first to reach their dazed captors. Each snatched an automatic rifle from the floor near the guards' bodies. Then, when the thugs appeared to be regaining their bearings, Noah rifle-butted one and then the second one on the forehead, knocking both out cold. It was a brute tactic Lexi would have taken if Noah hadn't beat her to it.

They removed the web belt from each man with full ammo pouches and placed them around their waists. Noah grabbed the tactical radio from one goon's hand while Lexi unholstered the Colt .45 from her belt. She then tossed it to Winslow. "We're in luck. Let's go."

"Go right," Winslow said. "Hand on my back at all times, Ken."

Noah pushed out the door that was speckled with plastic bottle shards. He first looked left toward the end of the hall before heading right. Their target direction was also home to the center of the mansion, where the mayhem and pickup game of baseball with tumblers had occurred earlier. It was also the likely source of impending resistance. But with any luck, most of the armed invaders were outside guarding the perimeter against attack, not inside.

Before Lexi cleared the doorway, Noah got off his first shots. He was well trained, firing in double-tap bursts twice to conserve ammunition. When she turned into the hallway, two Red Spades lay dead on the marble at the far end near the entry hall. The radio Noah had clipped to his web belt squawked something about the big bad bear escaping. That meant reinforcements were on the way.

Noah passed the second door, carrying his rifle in the low ready position, tight against his shoulder. Lexi did the same, nuzzling her cheek against the butt. Adrenaline kicked in. Her breathing went shallow, and her heart thumped hard. She split her attention between Noah and the rear, scanning for the appearance of threats as the group shuffled forward.

A three-second burst of gunfire came from Noah's side. A ceramic vase exploded into dozens of pieces. The glass of a museum-quality painting in the wall shattered, sending the section tumbling to the floor. Drywall dust puffed from the wall where bullets hit.

Reaching the staircase, Noah fired again, this time in a longer suppressive burst. "Go. Go. I'll hold them back." He used the stairwell as cover to let loose with a second volley.

Winslow rushed up the first few steps with his pistol held high at the stairs above him. Macalister stayed close behind after clutching the back of Winslow's jacket to maintain proper spacing.

Lexi looked over her shoulder before following. A door twenty feet down on the patio side opened. A man with the same rifle Lexi was carrying stepped out. She pressed the trigger twice before he could complete his turn, hitting him center mass. His body jerked, blood spatter following him to the floor.

When no one else followed out the open door, Lexi swung around toward Noah. Four bodies lay in the hallway with no one else in sight. He yelled out, "Go! Go! Take point."

Lexi churned her legs up the stairs, her stump sinking low into the socket and pinching the skin. If she weren't so amped, she was sure it would have hurt like a gut punch. But they had no time for her to shift it back in place.

"Go left!" Winslow yelled. "Third door on the right."

The pounding of boots on marble told Lexi that the group was following behind in a tight formation. At the top step, she paused before sticking her head around the corner. A sweat bead fell to her lip, sending saltiness to her mouth. *Please don't let this be the last thing I taste*, she thought.

Which direction to scan first was a dilemma. If Lexi chose wrong, she'd get a bullet in the head without seeing it coming. She should look right for the sake of economy, but her instinct told her to look left. She crouched low, hoping a shooter would look for someone taller, and eased her head out until her right eye had a view of the hallway. One man was there with his rifle leveled at the stairwell. She then looked right but saw no one.

Without time to weigh the soundness or consequences, she did the first thing that came to mind. She clicked her weapon to fully automatic mode, grabbed a small crystal candy bowl on a table near the entrance, and threw it as hard as she could down the far end of the hallway opposite the gunman.

He opened fire, directing his aim farther down and away from her side of the corridor. Lexi then plopped belly-down onto the hallway floor with her weapon pointed toward the shooter. Unsure of her aim, she pressed the trigger and maintained the pressure, releasing a barrage of bullets. Several hit him, including at least one in the face.

"Clear!" she yelled.

Winslow yanked her up by the elbow, urging her toward the man she killed a moment ago. Still holding on to her rifle, she stomped her left leg once to ensure the prosthetic was still working following that risky belly flop. It felt out of alignment on the second step and had considerably altered her gait.

She lumbered a few more steps when Noah whizzed past. He took point, setting up position a few feet beyond the governor's bedroom suite, using a chest made of thick, polished wood as protection. "Inside!" he yelled.

"Go! Go!" Lexi wouldn't keep up with her prosthetic off-kilter if they had to do stairs or slopes again, so she first pushed Winslow and the governor down the hallway. "I'll cover." Twenty feet was all they needed to get the governor to his bedroom. Lexi limped, checking behind them every time she dragged her left leg forward. The distance between her and the governor increased with her taking one stride to his two.

Winslow was steps from the suite entrance. Then, attackers emerged from the main stairwell. Six, Lexi counted, each firing in her direction. She glanced over her shoulder again, and two men appeared from the stairs they'd climbed moments earlier. Two bullets hit the wall inches in front of Lexi's head, sending a cloud of gypsum into the air. She crouched, but that only slowed her more.

Noah returned fire, and so did Lexi, but their attackers also took cover behind furniture. They were trapped with the bedroom as their one avenue of escape, but Lexi was the only one exposed.

"Come on, Lexi!" Noah yelled.

Unable to run, Lexi kept the trigger pressed, firing at the two men while she hobbled backward toward the governor's suite. With each drag of her leg, her prosthetic became more unstable. It gave out on the next step, sending Lexi's butt to the marble floor. She continued to fire until her clip was empty, making her a sitting duck.

Lexi closed her eyes, resolving herself to sure death. She thought of her mother's smile and her father's twinkly eyes. She thought of the sweet taste of Nita's lips against hers and the warmth from her tight embrace. She kept that image in her head, knowing it would be her last.

When another bullet whizzed past her ear, Lexi lowered her weapon but kept a firm grip, whispering still with her eyes closed, "I'll be waiting for you, Nita."

Then, she felt a tug on the back of her jacket collar. Her bottom slid backward toward the governor's suite. She sprang her lids open.

"I got you, Mills." Winslow was above her head, returning fire with his handgun at the two men. His shoes squeaked against the polished marble while they moved backward. Then, he stopped momentarily, grunting in apparent pain. He continued moving backward again.

As she slid, Lexi released the empty magazine from her rifle, dug out another one from her web belt, and popped it into place. She resumed firing. They reached the doorway and turned the corner.

"I'm empty," Winslow said.

Noah closed ranks, backing up with them.

"Pull me up," Lexi said. "I can hop." Winslow yanked her up with his right hand, holding his left close to his side. Blood streaked his light jacket at a hole near the bicep. Then, standing on one foot with her weight all on the right, Lexi handed Winslow her weapon.

"First right," Winslow said.

Lexi hopped toward the opening on the right, sensing Noah and Winslow backing up with her. She paused at the corner long enough to balance herself with a hand against the wall and glance over her shoulder. Several men appeared at the opening, including the devil man and General Calhoun. Noah got off a round, piercing Calhoun in the left thigh. He fell. Winslow fired, hitting devil man in the neck. He spun and fell atop Calhoun, blocking the entrance. That was the break they needed. The bottleneck could give them two or three precious seconds to make it to the safe room.

Noah and Winslow both turned toward Lexi and ran in her direction. She turned too. Before she took her second hop, Winslow had grabbed her left arm with his right, and Noah had held her right by his left. Both carried their weapons in their free hand. Winslow was wincing in pain.

They flew down the twenty-foot-long hallway, Lexi hopping on her good leg. At the end was the walk-in closet. Near a secondary opening, Governor Macalister was standing inside, frantically waving them forward.

Ten more feet, and they'd be safe.

Five more feet.

Two more.

Macalister moved farther inside.

The opening was wide enough for only one to fit through the doorway. Noah went through first. Lexi prepared to hop in next, but a shot rang out, sending Winslow tumbling and forcing her to the floor, blocking the entrance.

"Simon's down," she yelled while squirming toward the wall.

Noah and Macalister each grabbed an arm, pulling Winslow inside. When his feet cleared the doorjamb, Macalister slammed his hand against a silver wall plate. More bullets rang out, some hitting the metal inside the safe room. Then a thick metal door appeared from between the wall and slammed shut in one second. Plinking sounds from the outside followed in rapid succession.

Silence.

Only the heavy breathing of the four people inside pierced the air. They were safe.

36

Lexi scooted across the small safe room until her back hit the smooth metal wall. She finally realized her heart was pounding like pistons in the NASCAR engines she once built. Those things would bob up and down so fast they were a blur. Then, catching her breath, she looked across the eight-by-eight-foot room. The governor was down on both knees next to Winslow, cradling his head on his upper thigh.

"You did it, my friend." Macalister positioned Winslow into a comfortable position the best he could. "You saved us."

Winslow lay panting and bleeding. The gunshot wound to his left arm was terrible, but the one to his left shoulder looked more damaging. Then, between gasps, he choked out, "Are you hurt, sir?"

"What's this 'sir' crap?" Macalister smirked.

"I'll take that as a no." Winslow grimaced.

"We need to stop the bleeding," Noah said. "Where's your first aid kit, Governor?"

Macalister pointed to a wall cabinet near Lexi. "Over there."

"I'll get it." Lexi pulled herself up, using a small metal desk as leverage. A police radio base station, phone, and laptop were there. Above it was a flat-screen TV on one wall and the cabinet on the other. Balancing on one foot, Lexi opened the cupboard and located a red zippered soft-sided satchel with the medical symbol printed on its side. She snatched it and tossed it to Noah.

"This is going to hurt like hell," Noah said, "but I need to get your jacket off."

Something hit the door from the outside, causing a loud bang. Then another. The clank sounded like metal on metal, as if the attackers were trying to break through with a sledgehammer. Lexi and Noah cocked their heads instantly in its direction.

"Don't give it a second thought," Macalister said. "They'll be out there for days and not make a dent. They'd have to torch through it."

"Can you stay upright?" Noah asked. Winslow gritted his teeth when Noah eased his upper torso up and his jacket off.

"Yeah, I think so." Winslow's voice had lost its firm, confident tone. However, he still appeared invincible even with two bullet holes in his upper body. "You should get on the horn, sir."

The pounding stopped.

"I suppose so." Macalister struggled to get up from both knees. Lexi hopped over, held on to a wall-mounted metal shelf, and offered her hand. "Well, ain't this a hoot. The governor of the great state of Texas has to be helped up by a one-legged Elliot Ness."

"He was FBI. He needed both legs. We're more badass in the ATF."

"That's an understatement." Macalister clutched her hand and pulled himself up. "I owe you and Detective Black a debt of gratitude."

"Just doing our jobs, Governor." Lexi snapped her head in Noah's direction. "And don't you say anything about keeping a promise. We all did our jobs today to stay alive."

"Nevertheless," Macalister said, "you two are welcome at my home anytime. Unfortunately, I don't know if I'll have a home once these yahoos are done with it." He stepped to the desk, picked up the phone handset, and hit a single button. "Hello, Tom... Yes, we made it. Simon's been shot... No, the rest of us are unhurt... I have ATF Agent Mills and Detective Black with me... Send in the Rangers and get that son of a bitch out of my house."

While Noah dressed Simon's wounds with temporary bandages, Lexi hopped to the desk. "Can I get an outside line on that phone, sir? I'd like to call my girlfriend and tell her I'm all right. She was hit in that nightclub shooting the other night."

Macalister pulled out the desk chair for her. "By all means. Press the top button and have Tom connect you."

"Thank you." Lexi sat in the chair and picked up the handset but held it against her chin, thinking about what to say to Nita. Saying "I love you" didn't seem enough, but saying that she wanted to spend the rest of her life with her did.

After passing along Nita's number, Tom connected the call, but it went to voicemail. Then, calculating that her mother should have either been at the hospital or at her and Nita's apartment, Lexi asked Tom to connect her second call.

"Hello?" her mother answered.

"Mom, it's Lexi."

"My God, Peanut." Her mother's voice cracked with emotion. "Is it really you? Are you okay?"

"Yes, Mom. It's me. We made it to a safe room. We're waiting for the Rangers or the National Guard to rescue us. How's Nita? Can I talk to her?"

"She's sleeping. She got so worried when we figured out that you were in the middle of chaos at the governor's mansion that the doctor upped her pain medication to get her to calm down, but it put her right to sleep."

Lexi exhaled her uneasiness. Nita must have been in a lot of pain to take the opioids, and that must have terrified her. Then the faint sound of gunshots came through the metal walls of their secure room. "I gotta go, Mom. Tell Nita that I love her and that I'll be home as soon as I can."

Lexi's mother sniffled. "I love you, Lexi. Come home to us."

"I will, Mom. I love you, too."

Lexi hung up and remained focused. She and the others weren't entirely out of danger yet, so she couldn't give in to the emotion of the last few hours. Instead, she unzipped her pant leg to the knee, pushing the fabric out of the way to expose the socket and inspect her prosthetic. The pylon and the ankle attached to it appeared intact, but several bolts seemed loose and needed tightening with a hex key. In addition, her residual limb still felt pinched. She was likely swollen, but adjusting the sockets' position properly required time and patience. Alternatively, she gripped both hands around the plastic and shifted it to relieve some pressure.

When Macalister and Noah helped Winslow into the other chair, Lexi glanced at him. He appeared weak but alert. If they weren't rescued soon, he could bleed out despite Noah's bang-up first aid job.

An uncomfortable silence overtook the room while the gunfire grew louder. A battle was raging on the other side of the door and had reached an orchestra-like crescendo. Noah tossed Lexi her automatic rifle with a fresh magazine. She met Noah's eyes while he held his loaded weapon at the low ready position. They had the look of determination. That he would die with that rifle in his hands to protect the others in the room. Lexi then gave him a nod and readied her weapon, aiming at the door.

Then.

The pops stopped.

Silence.

Waiting.

A minute passed. Then two.

Then.

The phone rang.

"About damn time." The governor walked to the desk, reaching around Lexi. "Excuse me, young lady." He placed the receiver to his ear. "And...? Got it. Thank you, Tom." Returning the receiver to the base station, a smile grew on his lips. "The Red Spades are defeated. We should hear a double, triple knock."

Simultaneously, Lexi and Noah lowered their weapons to audible exhales. The next moment, someone knocked three times on the door and three times again. Macalister then pressed the silver wall plate, triggering the door to open. Lexi and Noah instinctively raised their weapons a second time until the familiar Lone Star patch on a Ranger's uniform sleeve came into view.

"Sergeant Mosley?" Lexi asked.

"We need to go, Governor," Mosley said. "The building is on fire."

"Help me with Simon." Macalister shifted his stare to Noah. "You help our very own MacGyver."

"Yes, sir." Noah slung the rifle over his back. Lexi did the same, sliding her right arm over his shoulder.

Mosley and Macalister helped Winslow out first. Lexi and Noah followed steps behind. When they reached the hallway outside the main suite, the smell of smoke was strong. Looking left and then right, Lexi saw flames at both ends of the hallway, making the central staircase their only way out.

Winslow grunted only twice while descending the swirling stairs. Meanwhile, Lexi was concerned about her prosthetic. If she couldn't repair it, she'd have to be on crutches until she got home to her spare.

Once at the bottom, Lexi took in the main room. The once-beautiful space with fine furnishings and a majestic view of Lake Travis through the floor-to-ceiling wall of windows was now a disaster. Everything was shredded or broken, including the windows.

Once out the main door, paramedics took over caring for Simon Winslow. They placed him on a gurney before checking his wounds and vitals.

"Hurry," Lexi said to Noah. "I want to say goodbye to Simon before they take him away."

Noah then picked up the pace. The front of the house looked like a war zone. The gate had been blown to pieces, several armored cars were scattered, and their shells were burning into a molten mess. National Guardsmen were standing watch around the perimeter with automatic weapons. A Texas Ranger SWAT van had pulled into the grassy round of the circular driveway. The twenty-foot flagpole was shamelessly flying the banner of the Red Spades. And firefighters were running about, leaping over large hoses that lay crisscrossed on the ground in a haphazard pattern.

It was utter chaos.

Noah stopped several yards shy of the gurney to allow the medics to attach monitors and new dressing to Simon's wounds. Lexi hopped the last few feet toward Simon's head when they were done. Simon's dark skin appeared dull as if covered by a waxy sheen, a sign he'd lost a lot of blood. She then used the gurney bar for balance and leaned closer so Simon could hear. "You saved my life. Thank you."

He looked up and met her eyes, reaching for her hand with his uninjured one. "You saved all of us. I'll always be in your debt for saving my dear friend."

"We have to take him, miss," a paramedic said.

Lexi squeezed his hand before letting go. "Get well, Simon."

While Simon was wheeled to a waiting ambulance, Lexi craned her neck, looking for her SUV. It was where she'd left it, past the portico, near the multi-car detached garage, but it had been battered. The tailgate was up, the windows were shattered, and the side panels and doors were riddled with bullet holes.

"Go to my car," Lexi said. "If my stuff is there, I can repair my leg."

Noah steered Lexi to the back of the war-beaten vehicle. Their suitcases and equipment bags had been torn open, and their things were strewn about the compartment. Even her blast suit had been ripped to shreds. Sitting in the back near the opening, Lexi sifted through the mess and finally came across the small, zippered bag containing her repair tools and spare socks and liner.

Lexi rarely took off her prosthetic in front of people, preferring not to show weakness. Though today's events had taught her that having a prosthetic could be challenging, it by no means made her appear weak. On the contrary, it made her seem tougher in the eyes of others.

While Noah stood by silently, Lexi removed the web belt from her waist, loosened her left pant leg, and rolled down the sleeve around her thigh that had kept the prosthetic in place. Lifting her residual limb from the socket relieved the pressure. But the real relief came when she removed the double layer of socks and the liner, feeling better than an hour-long massage. Her skin was beet red, but she didn't have time to apply the skin cream and let it dry.

"That looks like it hurts," Noah said.

"It does, but it should be much better by tomorrow." Lexi then used the spare hex key from her pack to tighten the bolts after aligning the pylon to the socket and ankle. A clean liner and double layer of socks made her feel fresh again.

A welcome, familiar face approached the car when she donned the socket. "You two are keeping my Rangers busy these days." Lieutenant Briscoe's utility uniform was no longer perfectly pressed, but she still looked like the poster image for professional law enforcement. The broad smile on her face said she was glad Lexi and Noah were safe.

"Sarah? How on earth did your team get down here so fast?"

"Simon arranged for a Texas Ranger jet to fly my team to the Spicewood airport. In case this went south, he wanted a team familiar with the players."

"I'm glad it was you," Lexi said. "But how did you get your equipment here?"

"The lessons learned from 9/11 showed us that pre-positioning assets was imperative in an attack, so the Rangers have staged equipment at the airport nearest to every governor's home since. Fortunately, this was the first time we've had to use it." Briscoe glanced toward Macalister from across the driveway. "Word has already spread about your MacGyver move, Lexi. The governor is calling you a real-life hero."

"It was a little chemistry and a lot of luck." Lexi finished adjusting her prosthetic and jumped from the back of her beat-up SUV. "Would you mind if we borrow your phone? Ours were tossed in the river, and we need to call family and our bosses."

"Of course." Briscoe dug her phone from a cargo pants pocket and handed it to Lexi. "Take as long as you need. I'll be at my command vehicle when you're done."

"Thanks, Sarah. We won't be long." When Briscoe walked away, Lexi turned her attention to Noah. "Why don't you call first? I'm sure your aunt would be relieved to hear from you. Besides, I need to look for something in my car."

"Thanks, Lexi. I'll be only a few minutes." Noah accepted the phone before stepping away for privacy.

Lexi swung around to the driver's side. It appeared someone had gone Carrie Underwood and taken a Louisville Slugger to the windows and doors. Pulling the door open to a loud creak, she was surprised it still worked. Once Lexi plopped down into the seat, she hoped the collection of pennies and nickels in the cup holder had served as camouflage. She ran an index finger through the layers of coins, eventually exposing what she'd been looking for. "Thank you. Thank you. Thank you."

Lexi carefully pulled out her grandmother's engagement ring using her thumb and index finger and kissed it. Hopefully, it would soon be Nita's. She then placed it on her right ring finger, promising to herself to never let it out of her sight until she put it on Nita's hand.

Lexi finally let her mind wander to something other than surviving. Surveying the damage to her car, she wondered if the ATF would pick up the bill for it or if she'd have to battle her insurance company. Either way, she needed to find another way back to Dallas and get Noah on a plane back to Tucson.

Minutes later, Noah returned. He had a sly grin on his face.

"I take it the talk with your chief went well," Lexi said.

"We've already made national news. The entire country knows how an ATF agent from Dallas and a police detective from Nogales saved the governor of Texas from execution." Noah snickered. "He's offering me a promotion. Surprisingly, he's gone from hiding me on the night shift to wanting to make this"—he pointed an index finger at his face in a circular motion—"the face of the department."

"Don't sell yourself short, Noah. I think you'd make an excellent ambassador for the department."

"Maybe." Noah handed her the phone. "I'll give you some privacy." He then walked toward Briscoe's command SUV.

Lexi couldn't remember her boss's direct line, so after an Internet search, she dialed the Dallas division main line. "This is Agent Lexi Mills. I need to reach my SRT commander, Special Agent Jack Carlson."

"Not *the* Lexi Mills who saved the governor of Texas?" the male operator asked.

Word had spread fast. And based on the glee in the operator's voice, Lexi guessed the news was taken well by most sectors in the division. But unfortunately, she doubted that would hold true for Carlson. She'd disobeyed his order by not reporting into the division first thing this morning and going off with Noah on a hunch.

"Yeah, that's me."

"You're quite the celebrity around here today."

"I don't feel like one. I'm tired and hungry and am sure my boss will chew my ass. Can you connect me to his cell?"

"Sure thing, Agent Mills. Let me put you on hold." The line went silent for a minute before the operator reconnected the call. "I'm sorry, Agent Mills, but Agent Carlson's line went to voicemail. Would you like to leave a message?"

"I'd rather wait. Can you ring Agent Kaplan Shaw in Intel?"

"I'm on it. Hold, please." A minute later, the operator returned. "Agent Mills, I have Agent Shaw on the line. Good luck, ma'am. I'm glad you're safe."

After the audible click, Lexi said, "Kaplan?"

"My God, Lexi. I can't believe what happened. Did you get hurt?"

"I have a few bruises, but the governor's head of security took a bullet in the arm to save my life."

"I hope he'll be okay."

"He should be," Lexi replied. "Hey, Kaplan, I tried to call Carlson, but he didn't answer. Can you let him know that I'm okay and will be in tomorrow?"

"That's right," Kaplan said. "You haven't heard. The Internal Affairs Chief questioned him after word about your capture hit the news. When I saw him, he stormed out and hasn't come back."

"Questioned? What for?"

"He didn't pass along our findings to the FBI until he got into the office this morning. But by then, all hell had broken loose. I'm not sure what IA was fishing for, but I think he was gunning for Carlson's shield."

"It wouldn't break my heart if he did." Lexi finished the call with the promise to stop by Kaplan's office first thing tomorrow.

Tomorrow, Lexi thought. First, she had to get through the rest of the day and make her way back to Dallas and into Nita's arms. That journey would begin by asking another favor. Lexi then walked toward the lieutenant's command vehicle.

After talking to the National Guard on-scene commander, Governor Macalister joined Briscoe, Mosley, Noah, and Lexi. "There's my personal MacGyver." Macalister smiled broadly. He looked down at Lexi's left leg. "Did you have a spare? Or did Amazon deliver?"

Lexi chuckled, rapping her knuckles against the socket twice. "It just needed a tune-up." She turned to Briscoe, returning her device. "Thanks for the phone. Any chance your team can get Noah and me home? My car was destroyed."

"Absolutely. My team will take you anywhere you need to go." Briscoe's gaze shifted toward the mansion. "Here he comes."

Lexi looked in the same direction. The sight made her breath hitch. "He's alive?"

Paramedics had General Calhoun handcuffed to a gurney and were wheeling him toward a waiting ambulance. Their path would bring them right past Briscoe's SUV. When the gurney was a few feet short of their group, the governor put up his hand in a stopping motion, bringing the medics to a halt.

"A word, please." Macalister then directed his attention to Calhoun, whose leg had been bandaged and chest decorated with monitor leads. "This is what you get when you mess with Texas, Mr. Calhoun. Even if you succeeded in killing me, you wouldn't have killed the Texas spirit. Now you'll spend the rest of your days in a Texas prison, waiting for your execution."

"This is just the beginning." Calhoun narrowed his eyes eerily like the devil man did when he had the governor in his crosshairs. "We're a snake with many heads. Cut off one, and more will rise."

"When they do, my Rangers will be there to cut them down," Macalister scoffed.

Lexi stepped forward. This might be her only opportunity for justice. "Tell me where Belcher is, and we won't tear apart the lives of your family during the investigation."

Calhoun laughed. "You'll never find him."

Macalister waved his hand dismissively. "Get this yahoo off my lawn."

After Calhoun disappeared into the rig, Sergeant Mosley stepped forward, carrying the Texas state flag that had been meticulously folded to display the lone star. "Would you care to do the honors, Governor?"

Macalister wrapped an arm around Lexi's shoulders. "I think Agent Mills and Detective Black have earned the honor."

"Thank you, sir," Lexi said. "I'd love to." She accepted the flag and led Noah to the flagpole. He loosened the halyard and quickly lowered the reprehensible Red Spades' banner, tossing it to the ground where it belonged.

While Noah ensured the state flag didn't touch the lawn, Lexi attached the upper corner to the first snap hook, then the lower corner to the second. She then offered the halyard to Noah, but he waved her off. "It should be raised by a Texan."

And with those words, Lexi raised her state flag proudly, knowing she'd kept Texas whole. She then glanced at the mansion as flames danced from the rooftop and out the windows in the early-afternoon sun. The charry remains of the ends were skeleton-like, and the center wasn't far behind from meeting the same dark fate.

The Red Spades and the Gatekeepers may have taken the governor's home, but Lexi wouldn't let them take anything more. If it was the last thing she did on this earth, she would hunt them down.

37

"Careful, Darby. Footing could be tricky."

Darby looked over his shoulder, giving Lexi a thumbs-up. His body then split in half, forming two men. Faces morphing into Calhoun and the devil man, their eyes were cold and angry like a blinding winter storm. Then, moving fast like a nor'easter, they leveled their guns at Lexi with a bright flash of light marking each bullet they'd sent hurtling toward her.

Lexi tried to run, but her legs were stuck in quicksand, and it was pulling her in deeper. Flashes continued. A bullet would surely strike her whether she leaned left or right. The only escape was to give in to the soupy sand.

Lexi closed her eyes and relaxed her shoulders, waiting for either instrument of death to take her into the darkness. Glancing to her left, her mother looked up at her from the kitchen counter while making pies. "It's all right, Peanut. Your grandparents will show you the way." But the journey she was about to take didn't feel right. So much business was still undone.

Lexi then glanced right, where Nita was sitting on the edge of their bed with a towel wrapped around her torso, applying cream to her tanned leg. "I tried to make it home, Nita." Lexi's heart ached as she reached out for one last touch.

Nita locked gazes briefly with her before resuming her task. "The chase isn't over, Lex. Remember that heroes aren't always what they seem."

A bump jolted Lexi awake to the sound of skidding tires on the tarmac.

The engines whined when the braking pressure forced Lexi's lower belly to push against the lap belt. While their plane slowed, she looked out the small window portal to the dark evening sky, focusing on the perimeter lights enveloping Dallas Love Field in an amber glow.

Lexi dug her new phone from her cargo pocket and powered it on. Swiping the screen, she discovered two unread text messages, one from Kaplan and the other from her mother. But the single missed phone call had grabbed her attention, so she pressed the voicemail icon. The following message from Noah played: *"Thanks for the airlift home. Call when you get a chance. Take care, Lexi."*

Lexi wasn't ready nor willing to let Noah fade from her life. In four short days, they'd chased madmen across multiple states, witnessed death and escaped it twice, and glimpsed into the other's life in a way that made them more family than friends. She thumbed Noah's name on the screen, returning his call.

"I meant for you to call in a few weeks." Noah laughed.

"I figured as much but couldn't help myself," Lexi said. "It felt weird not having you by my side the last few hours."

"I felt the same way." Noah cleared his throat. "My aunt says you have free street tacos for life whenever you're in Nogales for getting us out of that mess."

"I'll take her up on that offer the next time I visit. By the way, you still owe Nita a cooking lesson."

"The next time I'm in Dallas, I'll teach you two how to make a feast fit for royalty. But until then, I'm going to miss you, Lexi Mills."

"I'll miss you too, Noah Black." Lexi swallowed the emotion building in her throat. "But it's not over for me. I still have Belcher to track down."

"I wish you luck. Unfortunately, my job is done. But if you ever need someone to cover your back, I'm just a phone call away. Take care of yourself, Lexi."

"Same to you, Noah. Take care." Lexi ended the call, sensing she'd made a friend for life.

When the Texas Rangers' jet came to a stop near a hangar marked *Texas Department of Public Safety*, Sergeant Mosley popped up from his seat. "End of the line, boys and girls. We unload and inventory our gear before going home."

A chorus of moans and groans followed from the exhausted team of Rangers. Still, everyone unbuckled their seat belts, grabbed their bags, and deplaned down the stairs. Everyone but Lieutenant Briscoe. She approached Lexi's row, toting a backpack and a small personal bag.

"I'd be happy to take you home, Lexi," Briscoe said. "We could stop for a bite to eat on the way there."

Bells went off in Lexi's head. It had been a while since she'd been on the receiving end of a pickup line, but Sarah's offer was definitely flirting. "Thank you, Sarah, but I have to get home to my partner."

"Oh." Sarah's expression turned sheepish, but then she straightened her posture, resuming her air of confidence with a slight grin. "My apologies. I misread things. The offer for the lift home stands. If not me, I can ask one of my Rangers."

"That would be great. Ubers can be sketchy in town on a Saturday night, but I don't want to put anyone out of their way."

"Will you stop?" Sarah's tone was playful yet firm. "You've earned the gratitude of every Ranger in the state, including me. I'd be honored to get you home safely."

Lexi grabbed her two garbage bags of items she recovered from her totaled SUV and followed Sarah down the stairs. They entered the hangar, where the team was hauling and stacking bags and crates of equipment. Sarah whispered something to Mosley, who replied with a nod. She then returned to Lexi. "We're all set. My truck is close by."

Lexi and Sarah filled the drive with talk of the case, their jobs, and the promise to meet up at a shooting range when their schedules cleared. But with careers like theirs, that might not happen for months.

Sarah pulled up to the main entrance of Lexi's apartment building, hopped out, and retrieved the bags of goodies from the back row of the extended cab. A firm handshake to not blur the lines and a round of warm goodbyes marked their departure.

The two-hour nap on the plane had given Lexi the energy to make it inside and up the elevator. Still, once she was at the door, exhaustion from the harrowing day had kicked in with a vengeance. With her keys likely at the bottom of Lake Travis, Lexi knocked on the door, hoping Nita would be the one to greet her with open arms. Instead, the door swung open a minute later to the smell of fresh apple pie and her mother's worried expression.

"Thank goodness. You made it home." Her mother threw her arms around Lexi's torso the moment Lexi dropped her bags on the carpet. Her tight, loving embrace was the medicine she needed. The overpowering relief her mother was laying bare easily bulldozed the weariness Lexi had felt all the way home.

"You're going to crack a rib, Mom." Lexi gave her a tight squeeze before letting go.

"I can't help it. I'm so happy you made it home in one piece this time," her mother said with sad eyes. Clearly, Lexi being taken hostage, nearly executed, and escaping in a hail of bullets had bolstered her mother's dislike of her dangerous job.

"I'm starved. Is that your pie I smell?"

"She's been baking all day." Her father then appeared from the living room, causing Lexi to freeze.

"Dad? I wasn't expecting you." Why should she? Her father hadn't stepped foot in any of the places she'd rented since she came out as gay. But he was here, and he'd ditched his twill mechanic coveralls for his "going to town" clothes of slacks and a button-down blue shirt. That alone meant coming was important to him.

"I was worried about my baby girl. Of course I'd come. Besides, I needed to keep your mother plied with apples and flour until you came back."

"Thanks for coming." Lexi moved her bags of things against the entry table to not block the door.

Her father took several tentative steps toward Lexi and opened his arms to her. "Can you give your old man a hug?"

Lexi froze again. She'd waited fifteen years to hear those words, and now that she had, she didn't know how to react. Years of disappointment and months of tears had marked her journey after he'd turned his back on her, so much that a single hug couldn't possibly erase them. But the emotional pull was powerful enough to send her into his waiting arms.

He squeezed her tight like he used to when she was a little girl and had come running into his garage after scraping a knee. With every passing second, the sense that everything would be all right grew stronger. Then he wept, something he'd never done in front of her. His body quaking, he croaked, "I'm so glad you're okay. I love you, Peanut."

Peanut. He hadn't called her that in years, yet at this moment, it didn't feel long overdue. It felt genuine. She then squeezed him tight, letting tears track down her cheeks. "I love you too, Dad."

When they pulled apart, the hurt wasn't entirely gone, but it wasn't as palpable as it was in Ponder. This, at the very least, was a beginning.

Lexi glanced over her shoulder at her mother. "Where's Nita?"

"Sleeping, thankfully," her mother said. "When she woke earlier, she was relieved to hear that you were safe. But then she became upset that she'd missed your call. I got her to calm down by giving her another pain pill."

Lexi bit down on her back teeth. More opioids were the last thing Nita needed for peace of mind—hers and Nita's. "Thanks, Mom. I appreciate everything you've done today, but I've got her from here."

After sharing a surreal moment of eating pie with her mother and father at the dining table, they said their goodbyes at the door. They promised to visit each other in a few weeks once Nita was better.

Lexi locked the door, leaving her bags of things for the morning. She then padded down the hallway, easing their bedroom door open. The bathroom light had been left on, partially illuminating the space. Nita lay under the covers, sleeping among a bevy of pillows that were propping up her upper torso. Hence, her shoulder remained above her heart. Instead of waking her, Lexi went to the bathroom and freshened up, sponging herself off, brushing her teeth, and wetting her hair flat.

When Lexi went to her dresser for fresh sleeping clothes, she glanced at the folder positioned neatly in a corner. The documents she'd stored there represented every piece of intelligence she'd gathered on Belcher and the Gatekeepers before starting her first case back as a field agent. She'd have a lot to add to it in the coming days, but that would have to wait until she nursed Nita back to health.

Lexi slowly slid the top drawer open, retrieved her nightclothes, and sat on the chair in the corner that had become a de facto clothes hanger. She stripped, removed her prosthetic, and quickly applied some lotion, skipping the lengthy tissue massage to promote blood flow. Once dressed in shorts and a tank top, she leaned forward until her hand reached the side of the mattress, using it as leverage to quiet her hop into bed.

Lifting her side of the covers back, she slid beneath them, on Nita's right. The motion woke her. Lexi expected a broad smile but was met with tears when Nita turned her head. "You're back."

"Yes, I'm back." Lexi turned on the bedside lamp before shifting to her side and supporting herself with a bent elbow. She then kissed Nita on the lips. "I'm so sorry I couldn't be there this morning."

"You're back," Nita repeated, this time slurring her words.

Lexi looked into her eyes, finding her pupils small like pinheads, which broke her heart. The opioids had made them that way. Nita now had two long roads ahead of her. Lexi then laid her head atop her soft chest, silently swearing to focus on the important things in her life—Nita and her parents.

Nita softly caressed Lexi's hair. "I messed up, Lex."

Lexi reached her right hand up to meet Nita's and gave it a firm squeeze, feeling her grandmother's engagement ring on her finger. But unfortunately, that too would have to wait. "Nita, you're stronger than you realize."

EPILOGUE
THE FOLLOWING DAY

Walking into the Tucson Airport came with crushing disappointment. Every face he passed reminded him of their failure. He'd done his part by scouting the perfect locations in Nogales to set the stage for revolution. However, Fifty Calhoun and the Red Spades couldn't hold off a small-town detective and a one-legged ATF agent long enough to light the fuze. If they had, the country would be on its way back to glory. Every border station and airport from California to Texas would be closed, and the citizenry would be cowering in their homes. It was nothing short of a disgrace. Though, the fight wasn't over. The Gatekeepers had taken up the mantle and had sent him on his next mission.

Arriving at his gate, this time well before boarding, he selected a seat away from other waiting passengers for privacy. He thought about his latest trip to Nogales to observe the aftermath and concluded it wasn't a waste of time. He'd met the Gatekeepers' greatest enemy face-to-face and had learned her weakness. The next time they met, he would be ready to put Special Agent Lexi Mills where she belonged—in a pine box.

He then pulled out his tablet and brought up the documents Belcher's team had cobbled together over the last twenty-four humiliating hours. The plan was sound and would reconstitute the Gatekeepers' leadership.

But first, he had weeks of scouting to perform, gathering intelligence, documenting travel patterns, and looking for the perfect weak spot.

His phone buzzed from the pocket of his light jacket. He fished it out. The screen said the incoming call was from an unknown number. Everyone he dealt with who was associated with the Gatekeepers used a burner, so he answered. "Yes?"

"I think my cover was blown," the person on the other end of the line said. The voice was instantly recognizable. "I was grilled for two days."

"If they knew who you were working for, you'd be sitting in a jail cell, not calling me."

"What should I do?" Their voice contained the bitter taste of fear. Perhaps their usefulness had run its course, and they were now a loose end.

"Nothing. Let them fish around. There's nothing linking you to us. Wait for my next call. We might need you in the coming weeks." He disconnected the call before they could respond, realizing they had become a liability. He'd have to plan for their demise along with Lexi Mills's.

Soon, the gate agent announced, "Flight 362, nonstop to Sacramento, will board at gate B12 in ten minutes. If any passenger needs special assistance, please see the ticketing agent at the podium now."

I could use a little vacation to California, he thought. The Sacramento Valley spring temperatures would still be tolerable. And if he finished quickly, he could squeeze in a round or two of golf before he had to return to his cover job.

When the agent called his group, he picked up his bags and lined up with the others. The sheeple shuffled along orderly, showing their smartphones or printed boarding passes to the agent. Then the dance began. Passengers counted down the rows until they located their assigned seats and searched for an open space to store their luggage in the overhead compartments. He acted no differently and played the game.

Once seated on the aisle, he buckled and followed the flight attendant's instructions during takeoff. After the ding sounded through the intercom, he opened his satchel and pulled out the laptop issued to him through his day job. He'd been absent too long and needed to catch up on the annoying emails of his supervisor.

When the beverage cart came around, the attendant eyed him carefully.

"I remember you, sir. You flew with us a few days ago. What can I get you to drink?"

It was too early for tequila, so he said, "Coke would be fine."

The attendant placed an ice-filled cup on his tray table with the soda can. She winked before moving on, saying, "Genuine heroes get the full can."

PROXIMITY
Lexi Mills Book 2

An old foe has returned for revenge...but Lexi Mills never backs down from a fight.

When chaos erupts at a local grocery store in a quiet town near Sacramento, police arrive to discover a horrifying scene—explosive devices trapping a crowd of civilians inside the store, ready to detonate at the push of a button. After ATF explosives expert Lexi Mills arrives on the scene, she quickly realizes that this hostage situation runs far deeper than she imagined...

Locked in a desperate struggle with a vengeful madman while racing against the clock, Lexi must use all of her cunning to rescue the innocent hostages; a situation that forces her to grapple with impossible questions.

But her enemies aren't going down without a fight, and Lexi will need to put her life on the line and push her skills to their limits if she wants to get everybody out unscathed...

Get your copy today at
severnriverbooks.com/series/lexi-mills

ABOUT BRIAN SHEA

Brian Shea has spent most of his adult life in service to his country and local community. He honorably served as an officer in the U.S. Navy. In his civilian life, he reached the rank of Detective and accrued over eleven years of law enforcement experience between Texas and Connecticut. Somewhere in the mix he spent five years as a fifth-grade school teacher. Brian's myriad of life experience is woven into the tapestry of each character's design. He resides in New England and is blessed with an amazing wife and three beautiful daughters.

Sign up for the reader list at
severnriverbooks.com/series/lexi-mills

ABOUT STACY LYNN MILLER

A late bloomer, Stacy Lynn Miller took up writing after retiring from the Air Force. Her twenty years of toting a gun and police badge, tinkering with computers, and sleuthing for clues as an investigator form the foundation of her Lexi Mills thriller series, as well as her Manhattan Sloane novels. She is visually impaired, a proud stroke survivor, mother of two, tech nerd, chocolate lover, and terrible golfer with a hole-in-one. When you can't find her writing, she'll be golfing or drinking wine (sometimes both) with friends and family in Northern California.

Sign up for the reader list at
severnriverbooks.com/series/lexi-mills

Printed in the United States
by Baker & Taylor Publisher Services